THE
KING'S
ASSASSIN

STEPHEN DEAS

GOLLANCZ
LONDON

Copyright © Stephen Deas 2012

The right of Stephen Deas to be identified as the author
of this work has been asserted by him in accordance with
the Copyright, Designs and Patents Act 1988.

First published in Great Britain in 2012 by Gollancz
An imprint of the Orion Publishing Group
Orion House, 5 Upper St Martin's Lane,
London WC2H 9EA
An Hachette UK Company

A CIP catalogue record for this book
is available from the British Library

ISBN 978 0 575 09456 7

1 3 5 7 9 10 8 6 4 2

Typeset by Deltatype Ltd, Birkenhead, Merseyside

Printed in Great Britain by Clays Ltd, St Ives plc

The Orion Publishing Group's policy is to use papers
that are natural, renewable and recyclable products and
made from wood grown in sustainable forests. The logging
and manufacturing processes are expected to conform to
the environmental regulations of the country of origin.

www.stephendeas.com
www.orionbooks.co.uk

THE EDGE OF THE STORM

The ship drew into the estuary of the river Triere. Low-lying glades and salt marsh crept up out of the water on all sides, distant and barely visible. Ahead, the land rose abruptly into a line of cliffs, a solid wall a hundred feet high except for the wide canyon that the Triere had carved between them. Somewhere beyond lay a city, but Berren saw no sign of it at first, the cliffs obscuring everything beyond them; as the ship fought its way up the river through the mouth of the gorge though, the cliffs widened and then one side of the canyon fell away, curving into the shape of a horseshoe as though a giant hand had reached out from the sky and taken a scoop from the land. The ground inside the horseshoe sloped steadily upwards, away from the river to a far ridge that he could barely see. And here, nestled inside this colossal hollow, was the city of Kalda.

Beside the river the ground was flat; as it rose further from the sea, the streets grew steeper until around the edges of the bowl in which the city lay they were almost sheer. Opposite, the river widened into a lake where other ships pitched and rolled slowly back and forth. There were dozens of them, a hundred perhaps, and his own ship drew among them and threw out its anchor. He stared. Kalda. Home, once, to a man called Radek. The man he'd killed on the last terrible day of his old life.

1

From the deck where he stood he could see the whole city now, spread out across the fallen slopes. The sheer size reminded him of Deephaven, of standing atop the tower in Teacher Garrent's moon-temple and looking out across streets and houses stretched out as far as the eye could see. He'd done his best to forget his home, to forget everything about it: the loves he'd found and the fears and the loss. He'd tried to forget the master who'd dragged him out of the slums of Shipwrights', who'd taught him the art of thief-taking and then killed his first true love; now as that one memory opened the door, the rest came crashing out in a tidal wave of regret. A tear crept down his cheek. Tasahre was dead. Master Sy was likely dead too, hunted to the ends of the world by the sword-monks of Deephaven for what he'd done. They'd both become murderers and now he had nothing left, nothing at all except a remembered pain deep and bitter enough to make him gasp and stagger. Not that anyone paid him any attention.

The Deephaven press-gangs had taken him that very same day. He'd been easy for them, staggering around the old slums of the city in a daze amid the debris of the Festival of Flames. He had no idea what they'd got for selling him – a few crowns, maybe. They'd taken his sword, his boots, his purse, everything that might have been worth anything except the gold token he'd worn around his neck. They'd missed that, hidden under his shirt, but the sailors on his new ship had found it quickly enough and then he'd had nothing. It seemed fitting to wind up as a skag on some ship he barely knew after what he'd done. He'd killed a man he didn't know, murdered him in cold blood, staved in his skull with a waster – a wooden practice sword. Not that he'd wanted to but he'd had no choice. The warlock Saffran Kuy had ripped out a piece of his soul and made him do it. Compelled him with a terrible power the warlock still possessed even now, if he ever cared to use it.

Maybe he was lucky. In Deephaven, if they'd caught him, he'd have gone to the mines, a slow hard death far worse than being a rigging slave on a ship.

The absurdity made him laugh. Lucky? A week after they'd taken him, when they were far out to sea and days away from any land, the sailors had dragged him to the edge of the deck. He'd been certain they were all set to throw him overboard and watch him drown for the sheer fun of it. They hadn't, but that was just how life was when you were a ship's skag. Maybe since then he'd earned a grudging respect simply for still being alive, but even if he had it wasn't worth much. Yet in all the ports they'd visited since, he'd never once tried to escape. To what? What was the point? Back to what he was before the thief-taker had taken him in, a thief, a cutpurse? What did he have to look forward to? Nothing. A short life, vicious and pointless and a bad end, that was all. Well, he already had that.

He'd lost track of time, sailing across the oceans with only the seasons as his guide. He'd had two winters since he'd left Deephaven and so he supposed it was two years since he'd been taken; but for all the difference that made, it might as well have been one or it might as well have been ten.

The sailors lowered a longboat into the waters of the Triere and began loading it with travel-chests. Berren watched them with a distant interest. The ship's boatswain wouldn't let him ashore in a place like this, not where he might run away. So he watched; and as the boat strained its way further upriver and turned towards the city, all his possibilities and all the things that had been taken away from him seemed to go with it. He turned away, unable to bear the sight of land any more, and looked back through the towering mouth of the Triere cliffs at the uncaring sea beyond. The Bitch Queen, the sailors called her. That was his life now. They deserved each other.

He bowed his head and got to work. A ship in port had plenty of jobs that needed doing before it set sail again, and since he was the ship's skag, the worst of them were his. The longboat was long gone when another ship came by, catching the last wisps of wind that blew along the canyon to take it further up the estuary. It passed close and Berren stopped what he was doing to watch it, as he watched all ships as they passed.

On the deck stood a man.

It was him.

The thief-taker.

✶ PART ONE ✶

THE MASTER OF SWORDS

1

THE BITCH QUEEN'S HALL

The mob had come to watch three men die. Most of
them had no idea who the men were. Nor did they
particularly care. They'd come down to the Kalda
docks for the spectacle, for a bit of blood, for a Sun-Day
afternoon of shouting their anger and the riot that would
surely follow. They'd come for a bit of a fight, to throw
stones at the city officers and guardsmen and speakers.
They'd come for the cold rain and the wind of winter, for
everything the city had to offer, and that's what they got.

A man ran through the burgeoning brawls with practised ease. The mob barely noticed he was there. He slipped
between the larger fights around him like an eel between
a fisherman's fingers, finding space where none seemed to
exist. If anyone had asked him how old he was, he might
have said fifteen or he might have said twenty, depending
on who was doing the asking. The truth lay somewhere
in between. The truth was that he didn't know and didn't
much care. He was small for a man who wore his first
beard on his face and his name was Berren.

He hadn't come for the executions like everyone else,
nor for the rioting mob. A watcher perched on one of the
rooftops overlooking the sea and taking an interest in his
progress would have seen him pause now and then. With
each pause came a climb to higher ground: a wall, a crane,
an overturned cart, anywhere high enough to see over

7

the sprawling chaos. The watcher, if he'd stared for long enough, might have seen that through the heaving mass of people, amid the torches and the shouts and the fists and the sticks and, yes, the swords and the knives, Berren was making his way towards the far side of the docks. To a tavern called the Bitch Queen's Hall, where sailors and sell-swords were wont to gather, those of them that weren't already out amid the destruction on the dockside.

He paused beside a wagon that had been turned on its side. Broken boxes and hundreds of cabbage leaves littered the cobbles. He was hungry; but everything worth eating had already been taken and all that was left was crushed and trampled. He climbed up onto the wagon instead. The rain was getting worse, driving into his face. The iron-grey sky grew steadily darker. The storm blowing in off the sea and over the cliffs was a big one, the ships anchored in the river already putting up lights although it was still the middle of the afternoon. He shielded his eyes. In his rags he looked like one of the mob, but it wasn't the mob he was afraid of. At least one company of soldiers was already down from its barracks, laying waste to any rioters in its way.

The worst of the fighting was still around the gallows. Three men hung there, dead for five minutes now. The officers who'd hanged them had brought half a company of soldiers for protection. Now, too late, they knew they should have brought the other half too. The soldiers were breaking away from the scaffold in little knots of swinging swords, trying to force their way though the mob to some-where safe, scared enough to simply butcher anyone who got in their way. Berren kept well clear. He had no interest in any of this. From the top of the wagon he looked for where the worst of the fighting was to be had, and when he jumped down he did his best to avoid it. He had no idea who the three hanged men had been or why they were so important, nor did he care; what he cared about was the tavern, the Bitch Queen, where men of the waves said their prayers to the fickle sea in songs and ale and bawdy laughter. For that, here and now, was where the thief-taker would be.

A gang of men raced across his path, away from the gallows and towards the sea. Berren ran with them for a few seconds and then split away and resumed his course.

Master Sy. Memories filled his head and so did the anger he'd carried in him ever since Deephaven, the flames of fury that had smouldered in the dark for all this time. He let them. If there was one thing he'd learned as a skag, it was patience. Master Sy was supposed to be dead – or lost or drowned, or a slave in the imperial mines of Aria or something worse – anything, but not *here*, not *alive*. Yet today he was both of those things, and Berren had come to hunt him down.

The shops and the taverns and the storehouses at the edge of the docks gave a little shelter from the wind and the slanting rain. He eased his way along towards the Bitch Queen. Despite the downpour the rioters had set fire to something. Smoke drifted among them and out to sea. The gallows were rocking back and forth, about to be torn down. He couldn't see where the soldiers had gone and it was impossible to hear anything useful over the shouts and screams of the fighting, over the howl and hiss of the wind and rain.

A trio of snuffers lounged by the tavern doors. They were pressed against the wall and taking shelter as best they could. They looked bored, barely aware of the anarchy around them, but underneath their heavy leather coats Berren caught the flash of metal breastplates. They wore those coats loose too, the way Master Sy used to, and Berren could see where hidden scabbards bent their shape. Whenever anyone from the mob staggered too close, they tensed very slightly, and that was all that was needed. Men still came and went through the Bitch Queen's door but they walked slowly and upright and with their hands empty and easily seen. The snuffers glanced at Berren as he hurried in, but his rags were so torn he could barely have hidden a peeling knife. They gave a faint nod. Inside, warm stuffy air wrapped itself around him like a blanket. With the door closed behind him, the din of laughter and shouted conversation was almost as loud as the riot on the dockside.

A knife. He hadn't brought one because he didn't have one but there were knives everywhere in here. Daggers in scabbards, blades stuck into people's belts, knives cutting bread and meat, knives used for drinking games or simply sitting on tables. Berren moved among the knots and clusters of men looking for one that he could take. There were swords too, hatchets and makeshift clubs. He picked someone who was the worse for drink, waited until the man was jostled from the other side and, unseen, snatched the knife from the man's belt and melted away into the crowd. He clutched it tight. A cheap thing, blunt and savage, and for a moment he wondered what he meant to do with it; but then he closed his eyes and he could see the thief-taker's face again on that terrible last day as Tasahre lay bleeding on the deck of Radek's ship. He'd seen her face every night for nearly two and half years. The thief-taker had called Berren's name. To come with him? To flee? Or was it simply a cry of surprise at what each one of them had just done?

He should never have gone to the Emperor's Docks that day. Tasahre would be alive and maybe he'd have seen the thief-taker again or maybe not, but it could hardly have ended worse.

He looked about. The thief-taker was here somewhere. Today and only today. Berren's heart was already racing.

He'd had fights, more than his share of them. He'd taken beatings and he'd given them too. He'd broken men's bones and scarred their faces but he'd never killed, not until he'd smashed his waster into Radek of Kalda's head, and it had been the warlock Saffran Kuy who'd made him do *that*. His hands hadn't been his own. Today he would have no such excuse.

Across the floor and through the crowd he glimpsed the face he was looking for. The face of the thief-taker, the one-time Prince of Tethis. Master Sy. And now he couldn't move. He was back in Deephaven again and Tasahre was bleeding in his arms and Master Sy was on the edge of Radek's ship with a waiting boat below him and no other place to go, sword-monks and city soldiers closing in a ring around them both. The monks would take his head for what he'd done. The thief-taker of Deephaven was dead, he had to be!

The face shifted and vanished and now all he could see were sailors and a crowd of snuffers, all moving together as though they were about to leave. He started to push his way towards them, his fingers gripping his stolen knife too tightly.

A hand clamped onto his shoulder, spinning him around. 'Well well. If it isn't our wandering skag.'

2

THE BITCH QUEEN'S HALL

Berren tried to pull away but the hand on his shoulder held him fast. 'You made a fool of me, little bitch-boy. You know what we do to deserters, skag?'

Berren stared up into the face of a sailor. The sailor grinned and showed off his rotten teeth. Klaas. Klaas had been on watch the night Berren had slipped over the side with his empty barrel and floated and bobbed and half-drowned his way to shore. It took Berren a second to remember, and yes, he knew *exactly* what they did to deserters. They flogged them. A hundred lashes, and if by some miracle their man was still alive after that, they cut the tendons in his ankles and his wrists and threw him over the side to watch him drown. His eyes darted around the tavern. Klaas turned too, looking for his friends – sailors came ashore in packs and if Klaas was here then there would be others from Berren's old ship.

As Klaas moved, Berren caught sight of a silver token around his neck. It made him think of another, long lost now but made of gold and with the imperial eagle of Aria stamped on one side and a sword and shield on the other. A prince had given it to him once and it was the most precious thing he'd ever had. For months he'd seen it move from one sailor to the next as they'd gambled together, and in all that time he'd never lost the hope that he might somehow get it back. And then one day it was gone. Stolen from a sailor by a pickpocket in some port Berren couldn't even name. After that he'd toyed at nights with the thought of slipping through the decks in the dark, of finding a knife and slitting the throat of every man left aboard. A fantasy but they deserved it, the lot of them. There wasn't a single sailor on his ship that he would have spared or even given a second thought.

'Hey! Lads!' Klaas stank of sour wine and sweat. Berren still had his stolen knife in his hand. It was right there begging him to use it. And so he did. He stabbed Klaas in the gut.

'Why you . . .' Klaas's face twisted with fury. He clenched his other fist. Then he let go of Berren and looked down at himself. Blood darkened his shirt, spreading out in an enormous stain over his belly. The expression on his face changed. Anger turned to shock and then to fear. 'You stabbed me! You royal hunt! You piece of horse filth! Skag!' His voice grew louder. 'Skag!'

Berren stood frozen. Vengeance had become the engine of his life, keeping him going. Vengeance for Tasahre, his fallen sword-monk, his love. For the few months since he'd escaped ashore it had stolen him food when he was starving and taken the shelter he needed when he was cold. It had foraged for clothes and shoes to keep him warm even if they were little more than rags. It had bullied and fought him a place among the destitute of the docks and carved him a name that others had learned to fear. It wrapped its arms around him at night and whispered him to sleep, and in the mornings it roused him and drove him on. Vengeance was his lover, strong and terrible, who did what needed to be done while he looked and he asked wherever he went: *Syannis of Tethis, where can I find him?*

And now his lover suddenly wasn't with him. He'd stabbed a man – killed him – and vengeance was nowhere to be found. He felt suddenly small and stupid and very afraid that he was about to die.

I killed a man. No warlock this time, no Saffran Kuy screaming in his head. Just him and a knife and his own hand holding it. The old instincts of a boy thief took over. He kicked Klaas between the legs as hard as he could. As Klaas doubled over, the silver token around his neck dangled free in the air. Berren snatched it and tore it away and screamed, 'That's what you get, fat man! That's what you get.' He pushed his way between the sailors who were beginning to turn and stare; as soon as he had space around him, he ran. The crowd of snuffers and the thief-taker were gone now, out through a door into the streets behind the Bitch Queen. Berren followed. He didn't look back. Behind him Klaas had found his voice again and was screaming his lungs out. Klaas was a bastard and he'd deserved it. But then if you looked at it like that, so did every sailor on his ship. So did an awful lot of people.

I killed a man. His own hand. He'd been thinking it for weeks, thinking of Master Sy, turning the idea over and over in his head and seeing what it looked like, and all the time he knew that when he came face to face with the thief-taker, he'd never really do it.

Or so he'd thought.

The streets at the back of the Bitch Queen were quiet. Noise echoed from the riot on the docks; now and then clusters of people came running past, fleeing from whatever was happening there. The snuffers were ahead of him, seven of them. Master Sy was in the middle but all Berren could see of him was the back of his head.

He'd seen a man flogged to death for stealing once. Klaas was a bastard and Klaas had deserved it. But all that blood ... and Tasahre kept coming at him, lying on the Emperor's Docks in Deephaven after Master Sy's sword had ripped open her throat. She would have told him that what he'd done was wrong. Terribly, terribly wrong.

He quickened his pace. Master Sy was a murderer. Master Sy had killed Tasahre. He still had the knife, fingers clenched around it, Klaas's blood on his hands. He had no idea what he was going to do now, none at all.

One of the snuffers cracked a joke. Master Sy threw back his head and laughed and the sound of him laughing filled Berren with a rage. The thief-taker didn't deserve to laugh, not any more, not after what he'd done! Berren started to run. 'Syannis!' he screamed. The snuffers' pace faltered. They all turned to see him racing towards them, the bloody knife in his outstretched hand. But the man wasn't Syannis after all. Whoever he was, he stared at Berren in amazement and then mouthed some word that Berren didn't hear. The other snuffers drew their swords. Their blades were short. Familiar. Berren skidded to a stop, but too close. Two of them sprang at him. He turned and tried to run away but the first one tackled him and then the second one piled on top, pinning him down. 'Who are you, boy?' hissed one in his ear. 'Answer me before I fillet you like a herring!'

'Wait!' The man he'd thought was Master Sy spoke. He was younger than the thief-taker and looked far less bitter. His voice was different too. More commanding. 'Let him up! Let me see him!'

'He could be working for Meridian, Prince.' The soldiers got off and Berren scrambled to his feet. He stared at the men around him.

Sailors were spilling out of the Bitch Queen behind him. One of them pointed. 'Him!'

'Who are you?' asked the man who looked like Master Sy but wasn't. Berren pushed past and raced away down the street, fleeing the mob that was spilling out of the tavern and howling for his blood. The snuffers didn't try to stop him.

Who are you? The question chased him down the alleys as he ran with a dozen murderous sailors at his heels.

3

THE PRINCE OF SWORDS

He'd stolen to stay alive. He'd picked pockets, he'd cut purses, he'd been chased by more angry sailors than he could count. He'd done what it took to keep himself from starving while he looked: *Syannis of Tethis, where can I find him?* But he'd never killed a man, never, not of his own free will. Never even cut one with a knife.

Until now.

And after all that, Syannis hadn't been Syannis at all. Maybe that meant he hadn't seen Syannis on the ship either. Perhaps the thief-taker was the ghost he was supposed to be.

He wandered through the alleys behind the docks, among the slums all piled on top of each other, with blood still on his hands and no idea what to do any more. His feet took him unasked to the abandoned bakery where he'd sheltered for the last few weeks. A dozen more of Kalda's homeless had claimed the place for as long as it took for the city soldiers to find them and flush them out. The others turned away as he washed the blood off his hands in a bucket of rainwater. They were all as lost as he was, but they'd learned, since he'd taken a place among them, not to be fooled by his size. *Small means quick*, Master Sy used to tell him. *Big men think they're going to win because they're big. Big men are easy.* The rags of skin and bone sheltering here were more desperate than big, but they still looked at

16

Berren with hungry eyes. He wasn't one of them. He was a dark-skin from across the sea, a sailor weathered by the sun and they were afraid of him.

He hadn't eaten today but he wasn't hungry. Others dribbled back in ones and twos, flushed with spoils from the riot on the docks. Some were grinning, pleased with their work. Others limped or had the red weals of a beating on their backs. Berren sat apart, listening to their talk. It had been bloody towards the end by the sound of it. The city could thank the rain that half the port hadn't gone up in flames.

He stared at his hands. Even clean, all he saw was the blood. When he closed his eyes to sleep he saw Tasahre again, dying in front of him. Eventually he drifted away with the old silver token he'd taken from Klaas held tight in his fingers. That was money, that was. Silver, a crown at least. Food for a week and maybe some old shoes. Priceless now. If any of the others saw it, they'd kill him to take it if they could.

Shouts woke him up in the black of night, ripping him away from his restless dreams. A door smashed and he heard a strangled cry: 'Slavers!' And in a flash he was on his feet, running again. He pushed the silver token into his mouth and bolted for the roof. Kalda made no bones about selling its unwanted to Taiytakei slavers when they came. A cruel death at the oars, long and slow and hard; but he'd spent half his life running from men like these and he knew how to escape them. They'd come through the doors and he'd leave across the rooftops and it would be as easy as that because it always was. No one slept up in the old bakery attic because half the roof was missing. In the wind and rain of a Kalda winter you'd get better shelter sleeping in an alley. Half the roof missing had made for cold nights too, but it also made for an easy way out.

The shouts from below were getting louder. He thought he heard his name but that couldn't be right. They spoke with funny accents here; it must have been someone else. For a moment he stopped. If the thief-taker wasn't here, if the thief-taker had *never* been here, then what was he doing? If he ran, where to? For what? Why not just turn round and let them take him?

He reached the attic and entered. An arm wrapped around his face and then someone was on his back, bearing him to the ground. He struggled furiously but a second man quickly pinned his legs.

'We've got him!' shouted the man on his back. Berren struggled to turn and look but he was held fast. *We've got him?* These weren't slavers simply clearing out the slums. They'd come for *him*, not for just anyone. Because of the sailor in the Bitch Queen?

'And the rest?'

'If they look like they can swing a sword then take them to the arms-master. Otherwise let them go.' The voice came closer and hissed in Berren's ear. 'You! Keep still! I won't hurt you if you keep still, but I won't mind if it turns out that I have to. Got that?'

Berren couldn't even nod. 'Who are you? What do you want? I've done nothing!'

'You were out the back of the Bitch yesterday. You had a knife in your hand with fresh blood on it and you'd just killed a man. You call that nothing, do you?'

'I ... No! Not me!' No, he didn't call that nothing. He might have called it a mistake. Might have.

The man on his back pushed down harder, twisting Berren's arm. 'Oh,' he said. 'So that was some other dark-skin boy with his first fluff on his face who happened to look exactly like you *and* talks the same funny way, was it? Pillock.'

Sailors got stabbed in the Bitch Queen every week.

Maybe their shipmates came looking for you but not a gang of snuffers. Sailors didn't have the money to buy snuffers. 'No! I don't ... I didn't ... I wasn't ...'

The man squeezed and Berren whimpered. 'You count your lucky stars that we're not city men. The prince doesn't get on with the people who rule here.'

A fearful understanding gripped him. This wasn't about Klaas – these were the snuffers he'd met outside with the man he'd mistaken for Master Sy!

Another voice joined the first. The one he remembered. 'Tarn! Let him up.'

'You sure about that, Prince? He'll run.'

'No, he won't. Get off him.'

The weight came off Berren's back and then his arms were free. He started to get up, already glancing left and right for the quickest way out. There were two men behind him and then the snuffer who looked like Master Sy in front. From this close, even in the dark, it clearly wasn't his old master, but there *was* something familiar about him. Berren rose slowly to a crouch. He'd have to bolt past not-quite-Master-Sy. Then he could jump the alley between the bakery and the next row of run-down old houses. With a good lunge he'd get straight onto the roof. These snuffers with their armour and their swords, they wouldn't make it. If they jumped, they'd fall. He'd lured men to their deaths that way before. That wasn't killing though, not like in the Bitch Queen. No accounting for people being stupid.

Not-quite-Master-Sy was giving him a strange look. Intense. 'Syannis is right. You do look exactly like him.'

'I look like who, sir?' His legs tensed ready to bolt, but waited now. *Syannis?* The man didn't just look like the thief-taker, then? He *knew* him!

Not-quite-Master-Sy shook his head. 'If you want to run then run. Otherwise answer my questions and then maybe I'll answer yours. Tell me who you are.'

Berren hesitated. He had to ask. *Had* to. 'You know Syannis, sir?'

'Do *you*?'

'Is he ... is he alive?'

'Stop dancing with me, boy. You're Berren. From Deep-haven. You can't be anyone else. But why are you here in Kalda? Why are you looking for him all of a sudden?'

All of a sudden? Berren shook his head. 'I don't know who you mean, sir. I'm Jerrin. Jerrin Nine-Fingers.' He held up his hands so Not-quite-Master-Sy could see where the tip of one of his fingers was missing. It was the first name that came into his head.

The man looked past him. 'Tarn? Think you can find a good price for a slave? A slave who can handle a sword but happens to be really stupid? Apparently I made a mistake.' He turned away. Berren still didn't run; if he squinted then he could almost believe he was face to face with his old thief-taker master. *Why? Why did you kill Tasahre?* And then he'd either throw his arms around the thief-taker's neck with relief or stab him there and then and kill him. He just didn't know which it would be.

Not-quite-Master-Sy started to walk past him back towards the steps.

'You're right, sir,' said Berren slowly. 'My name *is* Berren, sir. Not Jerrin.'

'Imagine that. The surprise overwhelms me.' A grim smile spread across the man's face. It made him look even more like Master Sy, but he had a playfulness that the thief-taker had never had, and there was no anger there, no bit-terness. 'I don't know how you got here and I don't know how you found us, but I do know who you are, Berren. What matters to me most of all is that yesterday you had a knife in your hand when you called Syannis's name. What did you mean to do with it?'

Berren couldn't look him in the eye. He stared at his feet. 'I … I don't know.'

'I think you need to do a little better than that.'

'Honestly! Sometimes I …' Berren shook his head. 'I just don't know any more.'

'Syannis is my brother, Berren. I hope you'll understand. It wasn't easy or cheap tracking you back here after that nice little surprise you gave us outside the Bitch Queen. What am I to do with you, eh?'

'I have no quarrel with you, sir.'

'Really? But I might have one with you. So tell me again about that knife you were holding and what you meant to do with it.' He glanced behind Berren's back, mouth twitching. Berren sprang. He almost reached the edge of the open attic where he could have jumped but an arm caught him around the waist. He struggled, but there were three snuffers now and they were all stronger than him. He still managed to land a good punch or two. The man who looked like Syannis reeled away, his nose bloodied.

'Gods, man! Tarn, bag him! If he gives you any more trouble, hit him until he stops.' He shook his head. 'That what Syannis taught you, or was that your sword-monks?'

'Who are you!' Berren fought and squirmed but it was no use.

'Some people call me the Prince of Swords. Question is, Berren, who are *you*?'

4

BROTHERS

The snuffers forced a bag over Berren's head and tied it round his neck. When he kicked at them, they held him and punched him until he stopped; then they carried him down the steps of the bakery. On the street outside they put a rope around him and led him away. The night was quiet and everyone else had fled; the people who lived in the slums kept to themselves after dark and knew well enough to stay away from gangs of armed men. Still, even blind Berren could tell something about where they were taking him. They turned uphill, the roads growing steeper and steeper while the smell of the sea turned into the smell of smoke from the wood and the dung that the city folk burned to keep warm through the winter. The higher slopes then, where the rich folk lived.

They stopped. He was pushed across a threshold, almost tripping on it, then manhandled across a floor and up some steps. They sat him on a chair and took the bag off his head and he was sitting across a table from the man who looked like Master Sy. There were two snuffers beside the prince and two more standing by the only door. A lamp burned on the table. Lanterns hung around the room.

'More light!' said the man who looked like the thief-taker. 'And get some bread and some clean water. We can at least be civilised about this.' He took a deep breath and then stared hard at Berren. 'Well. What to do, eh? What to do? I thought about leaving you be, but Syannis wouldn't have it. You ran right past him in the Bitch Queen. Close enough to touch, he said. He thought you were a ghost.'

'He's really here?' Berren blurted out.

Not-quite-Master-Sy frowned. 'He was. He's gone now – left the city on the evening tide – but before he left he was kind enough to ask me to find you. So here we are, stuck with each other. I know who *you* are, Berren of Deephaven. You were once his apprentice. As for me, I'm his brother. Prince Talon of Tethis.' He paused. 'I would say "at your service" but under the circumstances,' he shrugged, 'probably not.'

Berren's mouth fell open. 'I knew he had a brother.' One door and he had to get past two men to be through it, plus the two snuffers behind the desk and the prince himself. His eyes searched for other ways.

'He had ... *has* ... two.' Prince Talon's brow furrowed; he shook himself. 'What in the name of the four gods, Berren of Deephaven, am I supposed to do with you?'

'Let me go, sir. I'm nothing to you.'

Talon laughed. 'Maybe so, but I can't just set you free. Tarn here thinks I should dump you in the sea with stones around your ankles and frankly I'm inclined to agree. But you did kill Radek of Kalda and I could kiss you for that. So. What do I do with you?'

Beside him the snuffer called Tarn scowled. 'He came at you with a knife, Prince.'

'He did. Be fair though – he thought I was Syannis.' Then he frowned. 'As if that really makes a difference.'

'But I was right! Master Sy really is alive then?' asked Berren.

'Well *you* seemed to think so.' Talon raised an eyebrow. 'You and your knife. The one that I keep coming back to in the hope you'll say something useful about what it was *for*.'

Berren hardly heard. 'I didn't believe it, not really. I

didn't see how he could get away. And after what he did ...
Even if they didn't catch him there and then, they'd never
let him escape. They'd have chased him to the end of the
world. They'd have taken his head or sent him to the mines
or something. They couldn't let him go, not after ...' He
couldn't finish. 'And then I saw him on a ship and so I came
looking, and I was looking and looking for months, and
then people said he'd be in the Bitch Queen, and there he
was, only then outside it wasn't him, it was you. I thought
I'd been seeing things. Ghosts. None of it real. But he *is*
alive. Right?'

Talon sighed. 'Yes, he is. Syannis left Deephaven just
like you did.' He exchanged a glance with Tarn. 'There
was some ... trouble, he said.'

'I didn't *leave*. I was jumped by a press-gang!'

Talon cocked his head. 'Really? Syannis said you ran
away after you killed Radek. Press-ganged? Explains
why he never found you.' He looked at Berren's face and
scowled. '*Did* you run away after you killed Radek? Not
that *I* much care but it does seem to trouble Syannis.'

'Sort of. Well I was going to. After ...'

'After ...?' Talon's eyes narrowed as if looking for
something inside Berren's head. 'Syannis thinks you killed
Radek for *him*, but you didn't, did you? I see no pride in
you at all. Just shame and fear.' He growled. 'I'm missing
a part of this story, aren't I? Something Syannis never
thought to mention. I think you'd better tell me what it is.'

Berren saw Tasahre again, covered in blood. He pinched
his lip. 'Master Sy killed ...' He couldn't make her name
come out. A quiver ran through him. 'Didn't he tell you
what he did?'

'He killed whom?'

'My teacher.' Gods but it was hard to talk about her
without screaming, even now.

Talon screwed up one eye and peered at Berren. 'He

24

didn't say anything about that. Just that you were the one who'd killed Radek. And that after that you ran away.'

'I ran because Master Sy ... killed my teacher.'

'I see. And he mattered to you, did he?'

Berren couldn't answer, could only look away and try to will back the tears. 'She,' he whispered.

'*She?*' Talon blinked. 'Oh dear gods. Your face ...' He sat back into his chair. 'I think I see.'

'She was my friend.' Friend wasn't the right word but it would do. No reason for anyone else to know any more. 'She was a sword-monk.'

'Sun and moon!' Talon stared at him in wonder. 'Well, there's a thing. Syannis has no idea. So Syannis killed your ... *friend* and you ran away straight into the arms of a press gang? Is that what I'm supposed to think?'

Berren nodded. 'Same night.'

'And that was all, what? A little over two years ago now. And how long have you been in Kalda looking for him?'

'Few months.'

Talon shook his head. He rocked forward in his chair. 'While I'm deciding what to do with you, you can tell me what you know of Saffran Kuy.'

The warlock. Berren shivered. He couldn't speak.

'You look like you just ate a lemon.' Talon didn't smile. 'Tarn, go and find out why it's taking so long to get some more candles! It's not as though they're mountain lilies, for pity's sake!'

While Tarn got up and left, Berren took a moment to gather himself, to push away Tasahre and everything that came with her. 'I used to think there were good men and there were bad men,' he said, 'and that most men, when it came down to it, were bad ones. But Saffran Kuy was something else. He was far more than bad. He was wicked. Evil ...' He pushed his lips together, struggling to find words for the warlock who'd made him cut out a piece of

25

his own soul, who'd made him murder a man he didn't even know. He held up the stump of the little finger on his left hand. 'That's the least of what he did to me.'

'Saffran Kuy is a monster, is he?' Berren nodded and Talon smiled. 'Well then, Berren of Deephaven, I suppose I won't be dumping your headless corpse in the sea tonight after all. But you'd best tell me the rest of your story while I decide what I *am* going to do with you. And you can end it with exactly what you were going to do with that knife. The truth, mind. Lie to me and I'll know it.'

So Berren told him about Master Sy, about how the Headsman had come to Deephaven and murdered the thief-taker's old friend Kasmin and how Master Sy had hunted him down no matter what he had to do. He told Talon about the priests and the sword-monks and Tasahre and what the warlock had done to them both. When he got to the coming of Radek and the fight aboard his ship, he had to push back the tears again. By the end, with Radek dead and Tasahre bleeding out at his feet, he couldn't stop them any more. Talon listened in silence. Outside, through the windows, the sky was starting to lighten. Dawn was coming. They'd been up all night.

'I'll tell you a bit more about Radek one day,' Talon said after a long silence. 'Let's go onto the roof and watch the sunrise. I always find that helps.' He stood up and Berren followed him out of the door into a hallway, and then through another to a balcony. The slope of the city faced south and east, and in winter the sun came up over the cliffs of the canyon. Talon stood beside Berren. The sky on the horizon was already turning pink. For a moment they were alone. 'And then you got press-ganged?'

Berren stared out over the water, lost in memories. There was more, but the rest was his own, to be held and cherished. He shrugged. 'We sailed into Kalda one day. I

26

saw a ship come by next to mine. There was a man on the deck. It was Master Sy. I couldn't just do *nothing*.'

'You were going to kill him?'

'It was all his fault, everything that happened to me.'

'Really?'

'And then I stabbed that man in the Bitch Queen. He was from my ship and he deserved it, but now ...' He stared across the city. He could run. Run right from here. Leap across the rooftops and down to the streets, into the alleys and away. They'd never catch him. But he didn't. Not yet. 'Now I don't know any more.' He bit his lip.

'It won't change anything.'

'I know.'

'They caught him. I'll tell you that much. Syannis, I mean. You were right: they did hunt him and they caught him and they sent him to the mines. He told me that and told me he deserved it too. I didn't understand what he meant and he wouldn't say, but I suppose perhaps now I do. Anyway he never got there. Someone helped him escape and put him on a ship and sent him back to me. He won't say who but I know it was Kuy. Warlocks.' He spat. 'The sooner someone puts an end to them the better.'

Berren nodded. 'Give me a sword and tell me how.' *Them? There's more than one?*

Orange fire burst across the horizon and the first brilliant rays of the sun struck the city. 'He's sorry,' said Talon after a while longer. 'Sorry for the way things ended between you.' Out across the estuary, the waves began to glitter. 'He doesn't say it, but I see it in his face.'

'That doesn't change anything either. She's still dead.'

'I suppose it doesn't.' Talon took a deep breath and let it out slowly. 'What now, Berren? I wish I'd never seen you. I wish I'd left you where you were. But I did neither of those things and so here we are. Syannis is my brother. I can't simply let you go, not if it's going to be with a knife in

27

your hand. I could murder you – that would be simple and quick but I think that would haunt me. If I could then I would make things back as they were, but I can't bring the dead back to life. I don't think anyone can do that. So what, then? What would be fair, do you think?'

Berren didn't answer. Talon was right about not bringing the dead back to life. Past that, he couldn't think.

'I'll send you home,' Talon said after a while. 'That's what I should do. I should put you on a ship back to Deephaven and in return you will swear to me that you will never cross the seas again.'

'There's nothing in Deephaven for me any more,' said Berren.

'There's nothing for you here either. I'll get you some proper clothes and send you off with a purse full of silver and the rest will be up to you. That's as right as I can make it. Start a new life and forget the old one. Yours if you want it. Otherwise I give you to Tarn and the sea.'

Berren shrugged. A purse and a set of clothes? Couldn't argue that wasn't better than being dumped in the sea with a rock tied around his ankles. As to what he did once he'd taken Talon's gifts, well, that was up to him.

'I don't know,' he said. 'But thank you.'

'No. Not "I don't know." I want your oath, boy, and I want it now.'

'Then I swear. When you send me away, I'll never come back.'

'Swear on the memory of your sword-monk.'

Berren swallowed hard. 'I swear. On her memory. I will not come back.' He clenched his fists.

'There won't be any ships crossing the ocean until spring now.' Talon turned to look at him. He met Berren's eyes with a stare that Berren couldn't answer. 'You'll be one of us for now, Berren of Deephaven, but understand this: I will be kind to you while you are here. I will look after you because it is a little right to set against what you have suffered. But do not mistake my kindness for trust. My brother is still my brother, and if you run from me with a knife in your hand then I will send Tarn and his company after you and I will not ask them to be kind.' The steel in his eyes twinkled to a grin and he slapped Berren on the shoulder. 'Now, in the name of the four gods, let's share a drink and get some damned sleep. Unless you'd prefer to return to where I found you?'

5

THE CITY WITH NO DOORS

B erren tried to sleep. He tossed and turned restlessly on a pallet of straw tucked in a tiny storeroom full of shelves and empty jars. The blankets Talon had given him scratched his skin. Light filtered in under the door. The silence of the early morning nagged at him and cold draughts of winter air danced across his face. Everything was *wrong* and all he could do was doze. Before long he heard the noises of men moving elsewhere in the house, and then the first smells of cooking slunk through the gap under the storeroom door and wrapped themselves around him. Hot fat! Warm bread! Butter! He couldn't remember the last time he'd eaten well.

No, that wasn't true. He could remember it exactly. It had been two years ago, give or take. The afternoon before the Festival of the Flames in Deephaven with nothing much to do and a pocket full of pennies. He'd eaten pickled fish and warm sour-bread and it had been delicious.

He got up and followed the smell. His nose led him to a hall with a table long enough to sit twenty men, although it was mostly empty. Talon was already there with a few others. They were tucking into the biggest breakfast Berren had ever seen.

'Berren! Berren of Deephaven!' Talon clapped his hands and waved Berren over. 'Sit! Eat! I bet it's been a while since you had a meal that left your belly bulging.'

Berren met his eye. 'Years.' He sat down at the end of the table.

'No, no, come over here.' Berren got up again. A part of him still wondered whether he should be running away, but a larger part was certain that, whatever the answer, it could wait until after breakfast. 'We're going to have to do something about you,' Talon said. 'Look at you!'

Berren looked. His feet were bare; so were his legs below the knees and his arms below the shoulders. The rest of him was covered with a mishmash of whatever he'd managed to get hold of, patched together with pieces of sacking. 'I look like a beggar,' he said. He'd not really thought about it before. All sailors looked worn and battered, didn't they?

'No,' said Talon. He pushed a trencher towards Berren and piled it with sliced sausage and pieces of fried fish, then waved at the pitchers on the table. 'There's goat milk and ale. And no, you don't look like a beggar, you look like what you are – a ship's skag. Beggars dress better. We'll have to do something about that if you're going to be one of us, and I can hardly send you back to Deephaven looking like that. Tarn, you can help.'

Tarn glowered at Berren. *One of us* – what did that mean? Who were *us*? Because the men he saw breakfasting around him were surely snuffers. Half a dozen were sitting here at the table, but Talon had had more with him in the night. What did a man do with so many snuffers?

He shrugged the question away. Whatever Talon wanted from him, it couldn't be worse than being a ship's skag. If it got him a good breakfast and some new clothes, so much the better. He gnawed at the slices of dried sausage. The last time he'd had sausage it had been a Mirrormere Hot, the day before Master Sy had sent him to live in the temple. The memory of its burn made his mouth water even more.

Tarn was giving Talon a dirty look. 'I have to buy him clothes now?' he grumbled. 'What am I, his mother?'

31

Talon paused between mouthfuls of egg mixed in with strips of meat and some sort of deep green vegetable that Berren had never seen before. 'Fine, fine. I'll take him.' He glanced up at Berren. 'You can tell me how Kalda compares to Deephaven. I travel a lot in this part of the world but I've never been across the Ocean of Storms. I hear they do things differently in Aria. Syannis told me some of it, but I'm sure he missed all the best parts. How many taverns did he take you to? Not one, I bet.'

'He took me to a few. There was one where we used to meet. I fell asleep the first time we went there.' The Eight, where the thief-takers used to gather behind the courthouse with the justicars and the witch-breakers. He pinched his mouth. Thinking about Deephaven only made him want to cry and shout and clench his fists. The Eight hadn't meant much back then, but now it made him think of the other thief-takers, of Justicar Kol and all the others, men who'd never exactly been his friends but had been the closest thing until he'd met Tasahre. And then there was the Barrow of Beer and surly old Kasmin ...

'Brothels?'

Berren shook his head. 'Master Sy didn't hold with them. I grew up next to one though.'

'You did? Lucky man.' Talon smiled.

Berren wondered about that. His memories were mostly of colours and of smells and of comfort. The women there had treated Master Hatchet's boys with a strange mixture of tolerance and scorn. He hadn't really understood what happened there. He knew what they did, but he didn't *understand* it. That had come much later. 'I suppose,' he muttered. Thoughts like that led straight to Tasahre. A gloom settled around him. He stared at his food while the snuffers came and went, sitting down to eat and getting up again when they were done. They moved with confidence and treated Talon with a casual deference, like he was their sergeant, not like he was a prince at all.

Talon smiled, a real grin dancing with mischief, and his eyes glittered. 'The past can be a terrible burden. You learn, Berren, to put it aside. It takes time but it comes.'

He chuckled. Berren's eyes snapped up. 'I don't *want* to put it aside and I don't *want* to forget.'

'I didn't say *forget*.' The air changed in an instant, Talon suddenly sharp as a knife with the air of a prowling tiger, filled with a menacing hunger. 'You know Syannis and I had to flee our home, don't you? Our father and most of our family were killed by Radek and his men. We lost our friends. Everything. I wonder sometimes which one of them has my old room. Does Meridian sleep in my father's bed? I imagine that he does, and then I wonder who has mine. Princess Gelisya? Or perhaps Radek slept there when he came by to rest from his hunting of us.' His grin grew wider, baring his teeth to show off a vicious glee. 'You put paid to that, though.' Then he shook his head as if throwing something off. 'No, I didn't say *forget*, but you can learn to put it to one side, Berren, and you better had because if you don't then it eats you. Syannis, he never threw it off. You've seen what it does. Find a new life and make that be the one that matters. You still remember the old one. You just learn to put it in its place.' Talon looked distant for a moment as though he was staring straight through Berren and the wall behind him, and through the cliffs too and far, far away out to sea. Then his eyes came crashing back. 'Eat up! We have clothes to buy!'

The days passed. Talon laughed and joked as though he and Berren had known each other for half their lives. He showed Berren around Kalda and taught him the ways of this part of the world. Somewhere very far away there was an emperor like the emperor in Aria, only this one was called the sun-king and he'd lived for ever and could never die. He was powerful beyond imagining and he ruled over half the world. Kalda belonged to him, and the city's king wasn't really a king at all, and changed depending on the whims of that faraway court. Talon waved a hand over all that – too boring to talk about; instead, he whispered glee-fully about the scandals that surrounded the high priests of the temples and the secret vices of the merchant princes. In the evenings they went drinking, and wherever they went, people knew him: the Prince of Swords. Men clapped him on the shoulder and bought him drinks or else glared at him from a distance. Women draped themselves over him. A handful of snuffers always came too, with Tarn never far from Talon's side. When Talon talked about soldiering, his eyes almost glowed. He might even have become a friend if Berren had been able to see Talon without seeing Syannis and, with the thief-taker, always Tasahre. That was the last gift that both Syannis and Deephaven had given him, and why he could never go back.

'Did Syannis bring Saffran Kuy back with him?' he asked one day. 'Was he here too?'

For a moment Talon looked as if Berren had pulled a knife and stabbed him. 'Syannis and I don't agree on much,' he said at last. 'We argue and bicker all the time. Sometimes we can't stand each other for weeks. But that's what brothers do, stand each other, and Syannis kept us alive. I was ten, you see. Syannis was fifteen. For three years we ran from city to city, country to country, looking for somewhere that would have us. Somewhere we could be safe when all we had were our names and what little we'd been able to carry. He kept me alive. I owe him a lot. And we would *both* like our kingdom back, even if it was only a little one. But Saffran Kuy...' He shook his head. 'No, as far as I know Syannis did not bring any warlocks back with him from Deephaven. I pray to the gods that it stays that way but I fear it probably won't. Something runs between those two. Some unpleasant cord that binds them.' He smiled and then laughed again. 'It's actually nice to have someone who doesn't think the sun shines out of his arse. You know we've got another brother? Or half-brother anyway.'

Berren nodded. 'The one who looks like me.'

'Aimes the idiot, yes. Looks a lot like you indeed. When he was little he got kicked in the head by a horse. Syannis acts like he was to blame. He has a mad idea that Saffran Kuy can find a way to make our little brother whole again.' He stopped and turned to look Berren up and down. 'In the end I think that's how you got to him. When he saw you, he saw Aimes. It's hard to imagine him wanting an apprentice. I can't see him being a very good master.'

'He was...' Berren didn't know what to say to that. 'He tried to be.' That was fair. Master Sy had always tried. Hadn't always managed it, but most of the time he hadn't been too bad at all. 'He taught me a lot.' And that was fair too, and yet all Berren could think of was Tasahre, of holding her hand. Of feeling her heartbeat stop.

Talon smiled, pushing the tension away. 'Oh, Syannis was always good at trying. The thing he never learned was how to stop, and the gods know how much of a pain in the arse it can be to live with someone who's constantly trying to be perfect.' He shook his head. 'Tethis isn't much more than a castle with a few fields around it. It's not worth much, but now that Syannis is back in the game, some tiny little thing will happen and the dam will break. Blood will flood our little kingdom once more. You'll see murder.' He sighed. Then he looked at Berren and pursed his lips. 'Well, *you* won't, if you've got any sense, because *you'll* be on a ship back to where you came from. You wouldn't like to take him with you, would you?' Talon's lips laughed as he spoke, but his eyes were still and dark and spoke of storms.

A week passed and then another and Berren found himself sitting on a jetty in the small hours one morning, looking across the water at the ships in the dark, his head full of beer-fog and a silly smile on his face. When he looked up into the horseshoe of the city rising around him, he could see the whole of it all at once, smudged among the cliffs, a stain floating where smoke from the night fires still hung in the air waiting for a morning breeze to pick it up and carry it away. Talon sat beside him.

'Makes you feel small, doesn't it?' murmured the prince. 'The only city in the world with no gates and no roads in and out, and look at the size of it. Oh, there are paths up the cliffs and paths along the coast, but the only way in or out for anything bigger than a mule is by sea. Kalda, the city with no doors. How she's grown.' He stretched and pointed across the docks to the forts by the river mouth. 'They have black-powder cannons there now – gifts from the Taiytakei. But who is it, do you think, that the merchant princes fear? It's people like us, and yet here we are, right in the middle of them.' He stood up and grinned and stared at the slope of the city. 'Do you think you could run all the way up there without stopping?'

Berren shook his head. 'Nah.' That sounded like a thing the sword-monks would have done.

'Spring Festival isn't far away. Another month and you get your ship home. There are things I need to do before then. The sort of things that would leave you so bored you'd probably drown yourself in the river to get away. There's a sword-master up near the cliffs who makes a happy living teaching the rich young men of Kalda how to kill each other. Tarn will be spending his days there now. I thought you might join him. Scrape some of the barnacles off your own edges before you leave. Seems more to your temperament than sitting around the house watching me bite my own arm off trying to get everything ready for us to move.' He put his hands on his hips. 'Or does reading great lists of goods and numbers strike more of a chord? What do you say?'

'That I'm grateful for everything,' said Berren carefully. Talon could say what he liked about a ship back to Deephaven. He'd already made his own decision about that.

'Really?' Talon arched an eyebrow. 'Thing is, Berren, I said you'd start first thing this morning, and then I forgot, and now we're down here and we're drunk and we've had no sleep.' He pointed up the slope of the city. 'And we need to be up there. For sunrise. And that's not far off now.'

He set off jogging down the jetty and across the open space of the docks out in front of the Bitch Queen. When he was halfway, he turned and waved at Berren.

'Well, are you coming?'

6

MEMORY AND A FLASH OF
UNDERSTANDING

Berren slowly caught up with Talon as they ran through the city, laughing. Talon led him up to a fine house, high on one of the steeper side slopes with a crossed-swords sign drawn by the doors. When they reached it, the Prince staggered to a stop and leaned against a wall, bent over, hands holding his knees and gasping for breath. Berren stood beside him, breathing heavily.

'You're not ... as out of breath ... as I am,' panted Talon. 'Not fair!'

Beside the house was a narrow alley, wide enough for one person but not for two. When Talon had his breath back, that's where he went. It led around the back and up some steps to a low building with no walls and a roof held up by two rows of ornate wooden pillars. Inside, men with swords were sparring – one of them was Tarn – but when Berren stopped to stare, Talon pulled him onwards. They walked past the edge of the fighting square towards the back of the house, and a man with silvery hair came out the other way clutching a handful of wasters. Wooden practice swords. Despite everything else, Berren felt a tiny surge of anticipation at the sight of them.

As soon as the silver-haired man saw Talon, he dropped the wasters and embraced him. 'The Prince of War!' he said. 'How's your brother?'

'I haven't seen him for weeks. He was well when I did. I'm surprised he didn't drop by.'

'Well, he didn't. Give him my good wishes when you see him.'

'I will.' Talon laughed. 'Any last lessons?'

The man with the silver hair laughed back. 'I should imagine he'd be teaching me by now!'

The prince pushed Berren forward. 'This is my ... This is Berren. Let's just say I'm keeping an eye on him. I'd like him instructed along with Tarn.'

The man with the silver hair peered at Berren and frowned. 'Berren, is it?' He snorted. 'Whatever you say. Doesn't look like a Berren to me. Sure he's not a relative?'

Talon's foot twitched. 'There's a passing resemblance, if you happen to overlook the colour of his skin. Berren is from Aria.'

'If you say so.' The man with the silver hair shrugged. 'So what do you want?'

'All day, every day. He's had training. He was squired to Syannis for a while and he worked with some sword-monks.'

The silver-haired man blinked. 'Now *that's* not some-thing I get to hear very often. Aria, eh? Why isn't he still there, then?' He shook his head. 'Not my business. Never mind. How long?'

'A month, same as Tarn. Do the best you can for him in that time.'

'And then he'll be joining you in the companies?'

'And then he'll be going back where he came from, but the world's a funny place. Who can say for sure what their future will be, eh?'

'I see. So ...'

'So you'll be teaching him how to fight in a battle, with real swords and armour and chaos and blood and chopped-off bits of people everywhere, as you so picturesquely put it. Where being alive at the end is what matters and never mind the rest.'

There was more, but Berren was too busy battling yawns and wrestling with the cloud of a hangover and exhaustion and digesting the bit about battles and swords. *Companies?* That wasn't the first time he'd heard that word around Talon, and hadn't Master Sy once said something about mercenaries? Talon had carefully not let on anything at all about what he was doing in Kalda, but that would explain why he had so many snuffers around him!

'Berren.' Talon was looking at him again. Berren brought himself to attention. 'This is Sword-Master Silvestre. He taught me how to fight. He was taught by the great Mistress Shalari herself, who also taught Syannis, and I know you've seen Syannis fight. Shalari was the best tutor in the Far Realms, and now Silvestre is the best tutor in Kalda.'

The sword-master snorted. 'You know that's not true.'

'The best for *my* purposes, then.'

Silvestre looked Berren up and down. 'So, have you ever used a sword properly before? And I don't mean farting about with a waster, I mean a proper sword. Steel on steel. Sparks flying. Losing the odd finger. That sort of thing.'

Berren shook his head. 'No. Always wasters.'

'In a month?' Silvestre turned back to Talon. Talon nod-ded but Silvestre shook his head. 'Take him somewhere else. I'm not going to teach him to get himself killed. If he ends up in a battle then put him in some proper armour and keep him away from cavalry and crossbows. I don't care who he's trained with or how; if it was all practice drills then I can't do anything in that time except make him a liability.'

Talon leaned forward. He whispered something in the sword-master's ear. Berren didn't hear what it was but from the way the man's face changed it must have been something startling – too startling to be a threat or a bribe. The sword-master was looking at him again with a new expression, more penetrating than the last.

'All right, all right, we'll take a look and see what he can do. No promises, mind. If he fights like a donkey then he's still going to be a donkey when you take him away.' He looked back to Talon. 'When?'

'Today. Now.'

'Now? He's drunk! And so are you!'

'Man needs to be able to defend himself even when he's a few sheets to the wind.'

Silvestre laughed. 'And don't I know it! Man needs to be able to defend himself when he's passed out in the street, but that's not to say I can teach him how to do it. Still, does he even have his own sword?' The sword-master didn't wait for an answer. 'Come on then, so-called-Berren. Go out to the practice yard. Someone will attend to you shortly.'

Berren jumped up. Real swords? It almost made him laugh to think how long he'd yearned for something like this, back when he'd been the thief-taker's apprentice in Deephaven. Now it was here, what did he feel? Nothing. He leaned against one of the wooden columns around the fighting square, watching two men he didn't know spar while Tarn shouted at them. The swords were wooden wasters like the ones he remembered, only here they were carved to look more like real swords. The fighters had helmets and heavy padding on their arms and down their front. 'Feet! Use your feet!' Tarn yelled. Berren sighed. He had clothes and boots of his own, shelter, good food, even a little money, and now it seemed he would be learning swords again. Two years it had taken, but the sun was starting to shine again at last, and yet he barely even felt it. What he felt, when he looked, was numb. What he felt was the hole where Tasahre used to be. A month from now, one way or another, he'd go chasing after Master Sy, not even sure any more why he was doing it, just sure beyond anything that he had to. Maybe by the time he left, he'd know what was driving him. A month to find an answer to that, then, and to gather his strength and some money and whatever else he might need. He wondered briefly what Talon had said to the sword-master to change his mind.

'Berren!' Tarn was beckoning him, holding a waster. He had a nasty smile on his face. The two men in the fighting square raised their swords to salute one another and then withdrew, sitting heavily down at the edge of the square and wiping their brows. Berren squinted and Tarn started to laugh. 'Come on! Or are you afraid of me?'

You're trying to make me angry? Berren rubbed his eyes. He walked smartly across to Tarn and snatched one of the wasters out of his hands. When he held it, he couldn't help but smile. It had been such a long time, and yet it felt like it was a part of him at once, an extension of his arm. He twirled it, wondering how much more he'd remember. Then he walked to the middle of the fighting square and held it out in front of him, straight and level. He pointed the tip of it at Tarn the way he used to practise with Tasahre. Either this waster was lighter than the one he'd used among the sword-monks or else the years at sea had made him stronger. All the weariness, the stuffiness inside his head, all of that was draining away. He felt sharp like lightning and as pitilessly cold as ice.

Tarn made a face. He stepped into the square too, holding his waster loose, peering at Berren and looking puzzled. 'What in the name of Kelm's dick are you doing? You think you're some sort of duellist? This is a battlefield, son. There are people fighting and dying all around you.' He pointed to Berren's left. 'There. You've got a friend there and he's face to face with someone you've never seen before who wants to kill both of you. Their hilts are locked together. They're pushing and snarling and there's a madness in

42

their eyes and – oh – someone else just skewered your friend with a spear and now he's dead.' Tarn paced back and forth outside Berren's reach. Berren tracked him with the point of his waster. 'On the other side of you, a man you've known for years has just had his arm hacked clean off. He's been doing this for longer than you, eight years with this his ninth. Each year he's put his pay somewhere safe. Like most of your friends here, he thinks he's going to stop this soldiering one day and buy himself a piece of land and start a farm. He'll marry a nice girl and raise a fistful of sons who'll never see a sword in their lives if he has anything to do with it. *Unlike* the rest of your friends, he means it. And now you've got his blood spraying over your face. One-armed farmers aren't much use. Neither are one-armed soldiers, but that probably doesn't matter since he's going to bleed out before your eyes. You could stop to finish him off. A mercy maybe, but no, you're standing there, doing nothing, pointing your sword out like some prick. Maybe it doesn't matter about your friends – you've got plenty more after all – but now there's arrows raining down and they're scurrying away, the ones who don't get skewered as they flee.'

Tarn stopped pacing. He stared at Berren, almost in disbelief. In all the time he'd been talking, Berren's sword hadn't wavered at all. Ten minutes a day, every day, rain or shine, Tasahre had made him do this and he'd never quite understood why. He'd thought it had been about building the strength in his arm. Maybe it was, but he could see now that it had been more than that. The look in Tarn's face showed him. This was a fight he'd already won.

He started to move, one slow step at a time, the end of the waster kept pointed right between Tarn's eyes. Tarn backed away and Berren moved after him. After all this time his footwork was sloppy. Tasahre would have scolded him.

Tarn circled, keeping space behind him and his waster up on guard, wise enough not to be backed into a corner. Berren lunged. He couldn't jump the way a sword-monk could jump, but it was still quick enough and far enough to take Tarn by surprise. He blocked Berren's waster awkwardly, tried a riposte but he was much too slow. Berren knocked it aside, tapped Tarn hard on the hip as he turned his parry into a cut and then, in the same motion, let the end of his waster come to rest touching the side of Tarn's neck.

'Your friend who taught you everything that matters lies at your feet,' he said. 'You have her blood on your hands. You watch as it pools on the wooden deck beneath your feet. She's dead because you interfered. Because you thought you could make something better. Because you couldn't stay out of what wasn't your business.' He let the sword stay touching Tarn's neck for another second and then backed away and gave the sword-monk salute. Tarn stared at him, eyes wide.

'Gods,' he murmured. 'Who are you?'

Berren took a deep breath and rubbed his head. Now the fight was done, his hangover was coming back.

'Well, Syannis didn't teach him that,' he heard Silvestre say behind him.

'No, he certainly didn't.'

There was awe in Talon's voice. The sword-master sniffed. 'Well he's clearly not a donkey. Feet were ropey but we can work on that.' He clapped Berren on the shoulder. 'Welcome to my house, Berren. When we're training, you can call me Sword-Master or Teacher. When we're done, then you can call me Master Silvestre and pay for my beer.'

Berren only half heard him. He was smiling. In the fight with Tarn he'd felt Tasahre beside him, watching him, guiding him, moulding his shape and his movement as she used to do. For a moment he'd found a feeling that he'd forgotten could exist. Inside his head he'd felt at peace.

7

THE COMPANY OF MERCENARIES

Berren got up early in the morning every day after that and trudged up the slope to the house of Silvestre, arriving before dawn. Tarn came with him. For two hours they exercised, sometimes on their own, sometimes with others. It was a familiar routine, like the one he'd grown used to among the sword-monks of Deephaven. After that came breakfast and then Silvestre would sit them all down and talk. Sometimes he'd talk about swords, sometimes he'd talk about wars, sometimes about anything at all. As a teacher he was all fire and passion and temper, as different from Tasahre as Berren could imagine. He'd fought in a dozen battles, he'd spent what sounded like half his life as a pirate, half of it as a thief, most of it as a soldier and almost all of it chasing after one woman or another. With the scraps and scrapes he'd been in, it was a wonder he was still alive; yet whenever they took a break to rest and drink, another story would come of how he'd been chased through the straits of somewhere or other by the sun-king's navy, or how he'd stolen the first farscope in Caladir from the Taiytakei emissary there, or how he'd almost been caught making love to some countess and had only escaped by wearing one of her dresses and hiding in a closet for an hour. Berren suspected much was simply made up, but he listened anyway. Silvestre was as good at telling his stories as he was with his sword: everything he did came with a little flourish. Even when he fought, he couldn't resist just a little bit of showing off.

'He was the closest thing Prince Talon had to a father for a while,' said Tarn, when Berren said something about the two of them being alike. 'At least he didn't turn out like Prince Syannis, thank the gods.' Then Tarn frowned as if he'd said too much.

'Did you know them before Syannis left?' Berren asked.

Tarn shook his head. 'Seven years we've been together, me and the Prince of Swords. I just know what I hear.' And he wouldn't say any more.

Berren soon saw that two kinds of student came to the sword-master. Most were the rich young men and women of Kalda. They came to learn how to strut, how to duel, how to hold themselves in a certain way and how to look the part of a lord-in-waiting. They were all much the same and they were young, younger even than Berren. They had fancy clothes which Silvestre let them keep and ornate swords which he made them throw away. They all knew each other, kept together, and regarded Silvestre's other students – those like Berren – with disdain and a little fear. Watching them felt strange. They were the people he'd wanted to be, back in Deephaven, but now he couldn't understand what he'd been thinking. All their talk was about drinking, gambling, racing, money, of who was getting married to whom and who their lovers were.

Berren and Tarn, on the other hand, were learning to fight so they could kill people. They weren't the only ones, and it was easy to tell the two groups apart. Tarn spelled it out one day.

'We're mercenaries,' he said. 'I'm with Talon, the Fighting Hawks.' He nodded towards the others. 'Lucama is with the duke of somewhere I can't remember but everyone knows him as the Mountain Panther. So are Remic and Alaxt. They'll be the Panther's regimental lieutenants next season. He sends three men every year, always three different ones, one from each regiment. Those two –' he gestured to a couple of other mercenaries '– Morric and Blatter, they're with the Company of the Fist. I don't know who owns them or who's paying. That's the way it works in this part of the world. No armies, just us. We work for whoever pays, but a good half of us winter in Kalda.'

Berren frowned. 'Isn't Kalda ... ?' He shook his head. 'Isn't Kalda full of Talon's enemies?'

Tarn shrugged. 'Good place to have a couple of dozen heavily armed men around you then, eh?' and Berren couldn't think of much to say to that.

In the mornings they all practised together, the soldiers and the rich city boys. Then Silvestre sent the mercenaries to run down into the heart of the city and back while the others stayed behind. The run down was easy enough, but running back was crippling, uphill against a slope that got steadily steeper. As soon as they returned, Silvestre put them to work in the practice yard. The *dilettantes*, as he called them, were gone by then, and Silvestre drove Berren and the other soldiers mercilessly hard. They had no pause for breath until they almost collapsed with exhaustion, because that, as Silvestre said, was how it was when you went to war. If someone showed signs of being tired, he'd attack them himself, raining blows onto their arms and legs.

'There's a difference between you and those others,' he told them. 'They're learning an art. They might as well be learning to paint or to sculpt. You're learning to stay alive. Which means you never, *never* drop your guard, even if your arms are cut to bloody stumps and you have to hold your sword between your teeth.' They soon learned. Fight and fight and fight until you drop.

The days wore into weeks. Berren saw Talon less and less, until one evening the prince caught him on his weary way to bed. 'We'll be gone in a few days now,' he said. 'The seasons are changing. We're forming up again. Our ship's here ready to take us to war. Yours is here too.' He clapped Berren on the shoulder. 'Don't forget to have some fun before you leave.'

Berren yawned and tried not to look interested. 'You're going straight off to fight?' Time was running out, then. Talon would ship him off to Deephaven. He'd have to slip away and that meant getting his things together. Getting some money. Inside, he frowned. This had been coming ever since Talon had taken him in but he'd grown comfortable in Kalda now. Despite their start, Tarn had become a friend; underneath his gruff mask he was an amiable man, generous and honest and Berren was going to miss him. He'd miss Talon too, with his flashing smile and his wit.

Talon's hand stayed on Berren's shoulder. 'Our ships sail on the same day. Yours will take you to Brons. From there you'll be able to get passage on a Taiytakei clipper through the storm-dark to Deephaven. I'll make sure of that. Or you could stay in Brons, I suppose. Brons is as close as the sea gets to the heart of the Dominion.' He laughed. 'It's warmer there and they're all dark-skinned short-arses like you. I think most of the first settlers who went to Aria came from Brons. You'd fit.'

Talon let him go and Berren knew better than to ask any more. They'd be going their separate ways, that was what mattered. He needed to find the thief-taker as much as ever, still gripped by the same pull that had made him jump ship and take his chances with the sea. He had no idea what he'd do when they met. The anger didn't burn like it used to, but it burned nevertheless.

When Berren rose the next morning, Tarn had already gone and so he made his way up to the sword-master's house alone; when he reached it, Talon and Tarn were already there, squatting in a corner of the yard and deep in conversation. Talon saw Berren and beckoned him over.

'You've practised with Tarn enough,' Talon said. 'What do you think of him?'

'The sword-master says—' he began, but Talon was already shaking his head.

'No, no, no. If I wanted to know what Silvestre thinks, I'd ask him. If I want to know how he fights, I'll stay and watch. I want to know what you think of him.'

'I like him,' Berren said. It felt odd talking about Tarn when he was standing right there.

'Would you have him at your side in a fight? Would you let your life depend on him?'

Berren cocked his head. 'I would,' he said. 'Yes.'

'Why?'

Tarn's frown was fierce. 'He's reliable,' said Berren slowly. 'He's slow on his feet a bit and I'd worry about that perhaps –' Tarn glared '– but I'd know I could depend on him. The two of us would work well. I'm quicker, he's stronger. Where I'm small, he's large. Between us we could do things that neither could do alone. If I was hurt, he'd help me. Probably do something foolish.' He had to smile. The look on Tarn's face was touching: he was trying so very hard to scowl.

'What about the others here?'

Berren peered at Talon. Tarn had asked him the same thing several times and so Talon surely already knew his answer. 'Why? Why are you asking?'

'Just answer, Berren of Deephaven.'

'Lucama then. He has a temper and can be made to lose it. He makes mistakes then but I think I'd fight beside him anyway. He's short and fast. Morric, Remic, Alaxt, they're all plodders.' He grimaced and flicked his eyes sideways in case one of them was close enough to hear. 'They'll stand as long as they think they have a good chance to win and they're cool-headed enough to know when they can't. Blatter ...' He wasn't sure what to say about Blatter.

'He's not as fast as Lucama but he thinks more. He tries to bait us. He's a bit of a shit really, and some of the stuff he comes out with ... well, makes you just want to strangle him. He and Lucama aren't allowed to practise together now.' Berren paused. 'There was one time ...' Talon must have known already because Tarn had seen it all, but the prince just looked at him. Berren shrugged. 'I like fighting with Lucama. Blatter used to say things. Call us names. Dark-skin, short-spear. That sort of thing. Doesn't bother me much but it got to Lucama. The sword-master didn't stop it either, he just said, "What, you think you won't get taunts when you fight for real?" And I know how it is. Was always like that where I grew up. So anyway, one day when he's running his mouth, we pick Blatter up and pin him to the dirt and tell him we'd prefer not to hear his voice for a while.' Berren coughed. He'd taken his time with his words while Lucama had pressed Blatter's face into the dirt and Silvestre had watched it all without stirring. They hadn't seen Blatter for two days after that. 'I'd be surprised if that's the end of it between those two.'

Talon shook his head. 'They'll save it for the battlefield if they know what's good for them. Things like that can set whole companies against each other.' He stopped, his attention drawn by something over Berren's shoulder. Lucama was walking across the practice yard towards them. He took a long hard look at Talon and began to practise his lunges.

'Excuse me,' said Talon. He got up.

Berren turned to Tarn. 'What's he like?' he asked. 'When you're fighting?'

'Who? Talon?'

'No, the sun-king. Of course Talon!'

Tarn smiled. 'He's a tiger. Lordly gentlemen get sent out for a season in the field with one of the companies now and then. Supposed to make men of them but mostly they're a nuisance. They don't know their arse from their elbow and you spend more time making sure they don't get anyone hurt than you do worrying about the enemy. The Prince of War, though, he's different. He's been with the Hawks for ten years. Put him in a battle, he's everywhere. Always shows up where he's most needed and never runs from anything. You wouldn't think it to look at him, but on the field ... On the field he's someone else, like he's possessed. Most men run when they see *him* coming. Pity you won't ever—'

In the practice yard a fight had broken out.

8

SOME FRIENDS FROM BACK HOME

In the middle of the fighting square Talon and Lucama had their swords out and were dancing around each other. Lucama was slashing and cursing, snarling with a fury which Talon had surely provoked. Berren started to stand, but Tarn put a hand on his shoulder and pushed him back down; so he watched instead, chewing on his knuckles while the palm of his other hand rested gently on the hilt of his sword.

'I've been around a lot longer than you have,' muttered Tarn. 'Just stay out of it. This sort of thing happens often enough, even in the same company. Usually it doesn't come to much. He's just trying Lucama out.'

Trying him out. Berren wondered if anyone had told Lucama that. He was driving Talon steadily into a corner with sheer violence and twice Berren thought he saw Lucama's blade cut Talon; but since the prince never seemed to notice and since there wasn't any blood, he supposed he must have been wrong.

Tarn's fists were clenched, Berren saw. 'Are you sure we shouldn't—'

'No,' Tarn snapped. Then he spoke more quietly. 'He does this every year, picks on someone from another company and tests him. I wish he wouldn't. Don't worry – he's got metal under that shirt.'

The fight stopped as abruptly as it had started. Silvestre

was standing at the edge of the practice yard. He didn't say anything but he didn't need to – his presence alone was enough. Talon saluted, first Lucama and then Silvestre, and walked away. Lucama glowered after him. For the rest of that day he was sullen and bad-tempered.

The next morning was Berren's last with the sword-master. It rained solidly and by the end he and Tarn were soaked to the skin. Talon came to meet them when they were done, promising a night to remember before they all sailed their separate ways. The sword-master gave them a lecture on the virtues of running away as soon as a fight started to go bad and then shooed them out of his house as if he was glad to be rid of them.

'Silvestre doesn't like farewells to linger,' Talon said as they walked through the drizzle down towards the docks. Berren turned and looked back at the city around him for what might be the last time. 'He likes you. He likes Tarn as well. Actually, Silvestre is one of those people who likes almost everybody, which I suppose is both his blessing and his curse. Every winter he teaches men and women to fight. Soldiers like us. By the end of the season half of them are dead. He told me it was always half, for some reason. If you last through the first year then there's some hope you'll survive to grow old. Chances are that you won't, though.'

'I will,' said Berren, with a force that surprised him. Talon gave him a puzzled look and then laughed.

'They all say that. But *you're* going to Deephaven. It's me and Tarn who should worry.'

'I don't ...' Now was the time to speak, now or never, before Talon drank himself stupid and they were both too muddled to think and he was suddenly on the run again, on his own, heading off to find Master Sy – wherever he was. It would be *easier*, wheedled a voice inside him, to find the thief-taker if he stayed with Talon. Then it would only be a matter of time, surely? But then maybe the right

53

time to say something *was* when Talon was deep into his cups, when maybe he wouldn't be thinking things through and they were all friends together in the way that only too much wine could forge.

'You don't what?' Talon was smiling but there was a hardness and a sadness there, as though he knew what Berren had been about to say and was ready to tell him no, that they would part tomorrow with the dawn and there was no other way for things to be.

'I don't know what I'm going to do in Deephaven,' said Berren quickly. 'I did a favour for a royal prince once. I doubt he'll remember and I lost the token he gave me when they took me onto the ship, but I reckon I'm not much use for anything except fighting now. Last I heard the empire was heading for another war. They'll be wanting soldiers if they haven't gone and had it without me.' He wiped the rain away from his eyes. The water here was cold, not like Deephaven rain which mostly came as a blessed relief from the baking summer sun. He shivered. All he was wearing was a wool shirt. Tarn and Talon had thick leather coats.

'I'd give that a lot of thinking,' said Talon softly. 'A soldier's life can eat you from the inside. You've seen Syannis. I'd find something else if I were you. Something *good*. A reason, a cause, an aspiration. *Build* something, Berren. Something for others to admire. Something that will make you proud.'

Yeh, but what? What else could he do? He could read and write but not very well. He was still a dab hand at cutting a purse or picking a pocket, but that was a sure way to the mines in the end. He'd never learned a trade and who would take him now? And to do what? Bake bread? Make clothes? Till fields? He couldn't, not after all he'd seen, not after all he'd done.

Master Sy, he reminded himself. He wasn't going to Deephaven anyway.

The air quietly changed. Talon and Tarn and the others were suddenly on edge. Berren looked up and saw the street was empty. And then, ahead, a gang of armed men emerged to block their path. When Berren looked over his shoulder there was another gang behind. He counted the numbers. Fourteen against six. Poor odds, and one of the men ahead was holding what looked like a ball of bright fire, a glass globe the size of a fist filled with brilliant swirling oranges and yellows. Berren had heard stories of such things, told through the nights at sea, of globes of glass made with exquisite care by the craftsmen of the far south, filled with fire by the High Mages of Brons and sold to the Taiytakei for the rockets that their ships carried to war. They were a myth, or so the sailors had said.

Slowly Tarn drew his sword. Talon put a calming hand on his shoulder.

'Gentlemen!' he called. 'Can we in any way assist you?'

The man holding the ball of fire shook his head. 'You can die,' he said, and he tossed the globe. Time seemed to slow. Berren watched it arc towards them. His feet wouldn't move; then someone shoved him in the back and he staggered forward and started to run. His hand reached for his sword only to remember that he didn't have one. The ball of trapped fire flew past him, coming down towards the stones where he'd been standing, and then the world shook and roared. A shock of wind took him from behind and threw him onward, burning hot and blinding bright. Flames seared his back. He stumbled, almost fell, barely stayed on his feet while their attackers cringed and reeled and tried to shield their eyes. For a moment all he could hear was a rushing in his ears. He saw Tarn stagger and Talon stumble beside him, both with swords drawn, and then they tumbled into the waiting men, themselves half-blinded. Berren bounced into and back out of a doorway, still hardly able to stay on his feet. He screamed. Dodged around a flailing sword, passed the first soldier and then tripped on a loose stone and fell, rolling across the cobbles. The air smelled of burning, of burned skin and scorched hair. His back and legs felt as though they were on fire and maybe they were. He screamed again as he landed and then slid into a puddle. Cold water soaked him, a momentary relief. When he looked up, the street was filled with a haze of fog or smoke or steam. Talon and Tarn and two others ran past him. The other men gave chase, all of them running past Berren without giving him a second glance. They left two bodies groaning on the ground.

A moment later, more men with swords in their hands raced out of the steam, blinking and rubbing their eyes. Berren lay still and these ones ran straight past too. Warm air wafted over him, filled with the stink of burning. As the last one came by, Berren jumped at him and wrapped his arms around the man's legs. The man went down like he'd been shot, flinging his arms out to catch himself but still cracking his face on the stones; he cried out and rolled onto his back, clutching his face, blood pouring from his nose. Berren sprang onto him, snarling, and bashed his head into the ground one more time. Then he grabbed the man's sword, one of the long curved weapons he was so used to seeing on Deephaven's snuffers. He stood for a moment, ready to use it, but stopped. The man was helpless now, unarmed. He was as tanned as Berren, not pale-skinned like most of the people who lived in Kalda.

He *was* a Deephaven snuffer.

'Slug-leavings! Sheet-stain!' Berren screamed at him. 'What was that for? Why?' Screaming took the edge off the pain.

The snuffer groaned and feebly rolled away. Berren left him to it and ran on down the street, but after a few dozen steps he staggered to a halt, gasping for breath. Gods, but his back hurt! And his shoulders too and the backs of his legs, a burning pain from the flames, soothed only a little by the rain. He looked up and down the street but Talon and the others were out of sight now. All he could see were the two bodies on the ground and the man whose sword he'd taken, slowly crawling away. Where would Talon go? The Bitch Queen, perhaps, although Berren wasn't sure he ever wanted to go back in there, not on his own.

His breathing was all wrong, too quick and too shallow. Everything still moved so nothing was broken, but the pain was excruciating. He could feel his strength ebbing away. He staggered back up the hill to Talon's house, the only place he could think to go, but when he got near he saw yet more armed men. They wore no colours to say who they were but their arms and armour were the same as the ones who'd attacked him in the street, and so was the colour of their skin. Deephaven snuffers. This time he was sure, although what a company from Aria was doing here across the ocean was anyone's guess. He watched for a while in case the snuffers left and then slunk away. The docks then. That was the place to look. The pain was all over him now, weighing him down. He needed to get off his feet. To rest. Sleep.

A hand grabbed his shoulder, yanking him back into the shadows of an alley. He yelped, and then another hand clamped across his mouth and Tarn's voice was whispering in his ear: 'Quiet!'

Tarn let go. Berren stood very still, panting and gasping at what felt like a hundred knives all flaying the skin off his shoulder where Tarn had held him.

'Path of the Sun, look at you!'

Berren closed his eyes. He couldn't pretend he wasn't hurt, that was too much to ask, but he was damned if he was going to let Tarn see how bad it was. He took a few deep breaths until he could trust himself to speak without whimpering. 'What's going on?'

Tarn shrugged. 'You've seen as much as I have. As to who or why, we're not short on choice. Campaign season's about to start. Could be another company trying to cripple us. Could be anyone. And Talon's got enemies all of his own; you know that. Turn round.' Gently, Tarn twisted Berren around and looked him up and down. 'That must hurt. You've been burned from top to toe.' He shook his head. 'I don't know what that soldier threw at us.'

'Talon?'

'He's fine. We only lost one man. That fire didn't do them any favours. Flash blinded them and we just cut through them and ran. They didn't chase after us for long. Rain and a good thick coat and most of us got away lightly.' Tarn glanced down. The back of his sword hand was bright red. 'Going to hurt in the morning, that, but it'll heal quick enough. You, though, you look bad.' He smirked. 'That'll teach you go around wearing nothing but a shirt. Armour, boy, that's what you need. Never be without it. Come on, I'll take you down to the ship. Gods! I thought we'd lost you, but when there was no body I reckoned you'd come back here if you could still walk.'

Berren followed Tarn down the slope of the city once more, breathing hard. By the time they reached the docks and the waterfront, it was all he could do to keep putting one foot in front of the other. There was a longboat waiting, filled with soldiers Berren didn't recognise but whom Tarn seemed to know. Berren sat with his head in his hands while they rowed out into the river. The back of his head hurt too. Most of his hair was gone.

'You're lucky it was raining.' As they turned towards one of the ships anchored in the Triere, Tarn pointed up to the flag fluttering atop the foremast, a diving silver hawk on a black field. 'That's us.'

'You've got your own ship?'

Tarn chuckled. 'You ask me, I'd have preferred one of

those sleek Taki ones for crossing the ocean. They're twice as fast but it turns out you can fit three times as much cargo into this flat-bellied monster and we've got a whole company to move.' He wrinkled his nose. 'You have no idea how much work goes into just getting from one place to another. It's all food and shelter and how good are the roads, and where will be able to get water and then more food again. Ugh! Talon's not going to thank me for bringing you aboard but I can't leave you running around like that.'

Berren stared at the ship as they drew closer. From a distance it didn't seem much different from the one that had brought him here, but as they came alongside he could see it was bigger, taller and fatter. A ladder made of short planks of wood and two long knotted ropes dropped down. Talon let the other soldiers in the boat climb up first, then gestured to Berren.

'You up to climbing that?'

'I spent two years on the sea as a skag. I've climbed worse than this half-dead before, when it was keep working or be thrown into the sea.' Weary, he hauled himself up.

As he reached the top of the ladder and almost fell over the rail, the ship rocked with such a noise that Berren stopped for a moment, trying to work out what it was. Not the usual shouting and swearing of surly sailors with empty pockets and sore heads. Cheering, that's what it was. Soldiers and sailors alike were cheering, while Talon held his hands aloft with the setting sun behind him. The deck was packed. There were soldiers everywhere, nearly all in black shirts with the emblem of a diving silver hawk on the front. Some were crude, painted on by an unskilled hand. Others were exquisite, embroidered with silver thread.

'The Hawks have new blood!' Talon shouted over the din. You wouldn't have known from looking at him that someone had tried to kill him only an hour ago. 'You'll see them among you, in your cohorts, in your tents. Treat them the way you were treated when you first joined us. Let them know what's what and what it means to be a Fighting Hawk. Take them with you to the best taverns wherever we go! See they have their fair shares of all that matters. Of food and water. Of boots and swords and arrows. Of the fighting and of the plunder!' Talon drew his sword and thrust it into the air. 'The Fighting Hawks!' he cried to another thunderous cheer.

'When the season's over and we go back to our homes, we're all different people,' Tarn said, standing at Berren's shoulder. 'But together we become something else. All here are equal, be they a prince or a peasant. That's the secret of the Prince of War.' He stopped and turned to face Berren. 'I'll take you to that ship he found for you if you ask me to, but I know this is what you wanted. While you're with us, you're no better and no worse than any other soldier here. You'll fight beside them. If it comes to it, you'll die beside them, so best you get to know them.'

Berren could barely keep his eyes open. The burns on his back hurt every bit as much as the floggings he'd had as a skag; this time though, he felt a warmth inside him. For the first time in his life he was part of a family. 'He won't like it,' he said. 'He'll send me away. Just like his brother did.'

'He might.' Tarn tapped him lightly – even that sent a jolt of pain through him enough to make him wince. 'But not today and tomorrow we'll be at sea. Come on. Let's get you seen to.'

PART TWO

THE PRINCE OF WAR

9
IT'S HARD TO KILL A WARLOCK

For three days Berren stayed below decks, lying flat on his front with some sweet-smelling salve lathered across his skin. He slept a lot and drank a lot. When he complained that he was bored, Tarn declared that he must be getting better and let him walk around the ship wearing a nightshirt. He had blisters the size of lobsters on his back and on his legs, but he hobbled up the ladder to the deck as eager as could be to get away from the sweat-stink below. He took a deep breath of cold fresh air and welcomed the wind into his hair, the stinging rain on his face. The ship was close to land, ploughing steadily through the waves with a good breeze from the stern. He strained his eyes, trying to see whether he could recognise the shape of the coastline. The misty rain blurred cliffs into grey shapes, while great fingers of dark rock pushed out into the sea, their sides sheer and marked only by the nests of birds and the occasional tuft of grass, their tops crowned with a scattering of windswept trees. Elsewhere, channels of water split the cliffs apart and wound away into the land.

'They run for miles,' Tarn told him when he pointed.

As the day went on he began to see that where each channel reached the sea, the water was dotted with tiny islands, little more than heaps of boulders. Strange animals sat on them – seals, Tarn called them. Berren watched it all roll past, savouring the feel of the wind and the taste of the salt spray on his tongue. He was on a ship. He wasn't a skag. He was on a ship and he was happy. He'd thought he'd never feel that again.

They followed the coast for two more days then slowed and turned, edging their way into one of the channels. With its boats launched to guide it, the ship crept between two vertical walls of rock that were twice as high as the tallest mast. Near the entrance to the inlet Berren watched fish eagles circle. Further in, he stared at the myriad of tiny waterfalls that plunged off the top of the cliffs and only managed to get halfway to the sea before being lost in clouds of white spray. By now he was wearing a light leather jerkin like the other soldiers, though the worst of his burns were still wrapped in bandages. Tarn had even managed to find him a black shirt with a crude silver hawk painted on it.

'You're one of us now,' he said. 'I won't ask you to take a turn at the oars just yet, but don't worry, we'll make up for it once your skin's healed. A good dose of latrine duty, I think.' He grinned.

The ship eased on through the channel for the rest of the day and into the early part of the night. When Berren next climbed up onto the deck they were anchored in the middle of a wide curving bay, shielded on all sides by steep rocky cliffs. Boatloads of soldiers were already being ferried to the shore. Talon stood poised at the prow, his eyes on everything. When he saw Berren and Tarn, he beckoned them closer and pointed to the slopes at the edge of the bay.

'Tarn, take your cohort up there. Find me a path to the top. Take a position on the ridge and send word to the rest of the company. You should find yourself looking down on another bay like this one and there should be a camp or a stronghold of some sort on the shore. There might even be a ship. We'll be taking both but most of all I need to know about the ship. Send a runner to report what you see. If you think it's safe to do so then scout ahead.' His eyes glanced across to Berren, unreadable. 'I'm still sending you back to Deephaven at the first chance we get, but you can go with Tarn for now. Unless he wants you kept out of the way, of course.' He nodded towards where men were already climbing over a net thrown down the side of the ship to a boat waiting in the water. 'That's yours. Quick now!'

Berren looked at Tarn, who shrugged his shoulders. 'Happy enough to have you,' he said. 'If you think you can fight.'

Berren followed Tarn to the boat and sat with him as it filled. There were another seventeen men in the cohort, too many for a single trip, and by the time they were together at the base of the cliff Tarn had already found the path that Talon had described. Berren ran ahead, up to where it dived into the wall of trees that lined the top of the ridge. He turned back, waved to show that the path was good and then loped on into the woods. From the outside, in the sunlight, the leaves on the trees were a verdant green. From the gloom beneath though, they seemed nearly black, and only a little light reached through them. The ground was covered in a soft layer of moss and leaf mould and little else. The path vanished but Berren plunged on, marking as straight a line as he could. A minute later he emerged on the other side where the ridge fell sharply away again. Spread out below him, a semicircular bowl filled with trees sloped down to the water's edge, and in the middle, close to the shore, three buildings sat in a clearing. A thin column of smoke rose from one. Out in the water a small ship lay at anchor. Everything as Talon had said. He stood still and listened. Far away someone was screaming.

Tarn came and settled next to him, the rest of the cohort arrayed at the edge of the trees. Berren scratched at the bandages on his shoulders. The skin underneath had started to itch and now it wouldn't stop. 'What are we doing here?'

More screams wafted up from below. 'Slavers,' said Tarn brusquely. He clenched and unclenched his fists, got up, paced for a bit and then sat down again. 'It could be an hour before the rest of the company gets up here,' he muttered. 'Is there another way down?'

'Not much cover on that slope,' said someone. 'Whole company goes down there at once, someone's bound to see us.'

'Bit steep too,' said someone else. 'Most likely someone will slip. Be a noise.'

'Shouldn't we wait for Talon?' asked Berren, but the others ignored him and went on. They'd already made up their minds.

'Aye. What you'd need is a small force to go in first. Can't be too many of them down there.'

'Take them by surprise before they can raise the alarm?'

'Maybe get to that ship.'

'About a cohort, I'd say.'

'Aye.'

Tarn cocked his head. 'Scout a path for the main force? Deal with the sentries? Is that us? You know what? I do seem to remember Talon said something about doing just that.'

A murmur of assent rose from the mercenaries. A moment later they were all on their feet, drawing straws to see who'd stay at the top and mark the path for Talon and the others when they came. That done, they began to pick their way down from the top of ridge. The first part was the worst, a sheet of rock a dozen feet high. Below that, a steep slope covered in springy tufts of grass fell away down towards the bottom of the bowl and more trees. Berren clambered down the rock face easily enough, while others simply jumped and then slid through the grass. From there, Tarn led them forward. The trees down here were different – the leaves lighter, sunlight streaming in through gaps in the foliage. The ground was covered with ferns and the soldiers crept among them, slow and silent.

Screams rang out again. The trees muffled the sound but everyone heard it. As they came closer, Tarn made a sudden gesture and the soldiers dropped. Berren did the same, although he had no idea what Tarn had seen. For a minute they stayed absolutely still. Then Tarn began to move again, hunched right down into the undergrowth. There was another short pause and he waved the rest of the cohort towards him.

'I can smell the smoke on the air,' he whispered. 'When we're close enough to see what this place is, we stay hidden unless I say otherwise. We stay out of sight until we see what's here.'

More screams. This time they were sharp and clear. Tarn winced.

'And once we've seen, then what?' asked someone. 'There can't be more than a cohort here.'

Tarn ran his thumb across his throat. The rest of the soldiers nodded and grinned. 'But we look first. No one moves until I say.'

At the edge of the trees Berren finally saw what the screaming was about. A crude wooden frame made from branches lashed together with ropes stood at the near end of the clearing. A man was tied to it, naked and spread-eagled. Three other men were clustered around him. They were untying him, and as they dragged him away back to the largest of the three buildings, Berren could see that the naked man's back was bloody and raw. A minute later the men emerged again, hauling another man with them, kicking and struggling. They beat him until he stopped and soon had him tied to the frame. Berren looked away. He'd been on the wrong end of enough floggings in his years as a skag. 'What is this?' he whispered. 'What is this place?'

Tarn shrugged. 'Talon didn't say. Could be all sorts of

things. My guess is White Water Reavers.' He spat. 'Don't see why anyone else would come all the way out into the middle of nowhere just to beat up a few slaves.'

Berren winced at the name. Pirates in small fast ships who sacked villages, killing the sick and the old and carrying away the rest to their ships to be sold as slaves to the insatiable Taiytakei. Word of them made veteran sailors turn pale and mutter words to the gods under their breath.

A sudden tension filled the air around him. Three more figures had appeared, walking towards the men at the whipping frame. One tall, two short, all three dressed from head to toe in grey. Berren could feel the silent snarls from the soldiers around him.

'Death-mages!' hissed Tarn, and almost as if he'd heard, the tallest of the three suddenly stopped. He turned and looked round, and now Berren saw his face.

Saffran Kuy. The warlock.

10
THE NECROMANCER AND THE PRINCESS

Time slowed. The warlock stared into the trees where Berren and Talon's swords were hiding. The two other figures with him turned to stare as well. They were little more than children, a boy and a girl, although what children might be doing in a place like this was beyond Berren. He felt sick. A strange taste filled the air around him. He struggled to breathe. A few yards away, one of the soldiers sprang to his feet. Steel scraped on steel, swords drawn, and as one the mercenaries leaped forward and hurled themselves out of the trees. Berren stayed frozen, pinned like a butterfly by his memories of Deephaven. Of the warlock driving Berren's own hand to cut out a piece of Berren's own soul. Of the same hand striking down Radek of Kalda. If Kuy knew he was here, Berren was bound to obey the warlock's every desire, just as he had when he'd murdered Radek.

Saffran Kuy turned to face the rush of soldiers. His hands twirled. Dark smoke boiled in the air around him and then broke into pieces, each piece darting outwards. The shadows struck Tarn and his men and coiled around their throats, yet Tarn and the others seemed not to notice. Then Kuy turned and hurried his two young charges away. The slavers who'd been flogging their prisoner ran with him.

Berren snapped out of his trance. He ran after the others,

after the cries and shouts of surprise. Slavers still blinking in the sunlight were cut down where they stood, too shocked by the suddenness of Tarn's onslaught to put up a fight. There were more men here than Tarn had thought. The soldiers seemed not to notice, though – they were after the warlock, chasing him down with a vicious certainty of purpose – sure of their victory; but Berren had seen those shadows before, wrapped around Radek's throat, paralysing him. They were all in terrible danger and they didn't even know it!

More slavers emerged, put to the sword before they understood what was happening. Kuy scuttled into the building from where the man on the whipping frame had been dragged. Tarn charged after him with his cohort; Berren followed more cautiously, skirting fallen bodies on the beaten earth. Some of the slavers weren't dead yet; some reached out for him with their hands or their eyes, silently pleading for help; those who were hurt but knew they might yet live watched him with fear, hobbling or crawling away as fast as they could. Still more of them spilled out into the light, shouting and squinting and waving clubs and axes. Berren ignored them. He ran after Tarn and the rest into the building that had swallowed Kuy.

It was dark, windowless, lit only by dim curtains of sunlight that crept between the cracks in the walls. The air stank, the rancid stench of too many men in too little space, covered in their own filth. Berren had smelled it before, when his ship had carried a hold full of slaves for a few weeks. The smell had lingered for months, but here there was something else as well, something even more familiar, the old smell of rotting fish that he knew from Deephaven.

His eyes began to adjust. The soldiers had stopped. They were right in front of him, clustered in the centre of the room, formed up in a semicircle. They looked like men who'd cornered a tiger and now weren't sure what to do with it. Each still had a swirl of dark mist coiling around him, and now that he was closer Berren could see the mist for what it was – the terrors that Kuy had summoned in Deephaven, the ones that he'd thrown at Tasahre until she'd called down the light of the sun and banished them.

Berren shivered. Couldn't they see what was wrapped around them? But if they did, they didn't show it.

His eyes shifted. Dozens and dozens of filthy naked men were fettered to the walls. In the corner the warlock was pressed among them. He had one hand reached out towards Tarn while the other clutched one of the prisoners. The boy and the girl in their robes – apprentices? – huddled next to him.

'No closer.' Kuy's voice was thin. The strength and the venom that Berren remembered were gone. 'Dance in the darkness with me and this life will be mine!'

'You!' One of the soldiers poked at Berren. 'Watch the door! Keep them out!'

'Sun and Moon protect us,' muttered another.

Tarn shook his head. 'Death-mage!' he hissed. He raised his sword and took one lunging step.

The shadow around Tarn's neck that only Berren could see drew tight. Tarn fell as though he'd been struck by an axe. A surge of anger swept over the others, but before they could throw themselves on Kuy and tear him to pieces, their terrors sprang to life too. The prisoner Kuy was clutching screamed. He began to spasm, twitching as black blood dribbled and then poured out of his mouth, until he finally slumped silent. A sudden darkness filled the room and a terrible keening wail began. Berren bolted, stricken with terror, too full of the memories of what he'd seen once before; but outside in the light a dozen slavers were waiting now, clustered together with swords and axes and spears drawn, watching from a distance. He skittered to a stop, not knowing which way to run. Behind him, the shouts and screams of soldiers and the chained slaves alike filled the room.

One of the slavers held a crossbow. He raised it. Berren dropped his sword. He didn't mean to, but his hands were shaking so much that it happened on its own.

Move, he told himself. *Move!* But his feet stayed frozen to the ground.

A soldier staggered out of the door. He had one hand stretched out in front of him, the other clutching at his throat. Two of Saffran Kuy's terrors were throttling him. He barged blindly into Berren, knocking him aside. The crossbow fired and the soldier fell to the ground. He hauled himself forward on his belly for a few feet, and then slumped over on his back, an arrow sticking from his chest in the middle of a circle of red. The terrors uncoiled themselves. The slaver with the crossbow bent forward to reload.

Berren ran now, as fast as his legs would carry him. He heard another crack as the bow fired again, heard the fizz of the bolt through the air, but he was still running and the slaver had missed – that was all that mattered. He looked over his shoulder as he reached the trees. No one was following him. He ran on until he was deep into the woods and then crouched down among the ferns to catch his breath. He'd thrown away his memories of Saffran Kuy long ago, wrapped them up and locked them down; now they were back, the full force of them, and they had him as helpless as he'd been back on that day in Kuy's House of Cats and Gulls, the old terror writhing like a snake inside him.

No. He couldn't just run, though. Couldn't. Couldn't leave Tarn and the others, but he couldn't go back either, not after what the warlock had done to him in Deephaven. If Kuy saw him here, one snap of his fingers was all it would take and Berren would be his slave, his puppet. *Three little slices. You! Obey! Me!* Did wounds like that ever heal? He had no idea. The priests at the temple had said yes, they did, but they'd never seemed entirely sure.

He looked back up the slope towards the ridge over which Talon and the rest of the Hawks would come. He could run for help, but it would take ages to climb back up, to explain to Talon what had happened and then get down again. By the time he did, Tarn and the rest might well be dead.

He skirted the edge of the camp and crept closer once more. Tarn and the other soldiers were out in the open now, in the space between the three buildings, grouped together and on their knees. Saffran Kuy was there too. As long as the warlock didn't see him, that was what mattered. Or maybe the years at sea had changed him enough – maybe Kuy wouldn't recognise him?

The smallest of the three buildings had a door that opened away from the middle of the camp. A path ran towards the sea where the ship was anchored. There was no one there. Berren slipped inside. The slavers clearly slept here. He counted the sets of bedding. Fifteen. And then he saw what he was looking for. Another crossbow. As quietly as he could, he loaded it and then peered through the door out into the central compound. Tarn's soldiers knelt in a circle, all together now, all except for Tarn himself who lay still on the ground. The slavers stood cautiously apart while Saffran Kuy paced in slow circles. Kuy was talking, but Berren couldn't hear what he was saying. The terrors were still there, wrapped around everyone's throats.

He held the crossbow tight. He'd never been good with one, never had much chance to learn, but Master Sy had taught him the basics. Now he aimed at the warlock. Until he fired, he wasn't quite sure what he was doing, or why, except that he wanted Saffran Kuy to be dead; but when he pulled the trigger, the bolt flew low and hit the warlock in the thigh, not killing him at all. Kuy lurched and shrieked and then his leg buckled under him and he fell. The slavers looked around, saw Berren and charged towards him, shouting and waving their swords. Berren fled down the path towards the ship. As he did he caught a glimpse of the terrors unwrapping themselves from Tarn's soldiers and flying back to the warlock. It seemed they shared his pain.

He glanced up at the slopes high above as he ran, hoping again to see the rest of Talon's men swarming down, but there was nothing. The slavers behind him were yelling dire threats and urging each other on. Somewhere not far ahead would be the beach, and that was no good. Out in the open they might catch him, but in the trees he was sure he could escape. It would be like the old times, racing through the alleys of Deephaven's Maze with a posse of militia at his back!

A stray thought came to him: if the warlock could brew a potion to see the future, as he'd claimed, how had Berren managed to shoot him? He didn't have an answer to that.

He rounded a turn in the path, ready to dive among the trees, but now Kuy's two startled apprentices were right in front of him. The boy was hurrying the girl towards the ship. She was crying. Unable to stop, Berren ploughed into the back of them, knocking them apart. His weight went into the boy, sending him sprawling. The girl staggered. She looked at him with big eyes. She was so young – eleven, twelve years old – and Berren could only wonder why she was here at all, what Kuy was doing to her. But other thoughts pressed him. He could see the beach now. There was a boat drawn up on the sand and the two men beside it were getting to their feet, roused by the hue and cry.

He seized the girl. 'Do you want to live?' She looked blankly back at him, then heaved a sob and stared with huge pleading eyes, and he knew straight away that it was

74

the warlock she was afraid of, not him; but before she could say anything, the boy was up again.

'I'll kill you,' he spat. 'Master Kuy will rip your soul out. We'll feast on it, just like we did—' His hands were turning black, the nails into claws. Fear stabbed at Berren – he'd seen this before – but this time he brushed it aside. Before the boy could finish, Berren punched him on the nose. He felt the bone crack beneath his knuckles, and suddenly the boy was just a boy again, fourteen years old maybe, sobbing and shaking. 'Please don't hurt me!'

Is this what I looked like to Master Sy when he found me in that alley? No time for that though: the soldiers would be on him in any moment – he could hear them – and the boy would tell them which way he'd gone. His hand went to his knife, but in the end the boy was just a boy, miserable and defenceless. Berren let the knife go, kicked him down instead and took the girl by the hand. 'Come with me.' He gave the boy one last look. 'You'll come to no good end following the likes of him. I should know.'

More shouts came from the camp, screams and battle sounds. Berren ran into the trees, half dragging, half carrying the girl. They hid, crouching deep under the cover of the ferns, still and silent, and yet even after the slavers didn't come, Berren couldn't shake a feeling of disquiet. However much he told himself otherwise, the warlock had done things to change him. The terrors. Neither the soldiers nor the slavers could see them. Only him.

'I see them too,' whispered the girl when they realised the slavers must have turned back to the fight in the camp. She squeezed his hand. 'I always did.'

Had he been thinking out loud? He must have been.

'He said it was a present but I don't like it. I like making potions though. I'm glad you came.'

Berren shivered uneasily. 'My friends are coming,' he said. 'They'll take you home.'

'I know.' Her eyes were wide and earnest. 'He told me. He said Prince Syannis would come. My shining prince.' She stared at him. 'But he's not here, is he? Not yet. It's all right, though.' She laid a hand on his cheek. 'I know who you are. You look like my cousin. You're Berren. We've done lots together. Lots and lots. It's nice to see you at last.'

Berren stared at her. He'd never met her before, not once in his life.

11
A MISSING PIECE RETURNED

On the ship Talon prowled his cabin and Berren had never seen a brow furrowed so deep. After he'd shot the warlock, whatever spell held the Hawks had been broken. They'd fought their way out, but now half the cohort were dead or badly hurt, and Tarn was in some sort of coma and no one could wake him. No one else had seen any sign of Saffran Kuy and his apprentice, and by the time Talon and the rest of his men had reached the beach, the little sloop had raised its anchor and was on its way back out to sea, taking with it the warlock and the slavers that survived.

Talon stopped for a moment to glare out of a porthole. They were back at sea themselves now, nosing their way out of the inlet towards the open ocean as fast as they could, but the sloop was smaller, lighter, faster and hours ahead of them. Short of a miracle, there was no chance they'd catch it. A little growl escaped his lips. 'Are you sure it was him?'

Berren nodded. Talon had asked the same thing three times now.

Tarn lay prostrate on the bed. Talon's other sergeants crowded into the corners of the room. The girl was there too, and she sat on the edge of the bed, watching everything with an air of distant contemplation. Berren found her calm unnerving, had done so ever since they'd left the camp. She had a name now: Gelisya. He tried to remember whether he'd ever heard of her in Deephaven. He thought not, but Talon knew her at once. *Princess* Gelisya, daughter to King Meridian of Tethis, and that troubled him every bit as much as discovering that the warlock was back. His thoughts were so loud that Berren could almost hear them. *What were you doing there? Why were you with Kuy? What do I do with you now? Do I take you home as I should or do I ... do something else? Where is the trap in this? For surely it is there ...*

The prince clenched his fists. 'We are hired this season to deal with slavers in the Duchy of Forgenver. There have always been pirates plaguing the duke's coast, but of late they have grown worse. The duke pays us to put an end to it.' He sighed. 'There are three ships involved and that sloop was one of them. I spent all bloody winter hunting them down. Bribes, threats, everything to find out where they were going to be. This is what I got and now we've lost her. We could have trapped their other ships in that channel, one after the other. Now we do it the hard way.' He stared at Gelisya. 'I have no idea what the duke's going to think if he hears there is a warlock at work and the royal house of Tethis is entwined with them as well, so perhaps we just won't tell him. But you,' he pointed at Gelisya, 'had better explain to me what you were doing there.'

Gelisya shook her head violently. She'd been largely silent since Berren had rescued her, and he was starting to wonder how much of a rescue it had been. *I know who you are.* She'd said it as though she'd been waiting for him. What if the warlock had lured them there? Was that possible? But if he had, what did he gain by it? It made no sense. Let himself be overrun and chased away? That wasn't the Saffran Kuy that Berren remembered.

'He took me,' she said. 'I want to go home.'

Talon turned to Berren. 'What about you? You saw him. Thoughts?'

Berren shrugged. He looked at Gelisya. 'She knows a lot more than she's saying. She said Kuy told her Syannis was coming for her.'

Gelisya nodded. 'He said you were coming as well. Both of you.'

'So you knew we were coming, and so did he! He knew and yet ...' Berren curled his toes. *And yet Kuy let all this happen! Why?*

'Enough!' Talon shook his head. 'I've seen how the minds of warlocks work. I've no love for the new kings of Tethis; indeed I would happily see them burn and, given the torch, I would merrily light the fire. But I will say one thing for them, and that is that they would have no dealings with one such as Saffran Kuy. He knew we would come here?' He nodded to Gelisya. 'Then he has placed himself in our path to give us this gift, and I will not be used in such a way. The intent is obvious – he wishes to restart the old war. I will not allow it.'

Talon surveyed his men. 'We sail for Tethis then, to return Princess Gelisya to her father. Whatever I think of Meridian, that is what is right. If Saffran Kuy wishes to make a war between us, he can do it when I'm damn well good and ready and when I've spent the time to pick our field of battle. I will disembark with one cohort. The rest of you will go directly on to Forgenver and report to the duke. You'll tell him we have destroyed a slaver camp and freed some of his subjects – that, at least, is both true and will please him. You will say nothing of warlocks or of Princess Gelisya's presence. If he asks the reason for my delay, you may as well tell him that I have tarried in Tethis and have not told you why. The truth is not to leave this room, not for anyone. I will tell the duke myself when I join you, but he will hear it all from me, not from rumours and whispers. Am I clear?' Talon met the eyes of each of his men in turn; they nodded, then one by one they stood up and left. As Berren rose too, Talon shook his head. 'Not you. Nor you, my lady.' He looked at Berren and grinned warily. 'Did you really shoot him?'

Berren nodded.

Talon turned to Gelisya. 'Once again, my lady, what did Kuy tell you? Every word if you please.'

Gelisya pointed at Berren. 'Master Kuy said he would come,' she said quietly. 'He said everything would be all right and you'd take me home. Only he said it would be Prince Syannis, not you.'

Talon snorted. 'Be thankful it wasn't, for Syannis would not have taken you home. He would take his warlock-given gift and had his war, whether the rest of us liked it or not.' He glanced at Tarn and then looked back at her. 'What did this?'

Gelisya shook her head. Berren sighed. 'Saffran Kuy did it.'

'I realise *that*. Can it be undone? Can he be saved?'

Now Gelisya nodded. She pointed at Berren. 'You have to make a potion.'

Berren snorted. 'Me? I have no idea what you're talking about.'

'Well *one* of us has to do it. You can't just let him die.'

'Then do it.'

'But I don't *want* to.'

'Listen, I was in Saffran Kuy's home in Deephaven for less than half a glass. I spent most of that watching a sword-monk try to kill him. *Helping* a sword-monk try to kill him. He never taught me anything except to be afraid. Certainly not anything about any potions.'

Gelisya pouted. 'He taught you lots,' she said. She slipped a hand under her shirt and pulled out a black stone held on a chain around her neck. 'See? It is a teacher. It shows how to do things.' She took it off and pressed it into Berren's hand. 'It has a piece of a person in it that remembers things

80

for you. So now you *can* do it.' She looked mournful for a moment, then closed Berren's fingers over the stone. 'I did *tell* you that we'd done lots and lots together. He shows you how to do things. I suppose I have to give him to you now. I don't really want to because he's my friend. But I suppose you want him back. He is yours after all.'

Berren started to say something, but his mouth fell open and he froze. He could feel a presence in the stone – more than that, it felt familiar. It felt *comfortable*, almost as though it fitted him, quite perfectly, like the missing piece of a puzzle.

Or was that simply what he wanted it to be? Just his imagination, and the stone was nothing but a stone? His fingers tightened around it. Visions flashed before his eyes – he was still sitting in Talon's cabin, on the edge of the bed with Talon in front of him and Gelisya to one side and Tarn lying behind him, but he was somewhere else too, watching Saffran Kuy at work somewhere that wasn't the House of Cats and Gulls but was colder, smaller, cramped and dark. The warlock was making potions. He was muttering to himself, and then he turned and seemed to look at Berren. *Watch, little Gelisya! Watch closely! Stir slowly! Heat carefully! Are you wearing the stone?* Then Kuy seemed to forget where he was again. He muttered to himself about this and that, idly throwing handfuls of powders into his cauldron without saying what they were.

The vision shifted. They were in the same place but on a different day and it was light outside now and Kuy was making something new. And then that faded too; another came and then another, faster and faster, until one clear memory began to emerge, hauling itself out of some far closet of the stone, shrugging off cobwebs and dusting itself down. *Are you wearing it? Are you wearing the stone? Do you have him, tucked safe and warm around your soft throat, girl? Watch this one carefully careful. The need will be great. It will bring you a friend and it will bring you suspicion and it will bring you hate. More important than any of the others, yet you will use them all when their time comes. I have spoken to you of the first principle of knowledge: that we are beings of two parts. Every man, from the lowest worm to the highest king, has two souls. More important than the light of the sun, to know this, but to know is but a scratch. To understand, yes, to understand, now that is the heart beneath. What priests would exalt, I shall call the Useless Part, the one that departs for far-off ideals, for the Sun or the Moon or the Stars. Or Xibaiya or elsewhere. Delights to taste some other day. What remains we shall call the Useful Part. Mindless thoughtless fodder for the living, but useful, yes, for they are the energy we draw on to work the tiny miracles that fill our lives, consumed and eaten. But what if one were to hold its form and keep its empty aimless hunger? What shall we call such a creature? Dangerous, I name it, and most potent ally too. Ephemeral pet-things, but while they remain they hunger for a life they cannot have, and they will fight to own a new coat of flesh. Men, sometimes, lifeless although they still live. Walking the streets with empty faces as though their spirits have long departed but who have yet to understand that they are dead. Or who lie still and cannot be roused yet do not pass away. In the murky places of this wretched land you will find such as these. Or strong men filled with woes they cannot explain. The housewife sapped of energy by a mystery. Crippled souls who seem as though they must fight a constant battle merely to live, and so, indeed, they do. Now you will know the cure for both. Watch carefully, for I will show you a draught to cast aside these usurpers. They will be your friends, your allies, your servants and your soldiers. One day they will crush worlds for you, little girl.*

Suddenly he turned and seemed to stare straight at Berren. *Listening are you, little ungrateful Berren-piece? Watching us now? Because it is not done between us, yet here I sense your fate is close to mine once more. You will have a want for this one too, I feel it. I see pain in our futures. Savour it! Relish it! Let it soak you through your skin and run ebullient through your veins, for if you hear these words, you have regained that which I took and I have given you a gift by it.*

He saw it all, with absolute clarity. Everything Kuy had done, every ingredient, every motion and every method. And he understood that these things Kuy described, *they* were the terrors he'd seen back among the slavers, the same nightmares that Kuy had called to him as he'd battled Tasahre. Most of all, he understood what lay inside Gelisya's teaching stone. It was him. It was the piece of his soul that Kuy had taken in the House of Cats and Gulls. When he spoke, his voice was hoarse.

'Yes,' he said, 'I do.'

Talon frowned. 'You do what?'

'I do want it back.'

Gelisya sniffed. 'Well then *you* have to do it.'

'Do *what*?' Talon was close to breaking.

Berren looked him in the eye. 'She's right. I do know how to save Tarn.'

12

THE KINDNESSES OF WARLOCKS

Three days later, the Fighting Hawks weighed anchor off the city of Tethis. Berren, Talon and half a dozen other mercenaries climbed down into a longboat. Tarn was lowered. Talon placed his little princess cousin carefully on his lap and the soldiers began to row. Before they were halfway to the shore, the ship was on its way back out to sea.

'How long will this take?' asked Talon.

In the days they'd been at sea, Tarn had wasted away. He was still alive, but for how much longer? Talon asked the same question at least once every day and Berren always gave the same answer, the only one he could: 'I don't know.' He wished that he hadn't said anything about it now; most of the time, he even wished that Gelisya had never given him the stone. He could feel how it changed him, how it made him whole and filled the tiny missing piece that had had been cut away in Deephaven. Yet at the same time what good ever came of a warlock's gift? What would Kuy take from him now? And how had the warlock known he would be there, in that place at that particular time? Had he known it even back in Deephaven? The thought made him shiver. If Saffran Kuy could see so much of the future then what did that mean? How did you fight a man who knew how everything would end before it even started? *Dragons for one of you. Queens for both! An empress!* Kuy even knew how he was going to die. *I saw my apprentice kill me.* That had been the golden-hafted knife, the one that cut souls. That was what showed him these things. The only thing a man could do, Berren thought, was to keep well away, and he'd have been more than happy with that. But he had to find Master Sy first. Had to, for Tasahre and her memory. And now he had to save Tarn.

'I don't know,' he said again. 'All I know is that Saffran Kuy is making all of this happen. We're being moved about like pieces in a game of Hak-Kanad.'

Talon shook his head and frowned. He didn't want to hear. And who would? What did you do with knowledge like that except weep?

Word had spread among the other mercenaries that Berren and the warlock at the camp had known each other once. The soldiers looked at him differently now, with suspicion and mistrust. More memories had begun to surface from the stone too. Memories of other potions, of Kuy brewing them, explaining carefully and clearly exactly what he was doing as if to a dullard apprentice. Sometimes the room around Kuy was empty, sometimes Gelisya was there, sometimes another boy – the boy from the slaver camp. Always Kuy spoke to his *little Berren-piece.* Mostly what he made were cures for this, that or the other; but there were other potions, and even knowing the ones that seemed harmless left Berren with a sense of dread. There would be a price for this, he was sure, a price heavier than he cared to imagine.

But he was going to save Tarn.

He shuddered. For *that* potion he didn't even know what half the ingredients did; all he could remember were the names. In Deephaven he might have known how to find some of them, but here he had no idea where to even begin; then, if he *did* manage to lay his hands on everything, how would he know if he'd made the potion properly?

He wouldn't. For all he knew, he'd end up feeding Tarn poison. How long would it take to work? What *else* might it do? What other marks might it leave? He didn't know anything except that it would cast the hungry spirit out, and that Saffran Kuy was leading him by the hand, step by cursed step. He was sinking inexorably into deep black water. Talon was right. He should have gone back home.

But still, he *was* going to save Tarn.

They reached the shore and men and women stopped to stare. The waterfront constables huddled together, wondering what to do. Talon tossed a purse full of money at Berren.

'At least *you* can make yourself useful. When you're done, I'll see to it that you're expected at the castle. The sooner we're out of here, the better.'

Berren snatched the purse out of the air and darted away into the thick of the town. Out of sight of Talon, he slowed to a walk and soaked in the air of the place. For once he was glad to see the back of the others. Princess Gelisya haunted him. She made him think of Saffran Kuy and Tarn and potions; or else she made him think of Radek, and *that* made him think of Deephaven and Tasahre and the sun-temple and Master Sy. And then he'd be thinking of all these things and Gelisya would turn and look at him with her child's face and her black hair and her wide unblinking eyes that seemed weary with knowledge. Talon took it for granted that Saffran Kuy had abducted her for his own ends, but Berren wasn't so sure. He couldn't shake the notion that Gelisya had been more a willing apprentice than a helpless hostage. A bit of both, perhaps?

He stopped in the street and looked around and, for a moment, forgot about everything else. He'd been here before! Not actually into the city, but as far as the harbour. When he'd been a skag, and there'd been some sort of drink that the sailors had found when they'd gone ashore.

Califrax, or something like that. He'd heard it for weeks. *It's Califraxed. He was Califraxed.* The word had stuck to the ship like a limpet.

He stopped sailors in the street and asked what it was and his questions led him to a sleazy sailors' hole, the Mermaid, a bit like the Bitch Queen of Kalda except a tenth of its size. The inside was gloomy, but made up for it through a vicious assault on all his other senses. Berren pushed his way through the crowd around the door. Lanterns were burning and the windows, such as they were, had heavy curtains drawn across them and a layer of black grime on their sills. The sun outside was high in the sky but inside it might just as easily have been midnight. As he moved through the crowd, he was bumped and battered and shouted over and occasionally splashed by raucous seamen. His nose registered the usual smell of cheap drink and drunks, but also something else. A fragrance that seemed quite out of keeping, but that he couldn't quite place. Califrax, he found, was a vicious brown ale. After what he'd grown used to in Kalda with Talon, it was cheap and vile; still, he felt better for a glass of it. Something he'd done for himself, at last. His choice, just his. When he was done, he raised the empty glass to all the sailors of his old ship and quietly hoped they were dead.

People were watching him. One tall man in particular, all elbows, bones sticking out of his wrists, long fingers that couldn't stay still and with restless darting eyes, but what Berren noticed most were the tattoos on his cheeks and his neck that ran down under his shirt. Berren couldn't see one, but he was quite sure the man was carrying a knife. People like this used to come to Master Hatchet with sacks full of things that weren't theirs. Old times, old ways. They would never quite leave him.

Outside he asked directions to the market and then ambled towards it, taking time to let the town soak into him. As best he'd been able to tell from the longboat, Tethis was built around the mouth of a small river valley. Its poorer districts spread up and down the shore either side of the river, perched beside the sea and crowding into the notches in the cliffs beyond. The richer parts ran up and onto the higher land on its rim, and the market lay on the border between these two parts of the city, at the place where the river valley first widened out before it reached the sea. From the centre of its square, Berren looked up towards the back of the town, where the valley became a gorge too narrow for people to build their houses. At the top of the slopes there, overlooking everything, were the low walls of the castle where Talon would take Gelisya.

He wandered through the market, buying the things he needed. Some of them were easy. Salt. Powdered bone. Clove oil. Others he recognised when he saw them. A few earned him frowns and directions to another cart. Now and then he'd get a blank look, as if the person he was talking to had never heard of what he was asking for. Once, in an apothecary, he got a very different look, a look that showed him that the woman he was talking to *had* heard of what he was asking for, but wished she hadn't.

The sun began to sink and the streets started to empty. Carts full of farmers from outside the town made their tired way up the hill beside the river, heading for home. He still had plenty of Talon's money left in his purse, so Berren found himself a tea house and sat down to wet his throat and rest his legs. He went through the list of what he needed in his mind and looked at all his packages and pouches. He had almost all of it now, only two things missing. The first would come from Tarn himself: blood. The other was the sap of a Funeral Tree, whatever that was. He hadn't the first idea what it looked like or what it did; neither, it seemed, did anyone else around the market. Which left the apothecary who'd claimed ignorance but whose eyes had said otherwise. He drained his tea and stood up and made his way back through the alleys to her tiny shop.

'Never heard of it.' Just as she had the first time, the apothecary clamped her mouth shut when she'd spoken and her fingers curled into fists. She set about putting her potions and powders away for the day. 'And now I'm shutting up. Goodbye.'

Berren didn't move. 'I don't know what all this is for,' he said. 'All I know is that a man I know, a friend, is desperately ill.'

'Well that won't help him,' said the apothecary, still taking care not to look at him.

'So you *do* know what it is then.' He put a single gold coin on the table in front of her. 'The sap of the Funeral Tree. Please.'

'I don't have any.'

'But you know what it is.'

She took a deep breath and then she took the gold and leaned into Berren and whispered, 'You come here asking me for poison? A drop of it will kill you. I know there's some who use it in potions and the like, but you'd have to be a master to know what you were doing.' She looked him up and down. 'Sick friend? My arse. I doubt I should be selling you anything, but thankfully I don't have any. There's one who might. He says he's a soap-maker, but everyone knows that's not all he makes. Back when the warlocks were here, he came with them.' She shuddered. 'Likely as not he'd have some sap for you, if you've got more gold.' She held up the piece he'd put on the counter and then closed her fingers around it. 'A lot more than this, I'd say.'

Her last words passed Berren by. 'What did you say about warlocks?'

The apothecary looked him up and down. 'Not from here, are you? Bad luck they were, but they're gone now.

Took a while before we knew them for what they were. What brought them here was death. And then ...' Berren found himself on the end of a long stare. 'Don't know what you'll have heard, but the old king was a fool letting the likes of them settle here. His Majesty Meridian did us all a service.'

Berren thought about that for a moment. 'This man. This soap-maker. Where will I find him? Who is he?'

Her voice dropped to a hiss. 'Like I said, he came with the warlocks. Maybe he's one of them, maybe he's not, but he's a wicked man. His heart decayed to nothing long ago. If you want to deal with people like that, on your own soul be it. There. I've told you what I know. Now get gone.'

'Who is he?' He was sure he already knew.

'Name he used was Vallas.' The apothecary backed away and stuffed Berren's gold deep into a pocket. 'He'll probably have what you're looking for. Over on the western edge of town in among the fishermen. Ask for the soap-maker, they'll know who you mean. But if I were you I'd stay far away from that place.'

Vallas. Berren thanked her for her time and walked out into the street with his head spinning. He'd heard that name before, back in Deephaven, from Saffran Kuy.

Ah, my poor brother Vallas.

13

INCANTATION AND MEMORY

He swore. Then he began to walk. The apothecary's directions hadn't been specific about the distance, and by time Berren reached the western edge of Tethis, the sun had set and night had fallen. By the smell and the nets strung out along the beaches, he'd reached the fishing quarter. What was someone who made soap doing living here?

A shiver ran through him and he stopped. Fish. It was as though Saffran Kuy had made all this happen simply to lure him back. He was doing exactly what was expected of him. And then what? Alone with a warlock? Maybe even two of them?

'No, Kuy. I'm not your puppet.' He turned round and began to walk back up the hill. Maybe if he came with Talon and a dozen armed men at his back, Vallas the soap-maker, or Saffran Kuy, or whoever was waiting for him, simply wouldn't be there. There would be no sap of the Funeral Tree. Tarn would die, but if this was all simply an elaborate trap then Tarn was meant to die anyway, and there was nothing he could do about it.

If that's what it is, why go to all this trouble? Kuy could have taken me at the camp if he knew I was there. Something else, then, but what? But still, he was *not* going alone. Not after the House of Cats and Gulls.

By the time he reached the top of the gorge, the stars

were up. He'd been walking since the middle of the day and his feet ached. The guards outside the castle took a long look at him and waved him in. When he found where the Hawks were quartered, Talon was still up, waiting for him, pacing.

'Did you find everything you need?'

Berren shook his head. 'There's one thing left.'

'There's something you can't find? I want this done and I want to be out of here.'

'I don't know if …' Berren stopped. The glare he got was like a slap in the face, and so he stood there and told Talon everything: the apothecary and what she'd said, the soap maker and who he really was, and how Berren feared it was a trap. By the time he'd finished, Talon was snarling like a wounded wolf.

'They still have a warlock in their midst? I'd like to …' He shook his head and the disgust in his voice was obvious. 'I'll see to it. A soap maker in the fishing district. Sap of a Funeral Tree.'

Berren watched him go, too tired to argue. The mercenaries had been given an outhouse to rest in, a damp windy shed that was good for keeping the rain off and not much else. From the smell it had spent most of its time as a hanging shed for meat and fish. It was small and there wasn't much space, but the others made room for him. They looked at him askance as Talon came back and led them out, but then they'd looked at him like that ever since the slaver camp, as if they weren't sure any more whether he was a friend. When they were gone, he found a corner and drifted into nightmares of Saffran Kuy and Tasahre and the thief-taker's golden-hilted knife, and only woke from them when the soldiers stomped and clattered back inside in the middle of the night, bored and surly. Half asleep, Berren heard them talking quietly, until the whispers faded into rasps of heavy breathing and snores. It sounded as though their expedition had been a waste of time.

He woke again early in the morning. While the rest were still sleeping, he crept out through the door and into the dawn light and walked slowly around the walls of the castle, watched by the sour-faced night guards. It wasn't really a castle at all. In Deephaven there was a fortified palace in the middle of the city, and this was more like that, except several hundred times smaller and less grand. Long ago, someone had built a solid stone house here. Other people had added to it later. Someone had started to turn it into a palace and then stopped. Someone else had aimed for a castle instead. Whoever the builders were, none had ever realised more than a small fraction of their ambition, and the result was an aimless shambles. Berren's idea of a castle came from the city walls of Deephaven, thick stone piled high with towers and siege weapons and lots of soldiers – or at least, that's what the walls had been back when there had been a use for them, before the city had swallowed them up. True, there *was* a wall of stone separating the castle of Tethis from the city on one side, the gorge on another and the countryside around the rest, but it wasn't much of one and a man with a mind to climb it would have no trouble at all. In some places it was made of wood, or dry stone, and towards the gorge and the city Berren could almost step over it. It seemed not so much a barrier as an idea of one. A pair of small towers faced out across the hills and fields with a palisade between them from which men could stand and shoot down on attackers. Berren walked its length. Seventy paces, that was all. An army came, they'd just go around it, easy as anything. They'd barely have to try. Like the palace itself, the walls had been started more than once, but they'd never come close to being finished.

No one stopped him as he climbed up. Next to this sorry excuse for a palace stood a barracks for a couple of cohorts of soldiers, stables for maybe forty horses, a few clusters of sheds and workshops, all arranged around a large muddy yard. In Deephaven any one of the rich merchants who lived around the city square would have had all this and much much more. He shook his head. On the other side, away from Tethis, the river gorge ran like a scar through mile upon mile of green fields. In the far distance he could see hills and then mountains.

In the year before he'd been born a war had come to Deephaven. He knew about this because the temple priests had told him. The whys and the whos had all been desperately dull, but one day they'd taken the novices up onto the old city walls. It was the first time he'd ever been up there, and the memory still felt fresh. One of the priests had pointed out a distant hill. *That's where Talsin's army came*, he'd said. *You could see them, stretched out from there to there …* And he'd pointed out two places that seemed to cover half of the horizon. *An army of forty or fifty thousand. Glorious to behold.* The priest had been there and seen it with his own eyes – you could hear the memory of it in his voice. There had been more, mostly about how the wicked general Kyra had used all manner of vicious tricks, even sorcery, to smash that army. But the memory that stayed with Berren was simply of standing there. He could see the army in his mind's eye, blackening the distant fields. An awesome sight, terrifying for the city defenders.

He looked out over the fields around Tethis now and tried to imagine such an army here. It didn't exist. It couldn't. It would walk through Tethis without even noticing. What would you need? A few hundred men? Surely not many more. And how many did Talon have? Two, three hundred? Enough to take the palace if they were clever about how they did it. Enough to hold it? Enough to take the city as well? Was that what Talon was doing, quietly building an army, ready to take back his home?

'Are you thinking what I'm thinking?' Berren jumped and almost fell off the palisade. Talon had climbed up next to him so quietly that Berren hadn't even noticed. They were being watched. Three men, armed and armoured, were down below. They were pretending to have nothing much to do, but they were watchers, no doubt about it. A thief-taker learned the difference. Further across the yard, as the sun rose higher, he saw a few men scurrying back and forth dressed in white. Priests? If they were then they were the first he'd seen in Tethis.

'I don't know. I was thinking about Deephaven and Master S— I mean Prince Syannis.'

Talon growled. 'Mostly I'm spending my time wondering whether Meridian will quietly cut all our throats while we're conveniently here, and how to make sure that he doesn't. But I'm also wondering whether the Hawks could take this city.' He shrugged. 'I shouldn't, but I can't seem to help myself.'

'I reckon you'd need a trick or two or a good few more men.'

'Meridian has enough to keep a free company at bay for a while. There might not be many proper soldiers here, but a city like Tethis can raise a militia of a thousand or more if it has warning. Not much use on an open field but give them a wall to hide behind and no place to run and their own homes to defend ... well, then a town militia can grow fierce.' He clapped Berren on the shoulder and held out a small phial. 'Is this what you needed?'

Berren took it out of Talon's hand. He'd seen it before, this very bottle or one exactly like it, carefully packed in a wooden box lined with straw, hidden in a bag in the Hall of Swords with Tasahre standing beside him. There were words carefully etched into the glass. He peered at them, but he already knew what they would say. *Poison. Blood of the Funeral Tree. Enough to kill six men. Secrete in food or drink*. He shuddered. 'I didn't think you'd find it. The soldiers made it sound like a waste of time.'

'We found the soap-maker's place but there was no one there.' Talon sniffed. 'Looked like it had been abandoned for days. Most of it was cleared out but we found this. It was sitting on a table in plain sight. There wasn't anything else.' He wrinkled his nose. 'The place stank of fish. It was as though we were *meant* to find it.'

Berren shivered. 'I keep saying it: Saffran Kuy is playing a game with us.'

'With us?' Talon cocked his head. 'Or with you?'

'I don't know.' Berren looked away. 'Does it matter? Master Sy's somewhere not far from here, isn't he?'

Talon twitched. 'Never you mind about him. First passage to Brons, you're on it.' He frowned. 'Not that you'll get a ship from here. Maybe from Forgenver, but the sooner the better. Anyway ...' He yawned and stretched and then waved cheerily down at the three watchers below. 'If this is all you need then we can get on and get out of here. Are you sure this will work?'

'Not really.' The memory of Kuy making the potion remained clear as crystal. Whatever the warlock had done, he could repeat it. How it worked and what it actually did, of that he had no idea.

'Tarn's dying.' Talon swung himself over the edge of the palisade and slid down the ladder to the ground. 'He's dying and he's my friend. *Make* it work.'

Berren followed him to the hanging shed. He set about getting ready while Talon shooed everyone else away until only the three of them remained: Berren, Talon and Tarn. Berren laid out the other ingredients the warlock had used. There was already a little fire going and a pot of steaming water hung above it. 'What if this kills him?'

'Then he'll die. But he'll also die if you do nothing.'

Berren began grinding the salt and the powdered bone

together and then mixing them in the boiling water with other powders and oils. He didn't even have to think about it, as though the warlock's recipe was in control and he was as much a tool of it as the pot or the pestle or the mortar. Time slipped by without him noticing.

'I need a little of his blood,' he said absently.

Talon frowned. 'Blood?'

'It is a warlock's potion, not a healer's.'

Talon's frown deepened, but he took a knife to fleshy part of Tarn's left hand and made a cut and held a cup to the wound. 'How much?'

'A thimble will do.' Berren stirred the pot. Once it was bubbling again, he reached into his pocket and pulled out Talon's phial. Poison. If anything was going to kill Tarn then it was this. He hesitated. *Sure? Am I really sure?*

A shadow loomed behind him. When he looked up, Gelisya looked back at him. Her black hair merged into the darkness of the hanging shed while the light of the fire on her face made her eyes seem enormous. The sight of her froze him stiff and the recipe fled from his mind.

'Two drops,' she said, after they'd stared at each other for what felt like an age. 'You need two drops. As soon as it boils.' She nodded earnestly and then added: 'It's boiling now.'

Berren shook himself, tipped in two drops of the poison and quickly put it away.

'Take it off the fire,' she said. 'Let it cool for a minute. It's nearly done now. It's very good for a first time.'

And how would you know that? But now there was another distraction: two soldiers at the door, men in shiny silver breastplates and long skirts made of leather strips covered in a deep green lacquer. They were the same soldiers he'd seen in Deephaven on Radek's ship, and between them stood a silhouette in gleaming white. A woman, slender and slight. He couldn't stop looking. In another world she could have been Tasahre.

'You need to put the blood in now,' said Gelisya in a matter-of-fact voice. Berren nodded, struck dumb, took the cup from Talon and did as he was told. She was right, he knew that. How old was she? He tried to look at her and found he couldn't meet her eyes.

'What's he done to you?' he whispered, as much to himself as to Gelisya.

'He showed me the hole in the world,' she whispered back. She stepped closer and touched Berren's face and then jumped away as if he'd stung her. 'Oh! It's you!' Her eyes went wide. 'What are you doing here? I thought you were inside! How did you get here?' Her bottom lip began to quiver as though she was about to burst into tears. Then a blankness passed across her face and her voice changed, went back to flat and toneless. 'You need to let it cool down. It goes into more of a paste when it's ready. You fill his mouth and his nose with it so he can't breathe. You bring him to the brink of death, you see, to drive the bad spirit out. You have to stay with him. You'll see it when it comes. Then you have to take the paste all out again so he can breathe. You have to do that quickly – and give him lots of water! He'll probably be sick a lot for a while and then he'll be better.'

'What do you mean "It's you"?' he asked. 'Who?'

'I'm sorry,' she said. 'I didn't realise. For a moment I didn't know who you were but now I do. You're Berren. You took me away from the bad wizard. I have to go now.' She skipped away towards the door. Berren made to go after her but he was too slow and the soldiers barred his way while Gelisya slipped between them. *Took me away.* Not *rescued*, but *took me away*.

'Come back!' he called.

The woman in white pushed between the soldiers. She

was robed and veiled and she slapped him in the face. The soldiers stepped away and Berren heard a sharp intake of breath from one of them. He stood there, mute and confused. The woman slapped him again. 'You bastard,' she hissed. 'What do you creatures want with her? She's just a girl! You make me sick, both of you!' Berren caught a flashing glimpse of her eyes beneath her veil and the venom glittering within them, and then she turned and walked quickly away.

14
THE LASH AND THE ELIXIR OF LIFE

'Hey!' Berren stepped forward but the soldiers stood in his way until she was gone. Behind him, Talon let out a long and exasperated sigh. 'Now I have to find Meridian, except since he and everyone else who matters are off hunting somewhere, I suppose it'll have to be my retard half-brother.'

'What?'

Talon came to stand beside him. 'You're not from these parts. I keep forgetting. But you can't stand for that. Even if you wanted to, you can't.' He shook his head. 'Not from a bondswoman.'

'What do you mean? What's a bondswoman?'

Now Talon looked at him in wonder. 'How long were you in Kalda? The ones in white, they're all bonded men or women. Do you not have slaves in Deephaven?'

'No.'

'Well the sun-king doesn't hold with them either, but this far from Caladir no one much cares. In Kalda the likes of Meridian call them bondsmen and bondswomen, but slaves is what they are. People who have been bought. Who are owned and traded and sold as if they were property. The children and family of debtors mostly. Although of course the merchants of Kalda have acquired some very inventive definitions of debt when it comes to the Taiytakei. The city sells its unwanted to the slavers, the Taiytakei train them and return them. In Kalda the guilds lend money to rich men to buy their "freedom." Then the loans are called in, the debt is passed on to the man who is now "free" and of course cannot be paid, and in the blink of an eye and the flash of a writ, a freed slaves become bondsmen. It's the same thing but with a different name.' Talon snorted. 'Aimes. *That* will be interesting. Excuse me, but as head of the visiting party I must now find our hosts and inform them that their property has offended one of my household.' He sighed, irritated. 'Since you're not a bondsman yourself, the proper response would be to allow you to punish her by whatever means you see fit. What on earth did you say?'

Berren shook his head. 'I don't know.' He was still trying to remember what Gelisya had said about the potion.

'Ah well.' Talon snapped his fingers and muttered something. 'The usual punishment is a flogging. If you wanted to you could ask to have her executed but I'd rather you didn't. I don't wish to offend King Meridian by killing a favoured bondswoman, if that's what she is.' He shook his head. 'Stupid woman. She can't possibly have thought she'd be allowed to get away with something like that. Someone put her up to this to test us.' He turned and let out a heavy sigh. 'You'll have to wield the lash yourself. Ever flogged anyone before? I don't suppose you have.'

'No! And I don't want to.' Berren shook his head. 'I've seen enough of that. I don't even know who she was.' He went back into the gloom of the shed and looked at the potion in the pot. It was thickening nicely. Talon clapped him on the shoulder but his voice stayed hard.

'Whoever she is, it has to be done. No one will despise you if you choose to go easy on her, but she is Meridian's property and she has struck a guest, a Fighting Hawk, and what you do now reflects on me. If you make yourself look weak or cruel or stupid, you make us all look that way. You will put her to the lash because that is the law, but no need to be harsh. Ten strokes will do and you may be soft with your hand, although not *too* soft. I'm sure after two years at sea you know how.' Talon looked away, glancing down at the congealing mess in the pot on the floor. 'Is that ready yet?'

Berren shrugged. 'It has to cool. Not long.'

'But soon, yes?'

'Yes.'

Talon looked pleased. 'We can leave tonight then.' He glanced at Tarn. 'Do you need any more help with him?'

'No. At least I don't think so.'

'Then I'll see you're left undisturbed until you're needed.' He walked out into the sunshine leaving Berren alone in the shadows and the gloom. Berren sat next to Tarn while the potion cooled. Why? Why did he have to whip someone if he didn't want to? He could hardly blame anyone for hating what he was doing. It was magic, dark magic. Warlock magic. Magic that wasn't meant to be used.

The potion cooled into a paste as Gelisya had said it would. Without thinking much about what he was doing, Berren prised Tarn's mouth open and forced in as much as would go. What was left he pressed into Tarn's nose. *I'm probably killing him*, he thought, but he did it anyway. When he was done, he watched and waited. Ten seconds passed, then twenty. Tarn twitched. Thirty seconds. Suddenly Tarn arched. Convulsions shook his body. A thin black mist began to form around his face.

'I can see it! He's almost ready,' said a voice behind him, quiet yet ripe with excitement. Gelisya again, and maybe that meant the soldiers and the slave woman too, but Berren didn't dare look around. He watched as Tarn bucked and spasmed and then went still.

'I wanted to see,' said Gelisya. 'I've never seen it work before.'

Berren hardly heard her. Tarn wasn't moving now, and

all he could think was that he'd killed his friend. He forced open Tarn's mouth and frantically clawed at the paste, flinging it out again.

'I'm sorry,' said Gelisya. 'I didn't realise it was you. But I went inside, and you *are* there, and you're here as well. How do you do that?'

'I don't have the first idea what you mean.'

She giggled. 'Silly! How can you be in two places at once?'

Berren growled at her but she didn't go away; instead she passed a jug of water.

'I like my maid,' she said. 'I'm sorry she hit you. I'll tell her not to. I'll tell her I'm cross.'

'I'm sorry too. Apparently I'm going to have to hurt her. And then I dare say we won't ever meet again.' He poured water between Tarn's lips. Tarn jerked, then coughed and spluttered. Alive, thank the four gods!

'You will.' Gelisya's voice sounded solemn. 'And I *am* sorry. But I know how to make it better.'

'Don't bother.'

'But you'll like her. And she'll like you. It's *important*. We're supposed to be *friends*.'

'You're just a child!' He said it as much for himself as for her. 'I don't even know who she is. I've never seen her before. I don't know anything about her and I don't know anything about *you*.' He had to stop, because as he spoke Tasahre flashed into his mind again. The slave, the shape of her, she reminded him of the sword-monk, which only made it all even worse. 'She slapped me, that's all. I hardly felt it, and for what I'm doing here, *I* might have slapped me too. She doesn't deserve to be punished. So don't.'

Gelisya didn't say anything. She twirled in circles on the spot behind him as Berren sat Tarn up and gave him a shake and slapped him on the back. 'He'd take you with us,' she said. 'I know he would if I asked him.'

103

'What? Who?'

'Saffran.' She leaned forward and whispered in his ear. 'I know you're going to keep the teaching stone, aren't you? I suppose I don't mind. But you have to keep it safe. You have to promise. He's my friend in there.'

Berren clenched his fists, Maybe if he wished hard enough, she'd read his mind and go away.

'It fills the hole, you see. Like the Black Moon and the Dead Goddess fill the hole in the world. He showed it to me. You have to keep it closed otherwise something will come through. Not yet, but one day. Before you both come back for the very last time. You have to keep it closed.' Even with her lips almost touching his ear, her whisper was so quiet that he could barely hear her. 'He's making us ready. To let it in when the Ice Witch brings the Black Moon down.'

Enough! Berren spun around, but before he could throw Gelisya out of the shed Tarn's eyes flew open. He sat bolt upright, was violently sick, then started thrashing about and screaming. Berren tried to hold him still but Tarn was a big man and strong with it, and Berren was neither. He swatted at Berren, trying to push him aside, eyes staring away into the distance.

'Petarl? Petarl!' Whatever he was seeing it wasn't Berren.

'I'll get some of father's soldiers,' said Gelisya in a sing-song voice. She danced out. Tarn finally cuffed Berren aside and staggered to his feet.

'Tarn! It's me! It's Berren!'

Tarn stared at him. 'Petarl? Have the Swords of the Sun struck camp yet? And where's the bear? I haven't seen him!'

Berren tried to sit him down but Tarn was having none of it. He scrabbled around for his sword, was sick for a second time and then went back to shouting and screaming. Other Hawks ran into the shed, eyes wide with surprise. It took three of them to wrestle Tarn down, but when he finally grew calm and the first glimmers of recognition flickered in his eyes, it was Berren he clung to. The others slowly backed away, drawing signs of protection in the air around them. The looks they gave Berren were a strange mix – fear and admiration, loathing and respect – but Berren ignored them all, holding's Tarn's face in his hands, talking about their days together under Sword-Master Silvestre; and as he did, Tarn seemed to come back, piece by piece from wherever he'd been. It was slow: one moment he was lucid, the next he had no idea who Berren was or where they were or why. He kept asking about Petarl and the bear and the Swords of the Sun, whoever they were.

By the time Talon came back, an hour later, Tarn was almost himself. He greeted Talon as though nothing had happened, and Talon told him about the slaving camp and everything that had followed. Somehow, from Talon's mouth, the words seemed to strike home.

'And what *did* a death-mage want with slavers?' asked Tarn when Talon was done.

'Nothing good, you can be sure of that. Berren here put a crossbow bolt into him, but we all know it takes a lot more to bring a warlock down. Old friends, those two.'

Old friends? Berren had been about to say something about Gelisya but now his tongue was numb.

'I was trapped,' said Tarn. 'In another place from a long time ago.' He shook his head and shivered. 'Horrible. All I remember is chasing the man in grey into a dark room, and then I was lying helpless and powerless and waiting to die, back among the worst days I ever had.' And he told them how years ago he'd been caught up in a vicious tale that wound around a sacked monastery, murderous monks, poisoned wells, starvation and desperation and desertion, and finally ended with Tarn, too weak from hunger to move and paralysed with fear, watching while the rest of his ruined company had had their throats slit in their sleep by zealot boys half his age.

'That was before the Hawks,' he said. 'I was young then. Very young.' His face was pale. 'I'd almost forgotten.'

They went outside and Talon got straight into an argument with the castle steward, something about about horses and wagons, the steward politely insisting that Talon take some of the castle horses and Talon politely declining. Berren and Tarn watched. It seemed a strange argument, since the steward clearly wanted Talon *not* to take up his offer, while Talon was clearly eyeing the horses with envy. Berren could hardly blame him for that, for the two beasts that had been brought out of the stables looked like fine Deephaven cavalry mounts, not draught horses for pulling wagons. Even the saddles that the steward had had put on their backs were exactly like those the Emperor's lancers used, right down to the flash of silver thread embroidered into the stirrup straps.

Berren frowned at that. They were a long way from Aria. What were Deephaven lancers doing out here? There had been men from Aria in Kalda too and they'd tried to kill Prince Talon. Were they the same? They had to be, didn't they?

Eventually a pair of horses and a hired wagon drove up from the town. Talon and the steward were still arguing even as the mercenaries loaded up what little they'd carried with them from the ship. For a minute Berren began to hope that he might not have to whip Gelisya's bondswoman after all, but then, even as Talon was walking back to the wagon, three of the castle soldiers came towards them, pushing a figure in white ahead.

Talon was right about one thing – Berren had been flogged more than once while he'd been a skag. It was a common enough punishment but always done with a certain ritual. The victim would be called out by name.

The two sailors who tied him to the mast wore special hats. Sentence would be read aloud and most of the ship's crew were called on deck to witness the punishment. None of that happened here. The soldiers tied the woman to a whipping post, tore the clothes from her back, gave Berren a lash and then lounged, obviously bored. Talon's Hawks waited impatiently to leave. Everyone else around the palace, bondsmen and soldiers alike, went about their business as though nothing was happening.

Without thinking, Berren looked for scars, for any signs that she'd been through this before, but there were none. He took a pace closer and touched her skin, feeling how soft it was. Again a sailor's ritual, judging how hard the stroke would need to be to draw blood. Anyone who'd been to sea would know from that touch that Berren meant to stay his hand as much as he could.

But those hands were shaking. He didn't want this. It was unfair, unjust. He leaned forward. 'I'm sorry,' he whispered, hoping no one else would hear. There was no reply. He stared at the back of her head looking for any kind of acknowledgement, any indication that she understood. 'I have to do this,' he said. 'I don't want to.' Out of the corner of his eye he could see Talon's foot beginning to twitch. *Get on with it!*

But no, he couldn't. He lifted the whip to strike and his arm was quivering so much that he couldn't keep it straight. He dropped the whip. 'No. I'm not doing this,' he said and stamped towards the wagon. Talon jumped down to block his path and Berren met his eyes. 'No,' he said again. 'I'm *not* doing it. Let her go.'

Talon hissed. 'Fool.' He strode past, pushing Berren hard, almost knocking him down, and picked up the whip himself.

The first three strokes were vicious. Berren heard the woman gasp as the first one struck and her skin split.

After the third, she was hanging from the whipping post by her wrists, whimpering uncontrollably. Talon turned to Berren. He held out the bloody whip. 'Ten strokes,' he said. 'Seven left. You or me. If it's me then I will make every one as hard as the first. Now do your duty, soldier.'

Berren stared, hating Talon at that moment because he knew the prince meant it. Savage. He shook his head. Talon clenched his teeth and lashed the woman again. Hard. She spasmed and screamed. Then he turned back to Berren and snarled and held out the whip again. 'Do you *want* me to kill her? You are not a boy now, Berren of Deephaven. You are a man and a soldier of the Fighting Hawks. Like it or not. Now do what must be done!'

Berren had tears in his eyes now. His feet felt like lead, the earth like quicksand sucking him down and holding him fast, but he forced himself to move. He walked to Talon and took the whip. His face was numb and his voice shook when he spoke. 'I'll remember that you made me do this.'

Talon pointed to the woman's back. 'And *I* will remember that you made *me* do *that*. Now finish!' He stalked back to the waiting wagon.

Berren closed his eyes. He tried to think what Tasahre would do, what she would say. She wouldn't do *this*, that was for sure. She would refuse and find a way to stop Talon too. She would stand up for what was right, no matter what. And he couldn't. Couldn't find that strength she had.

He howled as he cracked the whip. The stroke made the woman cry out and he felt her agony as deeply as his own. He was killing a part of himself by doing this. Stepping away from the man Tasahre had seen in him and towards Saffran Kuy. The last five strokes were weak, as light as he dared, but he made them, and each one left a bloody mark on her back. When he was done, he was sobbing. He moved closer and whispered in the woman's ear.

'I will kill any warlock I see. Always. I will do everything I can to stop them.' He didn't know if the woman was even conscious any more.

'Come on!' That was Talon rushing him back to the wagon. As he left, Berren couldn't take his eyes off the body, slumped and bloody against the whipping post. For all he knew she might even be dead. And when he closed his eyes, he kept seeing Tasahre with sadness on her face.

'And we're gone!' said Talon loudly as they sat down. 'Fighting Hawks on the march.' The wagon began to move. No one seemed to be in any hurry to cut the woman down. Berren stared transfixed until they rounded a corner and the whipping post passed out of sight.

15

THE BLOODY JUDGE

'We could have gone by sea,' Talon said. 'It would have been quicker, but I thought it might be useful to see the lie of the land.'

He said it on the second day out of Tethis, in a joking idle sort of way. Berren thought nothing of it at first, but as the days passed the words rattled around in his mind. Whether he'd meant it or not, Talon was thinking of coming back one day with the Fighting Hawks. All of them.

Forgenver lay one kingdom, one duchy, seven rivers and nine days away from Tethis. They arrived to find the rest of the Hawks already settled and barracked outside the city and in high spirits from a first skirmish with the enemy. By chance, a half-cohort sent to scout the coastal villages near the town had arrived as a raid was coming in. The raiders were caught in their longboats in choppy seas. The Hawks had rallied the villagers and together they'd repelled the boats with a mixture of stones and crossbow fire and a great deal of shouting from the beach. It hadn't amounted to much and from the sound of things no one on either side had even been seriously hurt, but the boats had been turned away and it had pleased the duke.

Word of Tarn's recovery spread too. No one said anything to Berren's face, but a rumour spread like wildfire that Tarn had been dead and that Berren had brought him back to life again. No matter how much Tarn told them that was all rubbish, when Berren came by, conversations ended. Soldiers who were supposed to be his comrades made a sign against evil and slipped away. When he carried the stone that Princess Gelisya had given him, the skill to make potions was lodged in his head, there whenever he sought it. If he put it aside then the memories went away, but a part of him went with them. He felt that much more now. He'd carried a numbness with him ever since Deephaven, a dull lack of feeling that came back to him now whenever he didn't carry the stone. As a ship's skag, he hadn't known any better – wasn't this how all skags felt? But now ... But he couldn't explain it, couldn't even begin to describe what Saffran Kuy had done to him, so all anyone saw was that he carried it with him wherever he went, whatever it was.

'They're afraid of you,' Tarn told him one day.

Berren shrugged. 'Maybe they're right.' The two of them drew their practice swords and for half an hour they fought, Berren losing himself in the pattern of the blades and the interplay between them. This, *this* was when he felt at peace, with a sword singing in his hand. Block and riposte, parry and strike, one motion to the next, and all with the calm stillness in his head that Tasahre had taught him. Action without thought. This, and never anything else.

While Talon's spies worked their way closer to where the raiders were coming from, the cohorts of the Hawks spread themselves in pairs along the coast and waited. In the mornings Berren and Tarn walked together some-times, exploring the lands nearby and the village they were watching. In the afternoons Tarn stayed in the camp, talking and joking with the other men. At first Berren joined them, hoping for their acceptance, but it never came, and so as the weeks passed he drew apart. He spent more time than the rest standing watch, staring out at the sea, and when he wasn't watching he practised alone. He taught himself to shoot a crossbow, quietly trying to forget the ten minutes he'd spent learning with Master Sy. He practised and practised until he was as good as any of them. He tried other weapons, learning their weight and their balance and how they felt in his hands, although the short stabbing sword that the thief-taker had taught him and the slightly longer cut-and-thrust blades of the sword-monks remained his first loves. Sometimes, when he was lucky, Tarn or one of the other soldiers would spar with him, but mostly he trained alone in the way of the monks of Deephaven. It took him a week or two to be sure, but one on one he could outfight every single one of them. Tasahre had given him that. A gift or a curse? He wasn't sure.

Sometimes, late at night when it was dark, he would slip away into the village alone and quietly drink himself into a stupor. More and more his night-time dreams filled with the bondswoman from Tethis and the bloody weals he'd given her. Except her face wasn't veiled and when he turned her towards him she was a stranger.

Talon came by twice, moving constantly up and down the coast to watch over his company. The second time he came, he sparred with Berren himself. By the end neither of them was quite sure who had won.

'Deephaven soon,' Talon said afterwards. 'I'll find you a ship just as quickly as I can, but it looks like you'll be fighting with us again first.' He bared his teeth. 'I've tracked the enemy down at last. Again. This time they'll not get away.'

'Where's Syannis?' asked Berren, but Talon only wagged a finger and shook his head.

They struck camp and set off back to Forgenver the next morning. Berren watched the first wave of excitement sweep through the soldiers as they packed their tents and loaded their mules. He looked at them, milling and laughing and drinking around him, strangers nearly all, and wondered why they were here. What brought a man to a foreign land, far away from the place of his birth? What made them want to pick up a sword or an axe or a spear? They had their reasons, each of them. For their last night together in Forgenver and the two days at sea that followed, he could only watch them and wonder: How could they sing and laugh and cheer and joke when some of them must soon die? Or was that exactly *why* they did it? Was it the thought of death that made them so full of life? A lot of him wanted to join them, raucous and crude and merry, but he couldn't. Wherever he looked, he felt the shadow of Saffran Kuy, standing at his shoulder, laughing at him.

They reached wherever it was they were going – the middle of nowhere by Berren's reckoning. The sails were furled and the ship eased as close to the shore as it could. Two, maybe three, hundred yards away a wide sandy beach rose gently into a thick green forest. It was a warm day, sunny and dry with a light breeze that kept Berren cool under his padded leather jerkin. The beach was empty but Talon still had a dozen of his best crossbows standing watch, bolts at the ready as the first boats were lowered over the side.

The Hawks went ashore two cohorts at a time. The first ones to land scattered quickly into the fringes of the woods while the boats struggled back through the surf to the ship. Then it was Berren's turn. He jumped in without hesitation, seized an oar and they all pulled hard together, conscious of how vulnerable they were, and Berren remembered another boat, crossing the river from Deephaven to Siltside, and the whistle of arrows and the shouts of soldiers. The longboat bucked and heaved in the breaking waves as they reached the shore as if trying to toss them into the sea. When they jumped out, the water was still up to Berren's waist.

Tarn yelled at them to move out of the surf and up onto the beach while he and the tallest of the soldiers helped to turn the boats around and back out again. The waves knocked Berren forward, almost made him fall, and he was still wading out of the water, dripping and soaked, when the fighting started. Maybe the first shouts from the scouts had come as they were climbing out of the boats, but if so no one had heard over the breaking surf. Now the skirmishers were running back out onto the beach, waving their arms. Tarn roared at them, and then there were other men coming from the trees, dozens of them in a ragged horde, yelling and waving swords and axes and spears and clubs. The skirmishers ran as far as Tarn and his cohort and then turned. There was nowhere else for them to go.

'Stand!' bellowed Tarn. 'Stand together! Hold firm!'

Berren could see the eyes of the first man charging at him now, wide and wild, full of fear and thoughtless rage. Those eyes terrified him. This wasn't fighting in Tasahre's circle or Silvestre's square; this was death coming at him, over in a flash, one swing, one stab and then one of them would be dead. The urge to run was almost overwhelming.

'Stand fast!' screamed Tarn.

Berren took a step back. The two cohorts had formed a single line of shields. All he had behind him was the sea, the boats still struggling through the waves back towards Talon's ship. A madman with an axe rushed at him. Out of the corner of his eye he saw someone fall, staggering back as though he'd been shot. He made himself stand firm and never mind how his heart was racing or how much he was sweating and his hands shaking. His mouth was dry with fear, his hands too tight on his sword, his legs had lost all strength and his feet had grown roots. It wasn't an axe coming at him, he realised, it was a cleaver and it looked big enough to fell a horse. He was going to die!

And then it was almost as though he stood and watched and it was someone else who calmly stepped aside. The man with the cleaver tore past and swung, but where Berren had been only his blade remained. The man took a few more steps, stumbled, then fell face down onto the sand, his guts spilling around him. Berren blinked. The world seemed to go quiet for a moment. He stared at the man on the sand behind him, doubled up, clutching at himself as he spread a red strain across the beach. Then he looked at his hand, already holding his sword straight out in front of him, aimed at the eyes of the next man racing towards him. He stared at the steel, at the blood dripping from it ...

... and snapped back to where the air was filled with shouts from so many voices that nothing made any sense, with the ringing sounds of steel on steel and with screams. The next man came at him with a sword. Berren didn't move, didn't flinch, just kept his own steel pointed straight at the man's face. The man's charge faltered. He slowed; the look in his eyes changed, fear winning out over fury, until he almost stopped, and it was the easiest thing in the world for Berren to step forward, lunge and stab him in the neck.

The Hawk to Berren's right fell, ribs smashed open by the blow of an axe. The force knocked him sideways and he clawed at Berren's arm as he died. The man who'd killed him was screaming bloody murder and already swinging again. Berren jumped out of the way of both of them. He stepped inside the swing of the axe, chopped the axeman's arm off with one blow, smashed him with his shield and then stabbed him between the ribs.

More raiders were emerging from the woods. Bodies littered the sand now, some of them dead, most still moving, the crippled and the dying simply trying to get away. Outnumbered like this the two cohorts of the Hawks were supposed to form a single circle of swords and shields that would simply shrink back into itself whenever a man fell. They all knew it but they hadn't drilled it, and Berren had no idea how it was supposed to work when the only thing you could do was jump out of the way of an axe and your own dying brother trying to drag you to the ground. They were all muddled together now, the mercenaries and the men from the woods, in a swirling melee where every man fought for himself with no idea of what was going on around him.

Berren danced amid the press of swords, dodging whichever way would keep space around him. Men fell, Hawks and raiders both. He had no idea how many there were, how hopeless the battle might be, whether they were on the brink of victory or defeat. All he could see was the space around him, the circle that marked the reach of his sword and anything that breached it. Another man with an axe came at Berren and lost his hand, and at the same time a heavy blow landed on his back. It knocked him forward but he was already spinning and pushing himself away. The man who'd attacked him had a club, raised for another blow. Berren split his face in half before he could bring it down.

Then he saw Tarn with three of the enemy around him. He leaped through the fight the way Tasahre had taught him, moving so fast that no one could touch him, chopped most of the way through the first man's neck and barged the second aside with his shield. Tarn finished the third. Berren lunged again, but then there was another coming at him and he had to jump away, back towards Tarn, except Tarn wasn't where he'd been, and now there was *another* man coming at him, this time with a spear, and all he could do was bat that aside and jump again, swinging at another raider as he did, missing, all the while feeling the sharpness seeping from his arms and his legs, the edge of speed draining away.

And then the raider in front of him turned his back and ran; and as Berren took a step after him, he saw that they were all running, twenty or thirty of them, fleeing back up the sand towards the woods. There were bodies everywhere.

'After them!' Berren felt a fresh surge of energy, his first rush of victory. He raced the other mercenaries, seeing which of them would be the first to bring a man down, but then they were at the edge of the woods and Tarn was screaming at them to stop, to hold, to watch for ambushes and archers. The hunger for more was strong, the urge to rush on and finish the enemy almost too much to resist. Berren tried to catch his breath and then, when he'd done that, he tried to work out what had actually happened.

'Hold! Hold here!' That was Tarn trying to sort out who was alive and who was dead, how many could still fight and how many were hurt. The men who'd made it to the woods were unscathed or else carried only small wounds, a nick or a sprain. There were others, though, left on the beach. You didn't get in the way of a man swinging an axe and come out with just a scratch, after all. The scouts had taken the worst of it. Most of Tarn's cohort was still standing as far as Berren could see, and so far they all had the usual number of arms and legs.

'You fought like a man possessed. Like a demon.' Tarn grinned as he passed. 'Hurt?'

Berren shook his head.

'How many did you send back to the sun?'

'Four, I think. Maybe five.'

'Maybe six or seven, more likely.' Tarn laughed. 'There's about twenty of them lying on the beach back there and there's six of us gone to the sun. Think about that.' He nodded. 'Glad to be your sergeant, soldier.'

They waited at the edge of the woods, tense and on their guard in case whoever had attacked them came back, but there was no more fighting. When the boats returned to the shore once more, Talon was with them with two fresh cohorts. There were a few hasty words with Tarn and then they were all at a run, Talon at the front, straight through the woods. The cohorts that followed would burn the dead and tend to the wounded, but for now Talon wanted to bring the raiders to bay before they had a chance to escape.

Ten minutes later they were standing in fields staring at a collection of huts that had been crudely thrown together from mud and wood. The Hawks swarmed through. Berren and Tarn kicked in door after door, shields raised and blades poised, but one after another the huts were empty. Berren was shaking: the excitement of the fight and then the charge through the woods and now the air of danger, the threat of every shadow, they all had a hold on him. His eyes flicked this way and that, and with every sign of movement, his hand flashed to his sword.

They passed a hut whose door was hanging broken from its frame. Tarn went straight past, but Berren thought he caught a flicker of movement, and when he stopped and looked again, he saw a pair of eyes looking back at him from the far corner of the floor. At first he couldn't understand what he was seeing, but when he took a step through the doorway, the eyes rose and a woman scrabbled to her feet, showering cold ashes everywhere. She was dressed in rags, old and with a bad leg. Someone who couldn't run. She had a knife and she was pointing it at him, holding it as far away from her as she could. She'd hidden in the firepit, covering herself with ash and half-burned wood and they'd almost missed her.

For a second they stared at each other and neither said a word, and then the woman lunged at him, stabbing at his face with her knife, hissing. Berren stepped around the knife and flicked the tip of his sword at her throat. Blood sprayed across the room and she collapsed where she stood. *A stroke of mercy*, he thought, but as he stared at her lying on the ground in a pool of blood all he saw was Tasahre on the deck of Radek's ship, and she was shaking her head at him, and the last light in her eyes as they died was full of sadness. Action without thought. An old woman with a blunt and pitted knife. There were so many ways he could have spared her and yet his instinct had killed her. He looked at his hands. They'd betrayed him. They'd shown him who he really was.

'What did you do that for?' asked Tarn behind him. Berren turned his back on both of them and walked out of the hut. Outside, the search of the village was largely over. He walked blindly through it. *I've become him*, he thought. *I've become Master Sy.*

'Hey!' Tarn came after him. 'Who made you the bloody judge of life and death?'

Berren didn't answer and the killing was forgotten before long, at least by everyone else, but the name would stick to him for ever. *The Bloody Judge.*

16
THE STONES BY THE SEA

The village was no raiders' camp after all. Women and children had lived there, though they'd fled before the Hawks arrived. They'd had livestock and poultry which they'd hurriedly driven away. There were farm tools. It had been a village, a living village and not some summer camp like the one the Hawks had left outside Forgenver. As the rest of the soldiers landed from the ship, Talon called a company council. This sounded like a grand thing to Berren until he saw that it was simply Talon and all the cohort sergeants getting together for a chat, and anyone else who wanted to join in was perfectly welcome. Berren left them to it. Slaughtering women and children, razing villages, salting the earth, all these things were anathema to a soldier, or at least they were supposed to be. Berren had no idea whose kingdom they were in but this place surely belonged to someone. There would be consequences for what the Hawks had done here.

The old woman he'd killed haunted him. He wandered away from the village looking for some solitude, and took a path that went back into the woods towards the beach. It led him to the sea by a cluster of boulders, some as big as a house. The ground underfoot was sandy and he could hear the waves and taste the salt in the air. He found himself a slab to lean against, warm in the sun, and stared out across the sea, out to the ship that had brought them here.

Why did you do it? Why? He couldn't even begin to answer. Before today he'd killed two men: Radek of Kalda because the warlock Saffran Kuy had made him do it, and he'd killed the sailor Klaas. Klaas had been a pig and a bully, a thief and a coward who'd got exactly what he deserved, but Berren had still thought about what he'd done for weeks afterwards, wondering if there could have been some other way. Maybe he could simply have run? Before that he'd barely even been in a fight, unless you counted the childhood fisticuffs with Master Hatchet's boys. And now, today, he'd killed half a dozen men he didn't even know, who didn't know him, and he'd killed a woman too.

What troubled him most was how he remembered it. Everything was a blur, even the woman. He remembered exactly what he'd done but as though he was watching someone else do it, the same way he'd felt in the battle. He'd killed her but he couldn't begin to say why. Because she'd come at him with a knife, yes, but what sort of reason was that when he was a soldier, armoured and with a sword, and she'd had almost nothing? Instinct, that's what it was. Simple instinct, and his had been to kill, because that's what they'd all taught him, one after the other: Master Sy, Master Silvestre, even Tasahre, although she would have wept at what he'd done today.

There'd been another man in the battle, too – he remembered now. They'd exchanged blows, and then Berren had lunged. He'd felt his sword hit something but then another soldier had barged into him, almost knocking him flat, and when Berren had looked up, the man he'd been fighting was gone. Now he was left not knowing whether the man was even injured, and the not-knowing bothered him. Was there someone out there who would forever see scars on his belly and think of that dark-skinned wiry short-arse on the beach?

A movement in the corner of his eye shattered his

thoughts. He dodged sideways in time to see a hammer smash into the rock where his head had been. He grabbed hold of the hand that held it and pulled, yanking a man even smaller than he was out into the open. For a few seconds they wrestled, Berren and a shrieking, swearing fireball of elbows, knees, feet and fists, until he managed to smack his attacker's head into a rock and put an end to it. Berren had his own dagger in his hand at once, then stopped. The stunned man groping in the sand at his feet wasn't a man at all – he was a boy, maybe eleven or twelve years old but no more.

Another figure appeared from a crack between the rocks – a woman, much older. 'Please, sir! Please!' The crack was tight and she was having trouble getting out. Berren watched her and all the while he rested one foot on the boy's neck to make sure he stayed on the ground. The flash of bloodlust that had made him draw his dagger was gone now.

The woman freed herself from the rocks and stopped where she was. 'Please don't hurt him! He's all I have. Oh please!' Berren cocked his head, waiting to see what she would say next. The woman's eyes glistened. Tears began to roll down her cheeks. 'We don't have anything. I swear! Nothing!'

'Is there a harbour here? A big one?'

She shook her head.

'But ships come here, yes?'

This time she nodded.

'What happens when they come?'

'The men go away.' As terrified as she was, Berren saw a moment of hesitation. She was wondering whether to pretend she didn't know or perhaps make up some lie about where they went. He put a little more pressure on the boy's neck, making him gasp. The woman bowed her head.

'And what do they do when they're away?'

She didn't answer until Berren forced another whimper out of the boy. 'They go fighting,' she said.

'They go looting, pillaging and plundering?' The woman wouldn't look at him. 'Slaving? Do they go slaving?' Yes, that got a flicker out of her. 'I'm not going to kill your boy for that,' he said. 'Lie to me and that's another matter. How long are the men gone?'

'Between planting and harvest time.'

'So the ship would be coming for them soon, then? Or has it already been?'

She shook her head, but no, of course the ship hadn't come already otherwise the men he'd fought this morning wouldn't have been here. It would come soon, then, to take them away to raid the Duke of Forgenver's coast. Had they been looking out for it? Was that why they'd been so quick to strike at Talon's company – because they'd been watching for a ship all along?

'How do you know when?'

'A man comes to the village and tells us.'

'What man?'

'I only saw him once.'

'When does he come?'

'He came already. Yesterday. He said you were coming. He said to be ready.'

'He told you *what*? That *we* were coming?' So it wasn't just a well-kept watch. And they'd not seen another ship on their whole trip up the coast, which meant that word had come from Forgenver before Talon had even set sail! Berren took his foot off the boy and walked briskly towards her. He grabbed her by the arm and dragged her towards the woods. 'This man, who is he? When was the first time he came here?'

'Winter before last,' she said. She didn't try to pull away from him. He saw her wave frantically at the boy though. *Run, run!* 'Was a hard winter and food was scarce ...'

'What does he wear? Big horse, fancy clothes, fancy sword, that sort of thing?' He looked at her, but that wasn't it. Something else then. A horrible thought struck him. 'Does he wear grey?'

His eyes drifted back towards the village. Glimpsed through the trees he could see galloping horses. Lots of them, with soldiers on their backs. He let the woman go and she and her boy were gone in a flash, running full pelt away across the beach. If she'd answered, Berren didn't hear, but he didn't bother chasing her; instead he raced to the edge of the woods and then stopped. A hundred yards of open field lay between the trees and the village. He'd meant to dash across it, taking his chances in the open to join his cohort, but the horsemen were too close now. The trees gave a measure of safety and so did the houses in the village, but the open ground between them? That was a killing field. At least there weren't as many riders as he'd feared. Perhaps thirty, certainly far fewer than Talon's company, but in the open they still had every advantage. Anyone who crossed the fields would be slaughtered.

They were from Aria, he realised. Soldiers from Deephaven. It wasn't just the armour they wore or the familiar way they carried their lances either; when they passed close to the woods, Berren could see their faces. Their skin was dark like his, used to the sun, not ghostly white like Tarn and almost every other face he'd seen since Kalda. They were the men who'd attacked Talon there, on the horses he'd seen in Tethis, but how did they come to be here?

He watched more closely. They'd claimed the ground between the village and the wood and split the Hawks in two, but they weren't doing anything more. They weren't charging in among the houses and burning out the men hidden there.

Then one rode out from the middle of them. He stopped

and turned his horse around on the spot, showing off, threw back his head and roared, 'Talon! Where are you?'

Berren froze. Talon came running out of the village waving his arms. The horseman jumped down, but not for a fight. Berren watched the two men embrace and knew he couldn't be wrong. It was a voice he'd recognise anywhere and it struck him like a thunderbolt. The thief-taker. Talon's brother. Master Sy.

17

BEER FIXES EVERYTHING

In Forgenver the Fighting Hawks had more than two hundred soldiers, with nearly another hundred camp followers, mostly boys desperately pretending to be old enough to fight, but also a smith and his apprentices, two cobblers and an ever-changing posse of women who served as seamstresses and nurses when required, but whose true purpose Berren had slowly come to understand. *Comforters*, Tarn called them. There was also a victualler and his boys, a sun-priest, a scribe and at least a dozen others. These were the people who mended swords and boots, bodies and souls. Most of them had stayed in Forgenver while Talon packed as many soldiers into his ship as it could carry.

On their way here they'd been cramped, men tripping over one another at every step. Now, on their way back, they were somehow to carry another thirty men and their horses and so there was a lot of grumbling and shouting and arguing; but Berren had eyes and ears for none of that. There was one thing on his mind and one thing alone. Master Sy. The thief-taker. The man who'd taught him so much and the man who'd cut down his Tasahre. He couldn't get close – didn't dare, he didn't know what he might do – but he couldn't keep away. Master Sy looked at him once or twice, but his gaze swept by with no flicker of recognition, and the two princes were constantly going back and forth from the shore to the ship, trying to arrange how everyone would fit. Berren paced restlessly while the rest of the Hawks lounged on the beach and twiddled their thumbs, all of them wondering what to do with themselves.

'Oi, Berren!' Tarn was standing beside a collection of barrels and boxes piled up in the middle of the beach, supplies taken off the ship to make room for Master Sy and his horsemen. Beside him was another soldier, taller than Berren but skinny, with a sharp pointy beard and an angry scowl on his face. Tarn waved Berren over. They were leaning against an open barrel of beer.

The other soldier looked Berren up and down. His scowl deepened. 'Well,' he said after a bit, 'I hardly expected a common peasant.'

He took a couple of steps closer and stared haughtily down his nose. Behind him, Tarn straightened. 'Um, Hain? Not a good—'

'Why don't you piss off back home where you came from, dark-skin? Why are you still here?'

Berren stared back at this soldier he'd never seen before. He cocked his head and then punched him on the nose. Hard. The soldier reeled, clutching his face.

'You cess-eater!'

Satisfaction spread through Berren. *Someone* had had this coming from the moment he'd seen Master Sy. He took another step forward. 'I'm Berren,' he said. 'I fought on this beach this morning. I killed six men. Did you?' He left a moment for his words to sink in while the other soldier stared at him in surprise, both hands clutching at his face. 'Who are you anyway?'

The soldier raised a finger at him. 'You can sit on this, you can, dark-skin.' He stormed off, wiping the blood from his nose. Tarn let out a great sigh.

'That was Hain of the Yorkan family,' he said. 'Probably not the best person to punch in the face. He's squired to

127

Prince Syannis of Tethis. I thought you two might want to get to know each other. Apparently not.'

'No.' Berren spat and rubbed his knuckles. He breathed out hard and slumped against the barrel. 'He was right, though. I should just leave. Get my things and go. Go home, wherever that is. I don't belong here.' He glanced across the beach. Master Sy and Talon had two clusters of soldiers around them now. Both were gesticulating angrily. 'But he's right here now! I need to know. I need to know why he did it.' His head was a whirl. First the fight on the beach, then the old woman he'd killed, now this. It was too much. Made him want to run. Run away long and far and just hide.

Tarn slid down the barrel to sit beside him and offered Berren a wooden beaker half filled with ale. 'You belong here as much as you belong anywhere, I reckon.'

'No, I don't. You're about the only person who doesn't wish I'd quietly disappear.'

'Not true.' Tarn shook his head. 'That might have been so this morning, but not now. Look, I know things have been hard. You don't mess with warlocks, you just don't, but you did it anyway, and it's thanks to you that I'm alive. I've seen the others giving you the evil eye, but that was before they saw you fight. You've stood with them now. You fought the enemy and some of us died and some of us didn't, but you didn't run. You proved yourself. Seen any of those warding signs since?'

'A few.' He'd felt a change in the air right after the battle, though, that was true. Right in the aftermath. Was that enough? Would they accept him now, the dark-skin, the necromancer's boy?

'Not from any who were on the beach with you, or I'll break their heads!' Tarn looked thoughtful for a moment. 'Hain had a bit to say that you might have liked to know, before you broke his nose.' He stood up and took another beaker and filled it from the barrel. The ale was good, brought all the way from Kalda, not the horse piss they'd had to endure in Forgenver. Pity to waste it, just leaving it on the beach to make space for some horses. Berren drained his cup and passed it up to Tarn for some more.

'Meridian's hired two companies to hunt us down. He brought these horsemen from across the ocean.'

'The same soldiers we met in Kalda?' Berren asked. 'The ones who tried to kill us with one of those glass balls of fire that the sun-priests make for the Taiytakei to put on the end of their rockets? Or didn't they happen to mention that.'

'Same ones, but Prince Syannis has turned them to *our* cause. Or bought them. Same difference, really.' He shook his head. 'Meridian must be desperate. Never mind the gold this must have cost him; if word ever reaches the courts of Brons and Caladir that someone is bringing in soldiers from Aria, there's bound to be trouble. After all, if an upstart like Meridian can hire a few dozen, what's to stop someone else hiring a few thousand. Or a few *tens* of thousands. The gods know there's certainly enough of you over there.' He chuckled. 'So you and Talon's brother – are you going to have a fight or how's this going to end? You can't keep looking at him like that and then not do anything about it, that's for sure.'

'I told you – he killed someone.'

'Yes, you did. Your sword-monk. You loved her. He didn't know. Harsh. Stop staring at him and do something about it. Say whatever needs to be said.'

'He let me down.' Berren stood up. Then he stopped. He still wasn't sure whether he wanted to murder his old master or cry at his feet. Gods be damned, and he still kept seeing Tasahre, only now she was all muddled with the slave he'd whipped in Tethis and the old woman he'd killed, and he couldn't see one without the others all

129

piling into his thoughts. He pressed his fists to his head and screwed up his eyes. 'I was a rubbish apprentice,' he said. 'All I wanted to do was learn how to fight. I couldn't leave things be. Didn't listen. Didn't see how good I had it.'

He downed another cup of beer in one long gulp. 'I've spent the best part of two years thinking about what Syannis did back in Deephaven. I wanted to kill him, slow and painful. Now? I don't know. Some of the things I blamed him for were more my fault than they were his. Even ...' He still couldn't say Tasahre's name without a pause to force it out. 'Even what he did at the end, that was Syannis being what he was and fate placing her in his path. All she was to him was another enemy, another thing in his way. I can't hate him for being evil or malicious because he wasn't, but that doesn't make everything right. Gods! Took me long enough to realise that, but when you're a skag, you have a lot of time on your own to think about how you got there. I still hate him for throwing me aside, but maybe even that's not fair.'

He refilled his cup again, thinking of the last time he'd seen Master Sy, standing on the edge of Radek's ship, one foot over the rail, hand out, calling to him to run. 'Thing is, the other thing you get to do as a skag is stare at death. I wanted to kill him and I wanted to loathe him, but in the end I couldn't. I hate him for letting Radek matter more than I did. I despise him for killing Tasahre. I'm afraid of him for the madness that drives him. I never knew, until now, that I wouldn't fly into a rage if I ever saw him. But we're not done, him and me. He was the closest thing I ever had to a father, and I need him to hear it, and I need to hear it back.' He raised his cup to the bemused-looking Tarn.

'Well,' said Tarn after a moment of silence. 'I don't think I really followed any of that. Just go. Say what needs to be said and get it done.'

Berren shrugged. 'Have another beer with me, Tarn.'

Getting drunk seemed the best thing. He'd never told anyone except Talon what had happened in Deephaven, and Talon had listened politely but he hadn't wanted to know, not most of it, not how it *felt*. When he'd been a skag, the sailors would only have laughed and jeered at him. But Tarn ... for some reason, Tarn needed to know. He filled both cups.

'It's all changed,' grumbled Tarn. 'This whole business with these slavers, that's not what's really happening at all. I don't understand any of this any more. I thought Prince Syannis and Prince Talon had made their peace with Meridian.' He laughed bitterly. 'I didn't even know Radek was dead until you showed up. Or rather, I did, but I didn't know how and I certainly didn't think Talon or Syannis had had anything to do with it. Now Meridian's hired two companies to hunt us, we've been suckered out here and they're probably only a day away. The lancers were supposed to take us by surprise and cut us off from the sea and then the others would finish the job. For all I know there never were any slavers and the Duke of Forgenver's in on it too.' Tarn scratched his chin. 'Hain said something else, something about Syannis seeing his future in the blade of a knife. Don't think that made any more sense to Hain than it does to me. Sounds like more death-magery.'

Berren sat very still. *I've seen that knife*, he thought. He smiled wanly. 'There are storms out in the deep ocean,' he said, 'terrible storms. They don't move – they're always in the same place – and to get from here to Aria, you have to pass through them. We did it three times. Always with other ships. Taiytakei ones, because they were the only ones who knew the way through, and we could only follow. They're not like other storms. Waves and winds, yes, and they got worse and worse, but in the middle the sky went black. Real black. Night-black with no stars or moon or any light at all, even when it should have been the middle

131

of the day. And the worst? There was a calm in there, once you reached the dark, a dead calm as though the sea was flat as a mirror and there was no wind at all, although with it being dark you couldn't tell if the sea was still even there. Some of the sailors used to see things then, in the middle of that calm. Flashes of things. Flashes of the future they reckoned. But not me, I never saw anything.'

Tarn poured them both another cup. 'Can we talk about something else? Women, maybe. Or ... I don't know. I know some nice women. Big ...' he held out his hands as if testing the weight of something.

Berren shook his head. That meant talking about Tasahre. 'And then the dark would break and you'd be right back in the heart of the storm with its waves and the lashing wind again, and you'd think that you'd only been inside that calm for a heartbeat or two, but the sun had always moved hours.' He shrugged. 'I spent the last two years a skag. Not much else to talk about, not that you'd want to hear. Certainly not any women. Before that?' He shrugged. 'Not a good idea. Oh, and the lightning in the storms, just before the calm. It was purple. Unnatural.' His head was buzzing from the beer now.

Tarn stretched his arms over his head. 'Prince Syannis ever tell you about his sword-mistress? Shalari? They shared a bed more than once before Radek and Meridian and their mercenaries came to Tethis, or so I hear. She died in the fighting. Whispers say that Prince Syannis never forgave Radek for that.'

'He was always a bit funny about women,' muttered Berren. He laughed, the drink in his head making his thoughts fuzzy. 'I thought this was all about losing his family and his kingdom and his birthright. On the whole that *did* seem enough.' He laughed again. 'Gods!' Maybe Syannis would understand then. Maybe, if he'd lost someone of his own, he'd understand why Berren could never forgive him for killing Tasahre. 'There's *one* lady I can tell you about.' He drained his cup again and grinned. 'I can tell you about the lady that gave birth to me. The lady of Deephaven.'

The evening wore on. Boats scurried back and forth from ship to shore and men ran about their business around them. Berren talked about Deephaven and everything that had happened there, of the older, happier times before Tasahre and the warlock. By the time he was done, the sun had set and it was dark and Berren's head was spinning and stuffed full of wool. He wasn't entirely sure what he'd told Tarn and what he hadn't, but they were laughing and leaning against one another like two drunk old men.

'I need a piss,' slurred Tarn. He stumbled up the beach, ignoring the grumbles from the men around them already trying to sleep in their tents.

'Me too.' Berren followed. 'Then I think I want to punch something.'

'Find yourself a new woman.' Tarn nodded sagely. 'Clear all that old rubbish out.' He lurched into a tree, staggered sideways and dropped his breeches. 'Ahhh. Better! Sunfire! I think I need to go to sleep now. Did I have a tent somewhere? I don't think I did. Bugger. And don't punch Hain again. It's not his fault he's a prick.'

'No, brother, no!' A raised voice cut through the quiet of the woods. Tarn wobbled. He put his fingers to his lips and made an exaggerated gesture to Berren. 'Shhh! What was that?' The two of them stood still, swaying gently from side to side. Then, with the clumsy stealth of the drunk, they tiptoed between the trees towards the voices. As Berren drew closer, he recognised them. One was Talon. The other, the quiet one, was Master Sy.

Tarn leaned against a tree. He flashed Berren a huge grin and set about making a great show of *listening*. Berren simply stood where he was, swaying.

'You know my opinion. Everything in our lives started to go wrong when father let that man into our kingdom.' Talon.

'He saved Aimes, remember.'

'Did he really? And even if he did, so what? He saved the idiot! Do you ever stop to think about what might have happened if he hadn't?'

There was a long pause. When Syannis spoke again, his voice was low and Berren only heard pieces of it. 'I know ... hated ... but ... ever speak like that again.'

'You can't have an idiot for a king! It doesn't work! But that aside, I'm talking about the here and now. I'm telling you that your warlock has been poking his nose around our homeland again. I thought he was gone, across the ocean for good, but no! And he's right up to his neck in this.'

'He came back, did he?'

'Yes! And have you not seen him?' Talon's voice rang with accusation, but if Syannis replied at all, Berren didn't hear. 'You have, haven't you? Don't! Don't say anything, brother! I can see it in your face. You sought him out when he crossed the ocean, and now that he's back, you've done so again!'

'*He* sought *me*.'

Talon was snarling like a wolf in chains. 'What hold *does* he have over you? Does he promise you that you'll be king one day? Is that what it is?'

A burst of scornful laughter. 'Is *that* what you think?'

Talon was almost growling. 'I will rejoice to see you on the throne, brother, and well you know it, but I *will* kill him if I see him, however much he is a friend of yours. Whatever he did, he did it for his own reasons, not for love of you or of anyone but himself!'

Tarn turned and mouthed something at Berren. *Do you know what they're talking about?*

'And what about my little protégé? Will you suffer *him* to live? Kuy has touched him too.'

Berren's blood quickened. Syannis was talking about *him*!

'I've kept him close and watched him well and I see no sign of taint in him. Which is more than I can say for *you*, brother. I begin to wonder, how did you find him? What made you choose him to be your apprentice all those years ago? Is it really just because he looks a bit like Aimes?'

'A *bit* like Aimes? I could find you a dozen men in Kalda who look a *bit* like Aimes. Probably a dozen in Tethis. I don't know what drew him to me.' Syannis paused. He muttered something too quietly for Berren to make out. 'But it's more than that. It's not what he looks like; it's what he *is*, inside. He *is* Aimes.'

Whatever else Talon and Syannis had to say, Berren missed it as Tarn tugged at his elbow, pulling him away. 'Hey! I've got an idea!'

Berren growled at him. 'Shh!'

Tarn lurched a little. 'There's still some barrel in that beer. Maybe if we empty it, we can sleep in it? Because I don't know where my tent is.' Syannis and Talon had fallen silent. Berren heard their footsteps moving away through the woods.

'I think it's on the ship,' muttered Berren. 'Because you never put it up.'

'Oh no, they took all the tents off to make space for the bloody horses.'

The two of them walked slowly back through the trees and staggered to Tarn's barrel. All around them the sands rang with snores in the darkness. The Hawks, drunk and happy, asleep.

'Oh, it's not so bad out here.' Tarn slumped down and yawned and a moment later he was snoring. Berren looked around the beach. There were men everywhere, soldiers lying in their bedrolls. There were piles of blankets, also evicted from the ship. He picked up a couple and threw one over Tarn, then walked back towards the woods. The trees would keep the wind off. He could already hear other snores coming from among them. He stumbled on, looking for a quiet place to call his own. He was about to throw his blanket down when a twig snapped behind him.

'Hello, Berren.' There was just a shape but the voice was unmistakeable. 'Just one thing: did you actually see her die?'

He shook his head. He was so drunk he wasn't sure he'd heard right. 'What?'

'Did you see her die, boy? Your sword-monk. Did you actually see her die? Did you see the moment her heart stopped?'

'Yes.' And now he could see it all over again and tears rolled down his cheeks. Stupid beer, making him cry.

'Are you sure?'

The apparition turned and walked away through the trees, silent. Berren stared after it.

There was a faint whiff of rotting fish in the air.

PART THREE

TETHIS AND THE
LOST KING

18

JUST ON A GRANDER SCALE

He crawled and dragged himself out of a hut he'd never seen, inch by inch out of a village he didn't know, to the reed beds on the edge of a lake he couldn't name. He was going to die and he wanted it to be outside under the stars, not in the dark. He reached the water's edge, rolled onto his back and waited. One by one the stars winked out. Tears filled his eyes. He wanted to live, not to die. He wanted to live but the choice had been taken away.

A man stood over him. The man's face, where it wasn't lost among the shadows of his cowl, was pale. One half was ruined, scarred ragged by disease or fire, with one blind eye milky white. He wore pale hooded robes the colour of moonlight.

'Are you death?' Berren asked.

'I bring the Black Moon,' the stranger said.

Berren woke up covered in sweat. For a moment he couldn't work out why he was in a room and in a bed instead of shivering on the beach. The hangover was real enough, though. Beside him Hain was snoring loudly.

He sat, head in his hands, wincing at the pain, putting the last few days back together, piece by piece. They'd returned to Forgenver. Master Sy had been on the same ship. They couldn't possibly have avoided each other and yet somehow they did. When they were back, Talon had come and dug him out of his tent. *My brother is heading south. He wants you with him. I think he's stupid and I think you shouldn't go. If you do, then you're stupid too. And you're not.* He'd sounded angry.

In the room next door he could hear Master Sy. The thief-taker was snoring too, just like he always used to back in Deephaven.

He didn't know why he'd said yes. Hadn't known then, still didn't know now. Just that he couldn't let it go, couldn't let the thief-taker vanish again, even if he had no idea of what to say to him. Talon hadn't said a word, but the look in his eye spoke volumes. *You deserve each other. Both of you.* They'd ridden out of Forgenver late that same day and headed south, him and Hain and the thief-taker. Day after day with hardly a word spoken between them.

His head was spinning. He could barely keep his eyes open and he couldn't get the dream out of his head. *I bring the Black Moon.* What did that mean?

He shook himself, wincing again. Dreams were stupid and it was much too early to be awake. He put on a night-shirt and went looking for some water. Moonlight robes made his dream-person a priest, didn't it? A moon-priest. He'd known a moon-priest back in Deephaven. Garrent. But a priest with a burned face and one eye? He didn't remember anyone like that.

When he got back, Hain was dressed. He gave Berren a sour look. They'd never really got past that punch on the nose. 'What happened to you?'

'Looking for water.'

Hain nodded at a jug on the table and mumbled something. Behind Berren the door opened and Master Sy came in. Except this wasn't *his* Master Sy any more. This Syannis was older, angrier, his face pinched tight in frustration. The heady mix of fear and awe Berren remembered as his apprentice was gone, not a trace of it left. What he saw now both made him feel pity and repelled him. And after all this time, after all that had gone between them, neither could think of a word to say to the other. He'd had so many questions – the warlock, the golden knife, the priests, Tasahre – so many questions and so much to say and so much anger … And ever since that night on the beach, all his questions had crumbled into ash and even his anger wouldn't burn.

Are you sure?

'Berren.' Master Sy gave him a nod. *I'm sorry about how it all ended.* That was as much as Berren ever got. And when Berren pestered him about what he'd said in the wood by the beach, about Tasahre being still alive, about that *Are you sure?* what did he get? Nothing. A shake of the head. *I saw the same as you did. I did not see what happened afterwards and I never spoke to you in the wood by the beach that night. You must have been dreaming.*

He should just leave, he knew it, and yet he couldn't. Because he had to know … *something*. He didn't even know what. Just needed to be with Master Sy for a while so he could finally be rid of him. 'Where are we?' he asked.

'Galsmouth, dark-skin,' muttered Hain.

'North of Tethis. Meridian's territory,' said Master Sy.

Berren rubbed his eyes. Yes, they'd crossed the river into Galsmouth yesterday. Today they'd set off for Tethis itself, a few more days down the south road. As far as Berren understood it, they were going to walk right up to King Meridian's castle and have a look around, spy on who was there for a bit, check on its defences, count soldiers, that sort of thing. Then they were going to sneak in, murder the king, sneak out again and slip away back to Forgenver. Just like that. They were going to get away with this because …

He had no idea. Because they were going to change their clothes and stop looking like swords for hire at some point? He'd assumed that the whole bit about murdering the king had been a joke, but the closer they got the less sure he became. Whatever Master Sy's plan was, he seemed to think it was going to work. And Berren? He was still here.

Somehow it was better than staying in Forgenver, knowing that he could have been with the thief-taker, talking to him and trying to understand ...

I loved her! She was everything that was right and good and you killed her! And why? She tried to stop you from murdering someone, that's all! She had you beaten! She tried to let you live! She gave you every chance! Why did you have to kill her? Why? Why did you do it?

But not a word would come out. Not a single one. The awkwardness between them was a physical thing. It would have been easy, Berren thought, for the thief-taker to have walked away, to have turned his shoulder and sniffed with disdain, to have ignored Berren completely. It would have made it easier for Berren too because it would have woken the anger again.

Sorry? You're sorry? And that's supposed to be enough?

Master Sy shifted from one foot to the other. He stood stiffly, almost as though he knew what Berren was thinking and didn't know what to say either. 'When we get to Tethis you will present yourselves to the castle,' he said. 'You will find a sergeant to one of the companies and you will offer yourselves as labour for the day for a penny and a supper apiece. You'll work and you'll do as you're told.' He glanced at Berren. 'Stay away from the castle and from any of the king's guard who might recognise you. Keep your eyes open and see what men of what companies are there. At the end of the day you will leave with the other labourers. Join me after dark on the river road beneath the castle, where the valley is steepest. We'll wait for three hours and then go into the castle together. Sun willing, we'll take Prince Aimes and return to Forgenver.'

'We will, will we?' Berren forced the words out through gritted teeth. 'And how will we get out again?'

'Leave that to me.' Syannis looked aimlessly around the room. 'Breakfast. Five minutes sharp.'

As he left, Hain leaned into Berren, the smell of last night's beer still strong on his breath. 'What *are* you doing here, dark-skin?'

Berren pushed him away. Five minutes later, the three of them sat in the same uncomfortable silence, eating with the ruthless efficiency of three men who'd do anything for a decent excuse not to talk to each other.

From Galsmouth to Tethis was two more days by mule. They stopped at villages on the way and Syannis traded their cloaks for some old farming clothes and a couple of well used axes. Over the next night they slept rough under the shelter of a copse of trees. They set out again early, pushing on along the coast road that ran all the way to Forgenver and beyond. In sight of Tethis, they stopped and camped another night. From the sea the town was laid out for all to see, sprawled along the shore beneath the line of hills and cliffs. From the land it was almost invisible: aside from the castle with its one piece of wall and its watchtowers, you'd hardly know it was there.

'Meridian's at home,' muttered Syannis as soon as they saw it. Berren wondered how he knew until the thief-taker pointed at the clusters of flags flying above the two towers. Among them was a red flag with four white ships. The flag of Radek of Kalda. Berren knew it at once – he'd spent years looking out for it, every day.

Syannis grunted, and for a moment Berren saw a glimpse of the old thief-taker who'd taught him most of what he knew, the Master Sy with the flashing eyes and the quick cutting tongue and the simmering rage buried beneath. For a moment and then it was gone. 'Come on.' The thief-taker led them off the road until he found a hole under a fallen tree. The three of them wrapped their swords and their armour in cloth and buried them along with anything else that marked them as men of war. When they were done, Syannis brushed himself down. 'See? Now we're farmers.'

With a flourish he produced a skin full of cider, and there it was again, a glimmer of the man Berren had once known.

Berren scratched his head and took a gulp. 'Talon led us along this road when we left Tethis the last time. Up to Galsmouth and through the next duchy.'

'Gorandale.'

'That's the one.'

Hain snorted. 'Nothing but hills and sheep. Mind you, Tethis isn't much better, nor Forgenver if it comes to it.'

'We came along this road.' Berren screwed up his face, trying to remember. 'We passed through a few villages on the first day. Once we were out of the town, everything was so empty. The hills got bigger. And yes –' he frowned '– there *were* a lot of sheep.'

Syannis shrugged. 'Can't be leaving the mules. Swords and stuff we can bury. Mules, they'll wander, or else someone will take them.' He swept his arm across the landscape. 'Look at this place. Almost deserted. Scraps of woodland. A few big rocks here and there. Sharp bends, steep valleys. A forgotten hut or two.' He shook his head. 'Outside Tethis itself, this country has its own laws. Especially inland. Hain's right. Hills and hills and more hills and nothing much else except bloody sheep.'

'Open country all the way to Galsmouth.'

'Yes.' Syannis made a face. 'Why?'

Berren handed back the cider. 'Nothing really. I was just thinking. I broke into your house once when you were in Deephaven. When you ...' He stopped. That was the night that Master Sy and the warlock Saffran Kuy had killed the Headsman. Hain probably wasn't supposed to know about that. 'Not long after you put a lock on the door.' He turned to Hain and grinned maliciously. 'And he was always so careful to bar the doors and the windows in case someone with a knife and a grudge slipped in at night. But he never thought to bar my room. It was always open. Even after I was gone.' Berren looked back at Syannis and then glanced away inland at the line of hills. 'I think this road is a bit like your front door, master thief-taker, and those hills, when they get closer, are like your unguarded upstairs window that no one's thought of. If, say, you wanted to move a few hundred armed men about. Like I said, I was just thinking. It's like breaking into someone's house, just on a grander scale.'

Hain looked at him. His face was a mask of questions, and then Berren watched as it filled with the glow of understanding. Slowly he nodded.

Syannis, Berren saw, was quietly chuckling to himself.

19

THE TIES OF THE PAST

The summer days were long and hot, the evenings and the nights pleasantly warm and the days started early. They rode their mules back to the roadside as the sun rose and then watched and waited until the first carts appeared on their way to the Tethis markets. Berren and Hain and Syannis sidled in among the traffic and settled alongside a couple of old farmhands driving a wagon full of hay. The men were surly, but they soon found their tongues when Hain offered to share his breakfast with them, and quickly got to chatting about the weather and their crops. Syannis let Hain do the talking. Berren's mind wandered. Coming here had seemed like a fine enough idea when he hadn't actually given it much thought, but now it was making him nervous. People in the castle would remember his face – the bondswoman, the two soldiers who'd barred his way, Princess Gelisya – and besides, Tethis was home to the soap-maker, Vallas, Saffran's brother.

As they came close to the town, two soldiers on horseback blocked the road ahead of them, stopping each cart in turn. When the wagon reached them, they poked their swords into the hay and took a good long look at Syannis and Berren.

'Business in Tethis?'

'Hay for them horses of yours,' grumbled one of the men on the wagon.

Hain smiled and patted the axe on his belt. 'New edges for me and my brothers,' he said. The soldiers muttered to each other, shook their heads and waved them on.

'Look at their colours,' murmured Syannis. 'The Mountain Panther. That tells you something in itself.'

'It does?' Berren shrugged.

'That Meridian has money,' said Hain.

They rode on until they reached the side of the Tethis valley opposite the castle. For a few minutes they stopped, but from there the castle was difficult to see.

'Can't stay here staring,' muttered Syannis. 'People will notice.'

'Another reason to come at the place through the hills,' said Berren.

'Or from the south instead of the north. Come on.'

The thief-taker led the way now. They reached the market where Berren had searched for what he'd needed to save Tarn. Instead of crossing the river bridge to the castle road, the thief-taker paused by the street down to the sea, towards the ships and the docks and the fishermen.

'A moment, Berren, if you please.'

Syannis and Hain left him there, holding the mules. Berren followed the progress of the street with his eyes. He'd walked it that day, all of it. It ran all the way down to the sea, past the Mermaid, around the bulk of the harbour to a shingle beach covered with nets hung up in ranks to dry. Somewhere down there was the soap-maker, Vallas Kuy. Berren's skin prickled. The stink of fish wafted up on the sea breeze. Gulls squawked and circled overhead. As soon as he looked for them, Berren started to see cats, here and there, hiding in shadows and nooks and crannies. He felt them watching him. His sword hand itched, but today he was a farmer and so he had nothing to grasp. He could almost feel the presence of the warlock.

It started to rain, a light warm summer rain that

reminded him of Deephaven. Dark clouds flitted back and forth across the sun. Berren looked out at the sea and the waves. *I can work on a ship*, he thought. *I could go anywhere. I could go home. What's to stop me?* He'd miss Tarn maybe. He wouldn't miss him much, though. Not enough to stay.

But go? Go where?

Syannis came back and he was on his own. 'Change of plan,' he said. 'Hain can go back and get our stuff. I'm coming with you.'

Berren blinked. *What?* 'But won't they recognise you?'

'Oh, I don't think so. It's been a very long time.' He bared his teeth. 'And you know what? I can't resist it. The temptation is too much.' He met Berren eye to eye for a moment, and there once more was the old thief-taker. 'Like walking the edge of a sword blade, eh? And what better place to say whatever needs to be said about Radek and your dead sword-monk than in the midst of our enemies, digging their privies?'

Syannis was mad. Utterly mad. Berren couldn't help himself – he started to laugh. 'You know I might just push you into one and bury you,' he said, and he meant it too.

'Yes,' the thief-taker's face gleamed, 'I know you might try.'

They led their mules from the market square, over the bridge and up the other side of the river valley and then back along the top of the cliffs. The open ground within the castle walls and palisades was filled with tents and makeshift huts and soldiers now. Even the castle itself had changed since Berren and Talon had come by some two months before. The buildings had been made gaudy with a riot of coloured paint and were festooned with flags and banners, as though some fading rainbow had fallen out of the sky and spilled its guts everywhere. As their mules picked a path between the tents, Berren spotted three different uniforms among the soldiers. He'd seen the castle soldiers before, the king's guard, but now there were also soldiers who looked like the two horsemen they'd met on the road, and then there were soldiers in polished silver and bright green with the strange double-headed pikes he remembered from Deephaven and Radek's ship.

They found a sergeant from one of the mercenary companies and Syannis begged for work. The castle was full. Berren could feel the tension in the air, too many men with too many swords, all pressed together with nothing much to do. The sergeant promised them a penny and a supper and set them to work. They filled old privies and dug new ones, cleaned boots, polished armour and stayed as far from the castle as it was possible to be. Berren looked up from time to time, but he never saw any sign of Gelisya or her bonds-maid, nor even Meridian or Prince Aimes or any of the rest of the court. The work was dull and dirty, but after years of being a ship's skag, he bore it easily enough. Simple hard work suited him. It let him empty his head, or it would have if Syannis hadn't been right there beside him. But Syannis *was* there, and Berren didn't know where to start.

'Stealing your half-brother sounds like a stupid idea,' he said at last, when he couldn't think of anything else. 'If you can get that close to him, you should just kill Meridian.' Come the evening, he thought he might just walk away and head back down to the docks and take up being a seaman again. Sail somewhere far away. Anywhere, really.

'And how is that any better?' whispered Syannis.

'You kill a man, he doesn't shout out, call for guards, raise the alarm, kick and struggle and scream. That's how.'

Syannis snorted. 'You sound like me. Well then maybe we will, but we can't kill Aimes. You know the only reason I took you was because you looked like him. Nothing else. I didn't want an apprentice. But there you were, my little brother, standing right in front of me, and this time I could actually do something. Later ... well, later there were other reasons. You weren't such a bad apprentice. Mostly.'

He is Aimes. Berren remembered that from the woods by the beach, the night after the battle against the slavers. Master Sy had meant something more than skin-deep. Berren couldn't imagine what, but the thought made the hairs on his arms prickle. 'This brother of yours, he's some sort of idiot, right?' He watched carefully as a cloud crossed the thief-taker's face.

'He was after he got kicked in the head by a horse.' Syannis sat down and wiped the sweat off his brow and took a sip of water, fresh from the river outside. In Deep-haven the river stank. Master Sy had sent Berren two miles every day, along the riverside to Sweetwater where the river was clean, but most people drank beer or weak wine. Here, though, they kept their rivers so you could drink from them.

Syannis passed the water skin to Berren. 'Talon and I are both bastards. Aimes was the true heir to Tethis. When Radek and Meridian came and our father was killed, Talon and I fled but I left Aimes behind. I just couldn't get to him. Everyone knew there was something wrong with him and maybe that's what saved him. Anyway, they didn't kill Aimes, even though they tried hard enough to get rid of me and Talon.' He leaned closer. 'Meridian declared Aimes king and then promptly sat on the throne and called himself regent. I suppose it gives him more of an air of authority in the kingdom. Meridian rules but strictly it's Aimes who wears the crown.' The thief-taker pursed his lips. 'He'd be a few years older than you. To look at him, he's in perfect health. They say he's a good rider and would probably be handy with a sword if he had the first idea what it was for. It's like something inside him is missing.'

'Something missing?' Berren almost choked. 'Like someone cut out a piece of his soul, maybe?'

150

Syannis looked at him long and hard. 'He was kicked in the head by a horse. It happens. He shouldn't have been playing in the stables.'

Berren took a long swig of water and burped loudly. That was one of those thief-taker answers he'd grown used to over the years. *Yes, there's more to it, but you'd better stop asking questions.* He laughed. Fine. He didn't care about Aimes and he didn't care about Syannis's stupid war either. He went back to digging. 'Sorry doesn't bring her back,' he said. 'Nice trick getting me to leave my sword outside the town though. Why did you tell me she was still alive?'

'I never said any such thing.'

'I didn't dream it. In the woods by the beach. You asked me if I saw her actually die and I said yes, and then you asked if I was sure as though you knew something that I didn't. Like maybe that other sword-monk got to her in time and did that thing that one of them did to you when she smashed up your knee. Why did you tell me that if it's not true?'

'I've told you before: I didn't tell you anything. If you didn't dream it then it must have been someone else.' Master Sy spat into the dirt and picked up his shovel.

'Did *you* see her die?'

'I saw the same as you. No one lives through a cut like that. She's dead, Berren. I'm sorry I had to kill her but I did. I didn't know she meant so much to you. Actually I thought you didn't like her.'

'Would it have changed anything?'

Syannis shook his head. 'In the heat of the moment? No, I don't think it would.'

'I'd never seen so much blood.' Berren looked away. He could see her again now, lying on Radek's ship with her throat torn open. He'd be able to see that moment whenever he wanted for the rest of his life. Everything else, the times they'd spent together in her fighting circle, the moments alone, the touch of her cheek on his hand, all those were slowly fading, but the last memory stayed as clear as though it was yesterday.

'Why did you stay here, Berren? Why didn't you go back to Deephaven?'

Berren stopped. He turned on the thief-taker and glared. 'Back to what? You took everything!' He shook his head. 'Being a soldier, even if it means digging privies for a twelvenight, is better than being a thief, never knowing where your next meal is coming from, never knowing when you might be caught and what will happen when you are — a beating, a branding, maybe a broken bone or two; maybe they'll take your hand off, or maybe they'll just stick a knife in you and roll you into the river. You don't know what it's like, because you've never had to do it.' He shook his head. 'I'm a foreigner, a dark-skin from across the sea and a warlock's boy too, so the other soldiers here don't like me much, but I still hear their stories. They're people who lost their homes, lost their families or never had anything in the first place. They dream of saving enough silver to buy a piece of land, build a home, raise a family ...' He chuckled, thinking of the Hawks who had other dreams. Tarn wanted to start his own fighting school and there were a couple who were set on buying their own forges. And then there was Divan, who wasn't quite right in the head, and who was firmly convinced that he'd stop being a Hawk one day and travel to the sandy wastes at the southern end of the world to live in a palace of gold and marble and be waited on by exactly three hundred and twelve concubines. The smile faded from his face. 'Even Talon's lost his home,' he said. 'They're wanderers. I fit.'

'You should go back, Berren.'

Berren started shovelling the contents of yet another old privy onto the back of a wagon. He was up to his knees in excrement and slime when he saw that Syannis had stopped and was standing over him.

'I'm sorry,' Syannis said again. 'But that's all. That's all I have for you. If that's not good enough then get on a ship and leave.'

'You should have told me,' Berren said, his voice dull. 'You should have let me help you. You should have let me be a part of it.'

'And you should have stayed where you were put, listened to what you were told and done what you were asked.'

Berren glared at him. 'Would you?'

'No. No, I doubt that I would.'

'Well then.' Berren climbed out of his hole and stood face to face with the thief-taker. His hands and his shoes and his trousers were covered in filth. Somehow, Syannis didn't seem to be nearly as dirty as he should be. 'Still shouldn't have.' He grabbed Syannis's shirt and pulled hard, throwing him into the privy. Then he looked down at his old master, up to his knees in shit, hands covered in filth and a face covered in outrage. He laughed, even as there were tears rolling down his cheeks. 'I can't forget her. I just can't.'

'Boy!' Syannis looked ready to explode.

'Not something that's supposed to happen to a king's son, eh?' Berren barked a bitter laugh. 'Where I grew up you could be stabbed in the street for a few pieces of copper. Life is cheaper than gold or silver and worth more than both. Nothing changes, wherever I go. And I'm not your *boy* any more.' Syannis opened his mouth to speak, but before any words could come out, Berren threw a bucket at him. 'This is what you wanted,' he said. 'Now dig, bastard prince.'

The thief-taker stared up at him. The anger in his face slowly changed and he started to laugh. 'You're a whore-son, Berren, you truly are.'

'It does seem likely.' Berren shrugged.

'You want to play it like this? Fine.' Syannis picked up a handful of filth and threw it. Berren ducked and it sailed past his face. The thief-taker started to climb out. 'You're going back in that hole, boy. One way or another.'

Berren picked up a spade and held it like an axe. 'You and who's army, king's bastard?'

Syannis was still laughing, but there was a glint in his eye of the old anger, that dangerous look just before he took someone's head off. This time Berren knew exactly how he felt, but halfway out of the pit, Syannis stopped. He pointed.

'Maybe that one.'

20

LESSONS IN BREAKING AND ENTERING

Berren followed the thief-taker's finger. Through the maze of tents, a posse of soldiers were weaving their way towards the castle. They weren't wearing the purple of the king's guard, the green of the men from Kalda, or the brown and black of the Mountain Panther.

'Come on! Help me out!' Syannis thrust a hand towards Berren. Berren pulled him out of the pit and then followed as Syannis ran to the palisade. They climbed up, ignoring the shouts of nearby soldiers. Down in the harbour two fat-bellied ships that hadn't been there in the morning now wallowed in the water. If he squinted, Berren thought he could see longboats inching their way towards the shore.

'Oi!' There was an angry shout from below and behind them. 'You two!' A soldier was staring up, waving his fist. 'What do you think you're doing up there? Get down and get back to work!'

Berren hurried down and ran back towards the privies with Syannis hot behind him, hoping the soldier would ignore them, but he followed. 'We were just—' started the thief-taker, but the soldier stopped him with a glare.

'I don't care what you was just – you want to work, you work!' He pointed at a patch of clear ground. 'A new one. There. When you've done that, this one needs filling in and that one needs digging out. Looks like there's going to be a lot of work for you two today, and you'd better put your backs into it if you don't want to go home hungry.'

'Ain't you got enough shit holes?' Berren laughed.

The soldier snorted. 'Got another company shipping in, haven't we?' The sneer in his words was clear. Not *his* company. He snatched up a shovel and tossed it at Berren. 'Dig, you oik! I'll be watching you.'

Berren dug, and Syannis too. They looked up now and then, watching what was happening. The castle yard grew busier. More tents sprouted up. New soldiers began to arrive, these ones in grey with a black sword, point down, emblazoned on their tunics. Now and then Berren caught sight of an archer or two, with longbows as tall as a man slung over their shoulders. They walked tall and proud, with a swagger as though they expected everyone else to move aside for them. Later in the afternoon came an even more startling sight. Six men armoured in shining metal plates came striding by. Even the king's guard stopped what they were doing to stare.

'The Black Swords!' whispered Syannis. 'All of them!'

Berren shrugged.

'That's nearly a thousand men. They usually split into separate companies and fight in two or three places at once. They've got archers and a few men in that Dominion armour. Everyone else is afraid of them.' He whistled softly and then grinned. 'Talon must really have put the wind up Meridian. Good.'

'Huh.' To Berren the men in their metal skins looked slow and clumsy. Difficult for a man with a spear or a short sword to find a way through it all maybe, but what did that matter if you could simply stand back and throw rocks at them? He shrugged and went back to his digging. Maybe no one had enough rocks to wear them down?

Once it was too dark to work, the sergeant who'd hired them sent them away, each with a penny and a burned end of bread. Berren wrapped his in cloth and put it inside his shirt for later, for when his hands weren't encrusted with other people's shit.

'Tomorrow?' asked Syannis, but the sergeant shook his head.

'I seen you two slacking off. Lazy. Got no place for lazy men here. Piss off and be glad you got paid.' He turned and left.

Outside the castle Syannis idly threw his crust of bread away. Berren shook his head. 'Duke's boy,' he muttered.

'What?'

'You come from where I come from, you wouldn't throw away perfectly good food, that's what. Old habits die hard.'

'I'm not eating like this!' The thief-taker raised his hands, every bit as filthy as Berren's.

'That's because you don't know what hungry is.' Berren shook his head and looked away. 'Bet you never have. Not once.' This could be where they went their separate ways. He'd done what needed to be done. Things would never be the same between them, but he'd said his piece now. The hole was still there inside him, but he didn't need the thief-taker any more. The itch was gone. 'It's all right. I don't want to fight. It's just funny, that's all.' He turned and started to walk away. There weren't going to be any goodbyes.

'Talon says you fought well,' said Syannis. 'What was it like?'

'Bloody,' muttered Berren. The fight on the beach still troubled him. Not because he'd been scared, which he had, but because in the fragments he remembered the strongest impression was of how much he'd *liked* it. And because of what he'd done afterwards to the old woman with the knife, while the buzz of it was still hot inside his head. Troubled him a lot when he thought about it, so mostly he didn't. 'I was too busy staying alive to notice much else. I expect I'd have a very different idea if I'd been watching from a distance.'

157

'There's going to be more. Berren?'

Berren paused. 'Master?' Even now the word came out with a will of its own. He could have punched himself.

'I can't do this without you. You're right about Meridian. He's here. I know a way to get close. But I have to deal with Aimes and so I need you. *You* have to do it. You have to get rid of Meridian.'

'Me? No. You've got Hain for that.' Berren turned away.

'Hain?' Syannis almost howled. 'You think *Hain* could do something like this? No. But you could. There's going to be a war, you see. A bloody one. Me and Talon against all the soldiers you saw in that castle. A lot of people will die. People like Tarn. Your friends. Kill Meridian, maybe you could stop it.'

Berren took a deep breath. 'You want to stop it, don't fight it,' he said. 'Let it go.'

'You always wanted to learn swords. I gave that to you. What was it for?'

'I don't know any more,' said Berren quietly. 'It wasn't for what happened in Deephaven, I know that.'

'What do you want?'

'Tasahre not to be dead, that's what I want.' To go back in time and make things different. Nothing that Master Sy could give. Yet he still didn't walk away.

'I gave you everything. Do I have to beg?'

'It would help.' *I shouldn't be here. This isn't my war and I shouldn't be fighting it. I should go home back to Deephaven. But back to what? Come on, there must be something. Some reason!*

The next thing he knew, Syannis was in front of him down on his knees. The tension in his face was obvious, obvious how much he loathed what he was doing, but he was doing it anyway. 'Please, Berren. Please help me. Just Meridian. Then do what you like.'

Berren bit his lip. This wasn't the Master Sy he knew.

Maybe what he'd done in Deephaven *had* changed him after all – maybe he really was sorry. 'I'll tell you what I want then,' he said slowly. 'There was a ... what's your name for it? Bonds-maid? In the castle. She belongs to Princess Gelisya. I had to whip her, and all because she stood up for what she thought was right. I want her to go free. Not to be mine. Just to go free.' There and then it was the only thing he could think of.

'Very well. When she's mine to give, she's yours. I promise.'

'No, I don't want you to give her to me. I just want you to let her go.'

Syannis shrugged. 'If that's really what you want.'

'It is. But you'd better do it. There'll be hell between us if you don't.' Why did she matter so much? He barely knew her, but then this wasn't about *her* at all. She was a symbol, that's what. A way to redeem himself for Tasahre. And perhaps to redeem the thief-taker too. It was a strangely fierce thing inside him, a reason. A purpose. It had been a long time since he'd had one of those. He offered Master Sy his hand. 'You're not my master any more.'

'I know.'

'Fine then.' He couldn't look at the thief-taker. So fallen from what he'd been. An idol almost. Everything he'd aspired to be once, long ago as a foolish boy. And still the closest thing he'd ever had to a father. 'Right then. Let's go kill your king.'

'Regent,' murmured Syannis. 'Not my king.'

They walked on down the road from the castle and into the town. The night-time streets were quiet and the market square was almost empty. A couple of soldiers lounged against a wall, pointedly ignoring a man taking a piss against someone's door. Syannis led the way past them, along a narrow street between small houses jammed up together along the side of the river, until the road became a track and the houses became huts, and then the track narrowed even more to a path, steep and uneven, and the huts came to an end. Before long they were clambering between rocks, while the river hissed and splashed beside them. They took a moment to clean the worst of the muck off their hands and clothes. A half-moon was rising.

'Doesn't anyone ever keep watch down here?' muttered Berren.

'Tethis doesn't have walls. No reason to watch the river. Well, none except the one that only Talon and Hain and I know about.' Ahead of them, a hooting call broke the quiet. Syannis stopped. 'That's Hain.'

Berren thought it sounded like a night bird, but since he'd been born and raised in a city, he supposed he didn't know too much about birds. *Apart from seagulls*, he thought sourly. Syannis set off again. Long grass and brambles tore at Berren's boots as he followed. The second time they stopped, Berren looked up. The top of the slope was maybe a dozen men standing on each others' shoulders above him, steep enough that a man would need his wits and both his hands free to climb it. He could just about make out the low castle wall that overlooked the gorge. The river was below them now, rushing and hissing. Its foam glinted in the moonlight. Another bird call hooted out, and this time they were close. Syannis eased his way between two tall thorn bushes and Berren followed. Behind the bushes was a hollow. It was so dark that Berren didn't see Hain until the thief-taker's squire spoke.

'All here,' breathed Hain.

'You found it then?'

'I could find it with my eyes closed.'

'Lamp?'

Hain reached down and lifted something. A dim light lit the floor of the hollow. Berren could see their boots. He could see that the hollow turned into a small hole in the side of the gorge. Large enough to crawl through. A cave.

'Muffle it!' hissed Syannis, and the light went out.

'Everything's inside.'

'Berren, follow me. Hands and knees into the cave. Hain, you take the rear.' In the darkness Berren barely saw Syannis drop to a crawl. He did as he was told and followed into the hillside. He couldn't see a thing, but then after a yard or two he felt space grow around him. Master Sy's hand fumbled at his shoulder and pulled him up, and then Hain was in as well. He unshuttered the lantern, and Berren could see the cave. It wasn't a big one, but large enough for half a dozen men to hide inside. At the far end was another tunnel, vanishing into darkness, old and rough hewn, and barring the tunnel was an iron grille. From the looks of it, it had rusted fast years ago.

His feet touched something. He looked down. On the floor were their swords and their armour, everything they'd left outside the city in the morning.

'You must be joking,' he said.

Syannis jingled a set of keys. 'Don't get dressed, lad, not yet. Just pick up your stuff and carry it.'

'You're not going to get through that!' Berren picked up his sword. He waited, watching.

The thief-taker jingled his keys again. 'It's been a dozen years and more since I was last inside these walls,' he murmured. 'Let's hope the locks are still the same as they were and that they haven't rusted as solid as they appear.' He put a key in the lock. It turned easily and the grille opened without a sound. 'Oh, look! Fancy that!'

'But that doesn't look like it's been used for years!' Berren squinted at the gate as he passed through. The rust was ancient. The lock should have welded itself solid by now. His head snapped up, peering into the darkness of the tunnel ahead. 'If they still use it, why isn't it guarded?'

'They don't,' hissed Syannis. 'They don't know it's there.'

'Well someone must—'

'Me, you dolt! Me and Hain! What do you think I've been doing for the last two months? While you and Talon were living the lives of princes in Kalda, I was here, squatting in flophouses, camping in the woods, digging holes for my own shit and eating bark! Turning those lancers so they were taking my coin instead of Meridian's. And while I was at that, Hain was here, hours and hours, night after night, picking at that lock, working it loose again for the day we'd need it. And no, Meridian really doesn't know it's here. You'll see why in a moment.'

They rounded a corner and the tunnel opened into another cave, larger than the first. The light from Hain's lantern gleamed off a wide pool of water.

'It's a sump,' said Syannis. He pointed across the pool. 'Swim down under the water there, you'll find a tunnel. It's narrow. Like the way in. It's not long though. Just a yard and then you'll come up into another pool. That's where the Pit is. We used to drain the tunnels every few months to keep the water down. It was our secret way out. By the time Meridian took the castle, it must have flooded again.'

'What's the Pit?'

'There are many more caves in these cliffs. When you get out of the pool, there's another tunnel. Wide enough that you can put your sword on before you go through it, and I suggest you do. It's steep and goes up about twice the height of a man. The Pit? People get thrown in it. People Meridian doesn't like. If he's got anyone in there, there's a chance he'll have a guard standing watch as well. I'll go first and wait for you on the other side. Take your time. Take this and follow it when you're ready. I'll give a tug when I'm through.'

Syannis handed the end of a rope to Hain and waded out into the pool, carrying his sword and his armour. As the water got deeper, he splashed and spluttered and then took a deep breath and vanished, simply sinking beneath the surface.

'You next, dark-skin,' growled Hain.

He pushed the rope into Berren's hand. Berren took it, but stopped for a moment. A tunnel under the water? 'Why me? Why not you?'

'Because I don't trust you not to run.'

The rope jerked. Berren took a deep breath and stepped into the pool. Cursed water was *freezing*, but at least it would wash the last of the shit off him. With one hand on the rope and the other clutching his sword and his leathers, he dived in.

21
DANCING IN THE DARK WITH KNIVES

The underwater tunnel wasn't as narrow as he'd feared, and before he was halfway though, Berren felt a hand on his shirt, pulling him on. Hain came quickly after. It took them a minute to light the lantern again, even though it had been wrapped in oilskin; when he did, Syannis shone it at a cleft in the cave.

'Up there.' He shuttered the lantern and squinted, then put it down. 'See,' he whispered. 'See how you can still see the cleft? Barely, but it's there. That means there's a torch lit beside the Pit.' He crept closer. 'Berren, you behind me. Hain take the rear. Keep back.'

The crack in the cave wall was wide enough, as Syannis had said, but the slope and the darkness and the thought that there might be an armed man standing not more than a dozen yards away made the climb agonisingly slow. At the top Syannis put a finger to his lips and gestured to Berren to ease closer. The cleft opened into a third cave. The walls were smooth, worn over time by water; the floor was flat, but most of it was a hole ringed by a low wall. The Pit. From where he stood, Berren couldn't see how deep it was. There was a pulley and some ropes, presumably for winching people out once they'd starved to death or whatever happened to them in there.

On the other side of the cave was an arch. Two torches

burned in sconces, one on either side. Beyond it, Berren could see two men with their backs to him.

Syannis began to ease his way around one side of the pit. He glanced at Berren, gestured to him to go the other way and then drew a finger across his throat. Berren looked down inside as he crept around the wall. The Pit was at least as deep as it was wide, but there wasn't anyone in it – at least, there wasn't anyone *moving*. The smell was terrible.

They reached the archway together. The thief-taker raised three fingers. *On the count of three.* Berren looked behind him. Hain had stayed back, lurking at the top of the cleft.

One finger. *One.* The thief-taker's eyes shifted from the guard to Berren. Buried in the gloom of the past was a man Berren had known as Jeklar the Throat, a friend of Master Hatchet. Jeklar had been called Jeklar the Throat for a reason, and he'd been happy to show anyone who'd listen exactly how you killed a man like this. Berren hadn't thought about Jeklar for at least a decade, but now the throat-cutter came back.

Two. He didn't have a knife though. He had a sword. Clumsy weapon for this sort of work. Too long. Syannis had a proper throat-cutter's knife, of course.

Three. He'd never done it before. Didn't know how. Didn't know if he even could. Kill a stranger, just like that? From behind? Without any warning?

He must have made a noise. The guard started at the last moment and stepped back straight into him. Without thinking too much about it, Berren clamped his free hand around the man's face and mouth. He dropped his sword, pulled the soldier's own dagger out of its scabbard and held it to the man's throat.

'Be quiet!' he whispered.

'What are you doing?' hissed Syannis. His own man was

slumping back. A wild fountain of blood sprayed across the roof of the arch and begin dripping to the floor. Syannis caught the body as it fell to muffle any sound. What was he doing? He didn't know. He was sweating and shaking and this was suddenly a lot harder than he'd thought it would be. Killing someone like this ... He couldn't just ... Sun and Moon, but it just wasn't that easy!

The guard flailed, pushing himself into Berren. He cried out, the sound muffled by Berren's hand, and pushed them both back further. They fell together. Berren closed his eyes and tried to twist his body. The two of them hit the ground at once, knocking the breath out of Berren's lungs. Then Syannis was there, driving his own knife into the back of the man's neck. The guard gurgled, reached out a hand and then lay still. Berren felt blood, still warm, running over his arms and his face like a river. He pushed the body away.

'Holy sun!' Syannis stared at him with eyes like saucers. 'What was that? What were you thinking?'

'That I've never cut a man's throat before!' hissed Berren savagely. 'And that maybe I didn't have to. Couldn't you have found a way to let them live?'

'Don't be absurd!'

Berren picked up the guard's helmet and jammed it on his head. 'I'll stay here on guard then.' He crouched down inside the arch out of sight, shaking. For a second he thought he was going to be sick.

One after the other, Syannis hoisted the dead men onto his shoulder and heaved them into the pit. Then he beckoned Hain closer and gave him the guard's helmet off Berren's head. 'Stay here for an hour,' he said. 'Make sure there's no alarm. Keep the exit clear. After that, we're either caught or we've escaped another way. At the top of the gorge by the river there are six horses. Wait for us there. If we get there first, we'll not wait for you but we'll

166

leave one horse behind. Follow us. We'll be heading north for Forgenver, and at speed.'

Hain looked aghast. Berren just nodded. This was the way it had always been, back in the old days. The two of them. It felt natural and his head wasn't thinking straight just now; it was still too full of the man whose blood was all over him, wondering who he was. Just another soldier like Tarn or any of the others.

Hain was beside himself. 'Sire!'

Syannis growled. 'He does this much better than you, Hain. He's a dark-skin thief, but that's what this needs.' He pulled Berren to his feet and slipped through the arch into a stone passage which turned and led up some steps and stopped at a door. They tiptoed in, feeling their way between barrels and crates and sacks filled with apples and other things – in the dark, Berren couldn't tell what.

'It's here somewhere,' muttered the thief-taker. They reached a wall and Syannis stopped. 'Door.' A line of golden torchlight lit up the floor. Syannis lifted a latch. 'You *will* have to kill, Berren. I hope you realise that.'

'If it comes to fighting then I will. But I can't just murder a man. That's not what I am.'

'Bugger,' said a voice from the other side. Wood scraped on stone, the sound of a chair being pushed back. 'That's three in a row.'

Syannis opened the door a crack. 'Then wait here!' he hissed. Torchlight filled the space beyond. The air was thick with smoke.

Another voice muttered something, then Syannis threw open the door and leaped out of the gloom, sword flashing. Three soldiers sat around a table. Over the reek of torch smoke, Berren could smell wine. There were dice, coins …

And blood. The thief-taker's short sword sliced through the first man's neck and stabbed the second straight through his gaping mouth. By the time Berren reached the table,

Syannis had done for the third too, opening his throat from ear to ear in a single slash. 'I told you to stay where you were!'

'And I didn't.'

Syannis nodded at Berren's sword. 'I hear you've finally learned how to use that.'

'You call me a dark-skin thief again, you'll learn a lot more.'

'That was for Hain, not for you.' Syannis dragged the bodies back into the cellar, then ran to a heavy locked door and took out his keys again.

'Now what?'

Syannis opened the door and stepped inside. Dozens of crossbows lined the walls and boxes full of bolts were stacked on the floor. An armoury. 'Not the sort of weapon you want people running around with most of the time.' He bared his teeth. 'Did Talon teach you to use one of these at last?'

'I taught myself.'

'Good.' The thief-taker closed the door and locked them inside. 'Take one and sabotage the rest.' While Berren cut nicks into the crossbow strings, Syannis set about clearing the back wall of the armoury. When he was done, he pressed his ear against it and began tapping the panelling. Then he stopped, pulled a hand axe from his belt and swung at it. Berren cringed. In the confined space of the armoury, the blow sounded like a clap of thunder.

A thought came to him: he was alone with the man who'd killed Tasahre. Alone where no one would see. He finished with the crossbows and took the last one for himself, cocking it softly while Syannis hacked at the wall. Then he held a bolt in his other hand and looked at it. Looked at it, and at the thief-taker.

No. Couldn't do that. Even though a part of him wanted to.

'My grandfather's grandfather built this armoury,' Syannis said as he tore at the thin veneer of wood, pulling it away. 'No one alive knows this door exists except me and Talon. And now you.' He finished and held up a candle so that Berren could see. Behind the wood was another wall, made of stone, and in the wall a door. Everything was covered in ancient cobwebs. The door had no lock, but it was heavy and the hinges were rusted almost solid. It took the two of them together to pull it ajar. Beyond was yet more wood.

'We put a panel over it,' muttered Syannis. 'It's a single piece of wood. A good hard ...' He rammed it with his shoulder. There was a loud crack, but the panel held. 'Damn! Stuck!'

'Stop!' hissed Berren.

'I felt it move! Another ...' Syannis made to charge the wall again. This time Berren held him back.

'Wait!' He took the bolt he was still holding and fitted it to the crossbow. For a moment, as it pointed at Syannis, he caught a flash of what it would feel like if he pulled the trigger right there and then. Exaltation, for a moment, and then sadness. Emptiness.

He fired the crossbow into the panel Syannis had been trying to knock down. 'You left Hain and brought me because I'm the thief, didn't you? When we're done here, you give me what you promised and then I want nothing more to do with any of you.' He held the crossbow bolt and nudged at the panel. As soon as he felt it give, he stopped and, using the bolt as a handle, moved it slowly aside. Silently, until there was gap large enough for him to squeeze through.

'See,' he whispered. 'That's how a cut-purse thief from Shipwrights' does it. He does it *quietly*.'

22
EXIT WOUNDS

B erren stepped cautiously through the space where the panel had been into a long wide passage that ran along the back of the castle. Here and there glimmers of light crept through narrow slits of windows.

'We used to call this the Long Gallery,' whispered Syannis. 'Go left. That way leads to the royal apartments. Meridian should be there. And Aimes.'

'You're never going to get him out. Not quietly enough. Not through all those doors and passages.'

'What if he *wants* to come?'

On either side pictures hung on the walls; in alcoves busts stood on pedestals. There was too little light to make out the faces staring down out of the shadows, but their presence made Berren's skin tingle. He felt himself being watched. Something didn't feel right. He stopped. In the gloom Syannis almost walked into him.

'What?'

'Listen!' Berren stood absolutely still and held his breath. Faint noises came from outside: the wind, the idle chatter of a pair of bored guards by the wall, even a distant hiss that might have been the sea. Within, everything was quiet.

'I hear nothing. Come on!' Syannis pushed passed him.

'Yeh. Nothing.' And that wasn't right, was it? Anxiously, Berren followed. At the end of the gallery an archway led into darkness.

'The king's apartments. Aimes' rooms will be here somewhere.'

Berren stopped again. The feeling in the pit of his stomach was getting worse. If these were the king's apartments, then where were the king's guard?

'The sun-chapel is to the left. Through the arch.' Syannis's voice was barely audible now. 'That's how we get out. There's another passage down to the caves. The rooms on the right will be the king's. Go straight on.'

'Where are the guards?'

'Guards?' Syannis snorted. '*I* never used to sleep with men at my door and neither does Meridian. We're past the guards. They're outside.'

The darkness was so complete that Berren had to hold his hands out in front of him not to walk into a wall. He took one careful step after another, dreading the moment he'd put a foot down and tread on a creaking board or a sleeping cat. But this was a castle, he told himself. The floors were made of stone; there wouldn't be any animals roaming free at night, nor would there be plates, mugs, bowls or any of the other things his feet had found while creeping through people's bedrooms.

I was younger then, he reminded himself. *Smaller and lighter and with agile feet. And I didn't have anyone with me.*

He fumbled his way through the darkness and into another long hallway. There were more narrow windows here, letting in just enough starlight to see by.

'The king will be at the far end,' whispered Syannis. 'The other rooms will be Meridian's and the princess's.'

'Gelisya?' The uncomfortable feeling turned sharp. He found himself thinking of Saffran Kuy. Saffran Kuy, who had his fingers all over Meridian's little princess, whether Meridian knew it or not. 'I'm telling you, this doesn't feel right. It shouldn't be so dark. If not guards then there should be pot boys. Maids. Night servants. *Someone*. And whoever comes this way at night would need some light.'

Syannis hissed between his teeth, 'What do you suggest? We can hardly come back again another day, not *now*. No, they're here. They have to be.' He put his hand to the nearest door. 'This one. These rooms were the finest. My father's. Meridian will be here.' He growled like a threatened wolf. 'Then we take Aimes.'

Time slowed. Berren lunged for Syannis, trying to pull him away, but his legs felt as though they were made of treacle. Syannis lifted the latch and pushed and then everything Berren had been afraid of began to happen.

'He's here!' shouted a voice behind the door. 'He's here! To arms!'

Old memories filled Berren's head of all the times he'd nearly been caught as a boy. When all you could do was run and dodge, dart down the narrowest, darkest, least used alleys. Some place narrow where big men would be slow, some place high where they couldn't reach, then some place dark where they wouldn't see you. You hid, and you prayed.

He's here? They knew Syannis was coming! They'd known all along!

'The sun-chapel!' snapped Syannis. He lunged with his sword into the darkness and roared. There was a grunt and a crash. Berren fled back to the chapel, but the archway was filled with men coming the other way now. Real terror gripped him – more soldiers, and they'd been lying in wait! He must have walked right past them without knowing!

'Master Sy!'

In the darkness he couldn't see how many there were. He had no idea even where Syannis was. He staggered. A hand clutched at his arm. He wrenched himself away.

'Run, boy!' The thief-taker's voice. He was already ahead. Berren bolted, bouncing off the walls as he ran. He caught a glimpse of the thief-taker in the shadows of the

Long Gallery. Other dark shapes were running through the far end of the hall. More soldiers!

Syannis skidded through the hidden doorway into the armoury. Berren skittered after him. There were guards only seconds behind him, coming from both ends of the gallery, but they *were* all behind him now, that was what mattered. After the armoury it was a quick sprint across the guardroom and then a long straight run all the way to the Pit and the sump and out with no one standing in their way. His eyes gleamed. They *would* get away!

He crashed into Syannis, who was fumbling at the guardroom door with a key. The thief-taker swore. Berren slammed the door into the Long Gallery shut behind him and put his shoulder to it. 'For the love of the sun! Keep your exit open! First rule of thieving you daft bastard!' The first soldiers crashed into the other side of the door and almost knocked Berren off his feet, forcing him slowly backwards. A sword stabbed through the gap, missing him by an inch.

'Got it!' Syannis had the other door open. Berren screwed up his eyes and leaped towards it. Soldiers sprawled into the armoury sending crossbows crashing all about. A hand caught his arm. The grip was strong, strong enough to spin him around before he broke free. He stumbled as he lurched out of the armoury.

'Get him! Get him!'

Syannis was ahead, darting down the steps to the cellar. Berren flashed past the dead guards slumped at their table, soldiers pouring after him. He felt the air move as someone threw a spear and missed the back of his head by a hair's breadth. He raced through the cellar, down the steps and round the corner towards the Pit. The soldiers' armour and swords slowed them down. He was gaining on them.

Almost there!

He unbuckled his belt and threw it to the floor, sword

and all, ready for the sump. With a bit of luck someone would trip over it. Syannis was right in front of him now, slowing him down. They reached the cave where Hain was waiting for them. Around the pit, Berren ran one way, Syannis the other. There must have been at least a dozen soldiers chasing him, but Berren felt like laughing again, because he knew they'd never catch him. He'd reach the sump and be in and they'd never—

Out of the darkness a figure stepped in front of him. Berren didn't even have time to see who it was, but there was only one person it could be: Hain. They smashed into each other. Something hit Berren's head. He stumbled a few steps, staggered into the low wall around the Pit, almost fell in, pushed himself away and then someone was on his back, bearing him down, pressing him into the ground with such force he could barely breathe. He thrashed and squirmed and watched, helpless, as Syannis reached the sump while more arms grabbed at his legs.

But the thief-taker didn't dive into the water; he kept coming. The soldiers holding Berren down suddenly let go and scrabbled away, and then Syannis was among them, slashing and stabbing like a wild thing. They fell back from his assault and for a moment Berren was free. He didn't pause. As soon as he was on his feet, he ran.

'Go! Go!'

He didn't have a sword any more, but even if he had there were too many guards. The last thing he saw before he hurled himself into the water was Syannis, backing after him, holding off half a dozen men, with more racing around the Pit to take him from behind.

The water was like ice. On the other side, he waited, dripping wet and freezing cold, but Syannis never came. Eventually, long after he knew there was no point in waiting any more, he left. The horses were exactly where Syannis had said they would be.

Hain. They'd all say it was Hain who'd betrayed Master Sy, who'd warned Meridian that the thief-taker was coming, the when and the how, but Berren wasn't so sure. Just at the very end, he'd seen a face lying in the darkness. Hain's dead eyes, open wide, staring at some unseen terror. And in that moment he thought he'd caught a smell of something that shouldn't have been there. A whiff of rotting fish.

23

THE PRINCESS AND THE SLAVE GIRL

Berren galloped through the kingdom of Tethis. He stopped at a farm, helped himself to a barn for the night and was gone with the dawn. He rode through the countryside, skirted Galsmouth with its garrison of fifty king's guard, crossed the river and entered Gorandale. For a few days he passed through rolling hills dotted with the occasional flock of sheep. He saw shepherds and a few quiet villages nestled in among the valleys, but little else. Syannis had left food with the horses. Hard bread, biscuits, dried meat and cheese. Enough to keep four men for two or three days; more than enough for Berren.

His head fluttered like a moth around Syannis's flame. They'd walked straight into a trap. Syannis could have dived into the sump and saved himself, but he'd hadn't and now he was probably dead. Berren had thoughts about selling the horses, about taking the money and finding a ship and never coming back. But for most of the time he thought about all the things that had happened since the day in Deephaven when they'd first met in a dingy alley that smelled of blood and piss, when Syannis had been nothing more than a thief-taker with three dead men scattered at his feet. He remembered how he'd wanted to be like that, to fight like that. He'd wanted it more than anything. He'd have given his soul.

Maybe he already had. The woman he'd murdered after

the battle on the beach still haunted his dreams.

Would Tarn have come back for him? Or Talon? Yes. But he'd never have thought Syannis would, because the thief-taker saw the world in a different way, where men and friends were sacrificed for some greater end. With regret, yes, but without remorse. The thief-taker had taught him that too. He'd taught Berren everything; now, too late, Berren found that that wasn't who he wanted to be.

All the things the thief-taker had done for him and all the things he'd taken away. Yet this time Syannis had come back.

He forded a river in the middle of nowhere. The road – not much more than a muddy line through the hills – wound back to the coast. He stayed for a night in a tiny town that smelled of fish and filled his belly with something that wasn't dry bread. Three days later he was outside Forgenver. Talon had always been decent to him. Talon deserved to know about Syannis. Then maybe he'd look for that ship.

'Hey! Berren!' he hadn't even reached the tents before Tarn was waving at him. The two of them embraced. 'Glad to be back?'

'Hard to answer, that.'

'Talon said you were in Tethis. He looked none too happy. So how's the enemy's strength?' He frowned. 'You know we're at war with Meridian now, right?'

'Yeh, I worked that one out.'

'I've heard he has the Mountain Panther and the Black Swords hired to his cause.' Tarn laughed. 'Throw in the king's guard, that's sixteen hundred men. So is it true? Is that what he's got?'

'Yeh. The Mountain Panther was in Tethis. The Black Swords shipped in the day we left.'

Tarn grinned and clapped Berren on the shoulder. 'Talon says they spent a week up the coast near Taycelmouth hunting for us until they realised we'd slipped away and taken their lancers too. Path of the Sun! That's too many to face in the field! And they have archers and heavy armour. I reckon Talon has to sit tight for the rest of the season then. Meridian will have to let at least one of them go, and by next year we could have a company of five hundred. That's what I'd do. At least the walls around Tethis aren't up to much.'

Berren snorted, thinking again of the vast half-hidden city walls of Deephaven. 'That's true enough.' Then he looked out of the camp, over to the town of Forgenver which had no walls at all. 'Better than here, though. An army coming at Tethis from the north by land would have to cross the gorge and the river. If you came by sea, you'd have to fight through the town.' He wrinkled his nose. 'There are some big ships in Tethis harbour. I'd be more worried about *them* coming *here*.'

'Don't you worry, soldier.' Tarn caught his eyes. 'They come here, we'll have a palisade wall up in no time and we'll shred them. Talon's promised us a hundred brand new crossbows.' He led Berren towards a large hut in the centre of the camp, half made of wood, half pieces of scavenged canvas.

'As long as they don't come from the armoury in Tethis.' Berren smirked. At least they'd done *something* useful.

'What we need is a hostage. But if it comes to fighting, we'll just have to rely on our swords as always. Talon's in the ...' He waved at the wood-and-canvas thing. 'That.'

Berren watched Tarn turn and walk away. The priests in Deephaven had tried to teach him things about warfare. Strategies and numbers of soldiers and how so-and-so had held such-and-such a place against an army of ten thousand for weeks or days or however long it was. Probably with six blind swordsmen and a one-armed archer who fired arrows with his teeth. Berren didn't remember too much of any of it, only that the heroically outnumbered defenders generally came to a bad end. But still ... They'd taught him about the civil war. How Khrozus Falandawn, with half Emperor Talsin's strength, had seized Deephaven despite its walls and Varr despite its armies. He'd wrestled the empire away from Talsin, and how had he done it? He was good with cavalry, he was brutal and ruthless, but mostly what Berren remembered was that Khrozus had had sorcerers, that he'd used magic. He smiled. He could still see the other novices shrinking and shrivelling into their stools, almost not wanting to hear what was to come. The priest banging on about the dangers of sorcery, how it was the path to wickedness, while Berren had sat wide-eyed, listening with rapt attention. Khrozus had won his battles with sorcery. He'd cheated. 'Hey, Tarn!' he shouted with a laugh. 'We need a wizard! Get us a wizard!'

Tarn turned back to Berren and made a sign to ward off evil. 'I'll trust my sword, thanks.'

Sterm. That was the priest's name. Sterm the Worm. Remembering made Berren smile for a while, and then the smile faded as he remembered how things gone for him when it came to wizards and their ilk, and the whiff of rotten fish he'd smelled as he'd plunged into the sump; and then other memories came too: the woman he'd killed, as always, and standing in the yard of Tethis castle with a whip in his hand and tears on his cheeks. Deephaven seemed so long ago. He'd been such a fool. So naive.

With a heavy sigh, he went and did what he'd come to do. Found Talon and told the Prince of War that his brother was gone. When he was done, Talon shook his head and sent him away without a word, though his face was pale and stony and his eyes were cold and hard. No blame, no pointed finger demanding to know how it was that Berren and Berren alone had returned. Almost as though Talon had expected it.

'Meridian won't kill him. Not while Talon's here,' said Tarn when the news finally spread around the camp. 'But he'll be happy enough to hold a hostage.'

The weeks passed and dragged into months. Berren stared out at the sea, watching ships come and go from Forgenver, telling himself that the next one, always the next one, would take him away. Talon recruited every man he could get. Each day wagons went back and forth, full of supplies. Most of it was food, but sometimes there were arrows or spearheads or boots, and when a hundred brand new crossbows arrived just as Talon had promised, the camp buzzed with the news for days and even Berren slunk across the camp to look at them. Every morning, as he woke up, he wondered if that would be the day he'd finally vanish back to Aria; and every night as he fell asleep in the same place once more, he realised that he had nowhere else to go; until, as the weeks rolled by, the thoughts began to fade and he knew, for better or for worse, that this was his home now, and the men around him were his family.

News came from Tethis now and then. Talon spoke of it with glee. Meridian had prepared an attack. He'd sailed two fat-bellied ships into Tethis harbour and filled them up with soldiers. They'd been ready to sail when the skies had darkened and the worst storm for twenty years had struck. One ship had broken apart and sunk right where it was, and the other needed months of repair. Dozens of soldiers, perhaps a hundred, had drowned. They heard too that Syannis wasn't dead and was Meridian's hostage, just as Tarn had said. Rumours shot through the camp like wildfire after this: every week there was a new story about how Syannis had escaped, or which bit of him had been cut off and sent to Talon as a warning *this* time.

Meridian tried again late in the summer, sending his soldiers northwards on foot. His army marched a day past

180

Galsmouth and then found their food infested with rats, rot and blight. They had no choice but to turn back. From the accounts that reached Forgenver, Meridian had been so furious that he'd had the quartermasters from each company hanged.

The seasons turned and the weather began to change. The days grew cold and wet, the nights dark and long. In Tethis the Black Swords were rumoured to have sailed south for the winter, leaving only two cohorts of archers. Outside Forgenver the Hawks had swelled their numbers close to the five hundred that Tarn had predicted. The autumn rains set in, driven by a biting wind while Talon drilled them ever harder; unrest spread among the older soldiers, used to spending their winters in milder climes. Day after day of rain turned their camp into a sea of mud, and still Talon ordered his grumbling companies out of their tents to march back and forth until they were soaked, to practise their formations until mud covered everything and no one knew who was who any more. Berren began to think there might be a mutiny, but just when he thought that even *he* might revolt and run away, Tarn barged into their tent, shook the rain off his coat and beamed with glee. He threw a coin at Berren.

'Two rest days and five silver crowns for each man.' He hauled Berren up off his pile of blankets, where he'd been savouring the ever-present smell of sodden earth and listening to the thrum of rain on canvas, the pitter-patter of drips where it found its way inside their tent. Tarn was still grinning. 'And then we march!' He rubbed his hands. 'Forgenver's not going to know what hit it. We'll drink the whole town dry!'

'What do you mean we march?'

'Get your coat on! We've got a shipment of blankets and boots and other things to get from the docks to the camp without there being any pilfering, and then...' Berren threw on his long leather coat, the coat Master Sy had once worn in Deephaven. Outside they trudged, heads down through the mud. 'Tethis, Berren.' Tarn slapped him on the back but his tone was serious. 'We're going to Tethis! We're going to war! Whatever words have never been spoken, speak them soon. A winter war takes far more lives than a summer one.'

The road into Forgenver was churned to a thick gooey mud that sucked at Berren's boots. The rain was relentless. Even under his cloak and his coat, he was soaked to the skin when they reached the docks. Crates lay piled up by the waterfront; men were swearing and shouting at each other over the hiss of water falling on stone. Puddles lay ankle deep. Everything was sodden and faded to a haze of grey, and in the midst of it all, barking orders and cursing, stood Talon, waving his arm over some crates stacked beside him.

'Tarn! These! Get these to the camp. I don't care how, but get them there. *Don't* drop them.'

'What are they?'

Talon glanced at Berren. He shook his head. 'Fragile, that's what.' Berren saw firelight flickering through the cracks in the wooden crate. Were they ... ? He bent down to peer closer and then stopped. Talon had drawn his sword, fast as a snake, and the tip of it was hovering in front of Berren's face. 'Fragile. Like glass. That's all you need to know,' he said to Tarn, then turned his eye on Berren. '*You* I brought here for a different reason.' His voice softened a notch. 'You'll know what they are when you see them.'

Berren stepped back. He knew already. He'd seen that flickering light before. In Kalda, a bright ball of flame in the hands of a Deephaven lancer.

Talon's stare was strong enough to flay skin. 'Sergeant Tarn, I suggest you put a covering over those crates when you get them to the armoury. You will take them yourself

and you will let no one else come near them. Do you understand? What they hold will change the course of a battle, if
used well.'

Tarn nodded.

'There's a handcart here for you. Let no one else see
them.' Talon turned back to Berren. 'Well, you might as
well help him now.'

The two of them gingerly loaded the crates. Berren
tried to guess how many fire-globes Talon had. A dozen
crates and a handful in each one, so perhaps fifty, perhaps a
hundred? Enough to change a battle, yes, unless the enemy
had them too. They set the crates down on a bed of straw,
carefully apart from one another. When they were done,
Tarn helped himself to a piece of sailcloth and wedged
it down on top. Further along the waterfront, a heavily
loaded wagon was being forced through the mud by a team
of beasts pulling from the front and a cohort of sodden
swearing soldiers pushing behind.

'We'll follow them,' said Tarn. 'They'll go nice and slow
and find all the bumps for us,' but Talon was shaking his
head and looking at Berren.

'Take them back on your own, Sergeant Tarn. Berren
stays here.' When Tarn cocked his head as if to ask why,
Talon laughed. 'Because I'm going to ask him to help
me kill a warlock, that's why.' He turned to Berren. Half
a smile played around the corners of his mouth. 'I know
what Syannis offered you in Tethis. She's here. She wants
to talk to you. She wants you to kill Saffran Kuy. Can't say
as I'd object.' He turned back to Tarn. 'Does that satisfy
you, Sergeant?'

Tarn wrinkled his nose. He nodded. Then, when Berren
didn't say anything, he shrugged and pulled his cart slowly
away into the rain. Talon watched him go.

'We both have a lot to be sorry for,' he said without
looking at Berren. 'Syannis couldn't bring back your

sword-monk and you can't bring back Syannis. You said Saffran Kuy made you kill Radek?'

'Yeh.' Berren spoke softly, words almost lost in the rain. He remembered perfectly how the warlock had come, a thing made of shadows, how he'd wrapped a part of himself around Radek's neck, and the voice inside Berren's head: *Kill! Kill him now!* A voice he'd had no choice but to obey.

'Princess Gelisya's bondswoman is here of her own accord. She ran away. If we lose, she'll be hanged. She ran away because, she says, Saffran Kuy is turning her mistress into something terrible.' He wrenched his eyes away from wherever they were and looked at Berren instead. 'I've not forgotten that you once said the same. If it were down to me, I'd make peace with Meridian long enough to have Kuy and his like hunted down and strung up. Too late for that now, but Kuy still has to be stopped.'

'Tell me how!' said Berren. 'I'll hunt him down and I'll kill him.'

Talon's eyes strayed back to the horizon. 'It won't be easy. I know he's touched you. He'll feel you coming.'

'So be it.'

The Prince of Swords nodded and sniffed. 'Meridian is no fool. Beating him will be difficult. But it's my homeland. I will know the battlefield. But I do not know which side Saffran Kuy will be on. I do not want him on mine. But I do not want him on Meridian's either. If he's near when we come to battle, I want him gone. Forever.'

'I'm a thief,' whispered Berren. 'I'll slip in like a shadow, put a knife through his eye and slip away again.'

Talon half-smiled. He slipped his sword out of its scabbard and stared at the blade. 'Killing a warlock isn't such an easy thing. I thought you knew that already. And I have little advice to offer. Come with me!'

He jerked his head towards the town and strode away

from the cursing men on the waterfront, through the Forgenver streets.

'The bondswoman is in here. Make whatever deal you like with her. Maybe she can help you. When Meridian is dead you can have her if you want her. Do with her what you will. Release her if you wish. I will see to it she doesn't hang for abandoning her mistress.' His restless eyes settled on Berren again as he stopped at a travellers' tavern and pushed open the door. 'When this war is over, Aimes will still be king of Tethis. She will belong to him. He's simple and will be easily swayed.'

He led Berren inside, through the commons and up some stairs. There were soldiers here, lots of them, not all in their armour or carrying their spears, but he saw them nonetheless. Lancers from Aria. Talon stopped at an arched door.

'Here. I don't know what she wants, save that Saffran Kuy's head on a pike is a part of it. Freedom, I suppose. Her life. Don't we all?' His eyes glittered. 'Although it's possible she wants to murder you for that flogging you gave her, so keep your on guard and keep your wits with you in there, Berren of Deephaven.'

With that he left. Berren watched him go, and when Talon was out of sight, he pushed on the door. He knew this place. The rooms were comfortable, the sort used by traders come to Forgenver for a few days to buy and sell before moving on to the next port up the coast. A hovel beside the Captains' Rest and the Watchman's Arms of Deephaven, but immeasurably better than a soldier's tent. It even had a bathtub.

Gelisya's bonds-maid was sitting on the bed. Clad in white with a veil over her face, she could have been anyone. Berren took off his cloak and his coat, shaking rain onto the floor; as he did, she turned to look at him. Between the dark of the room and her veil, all Berren could see of her was a sinuous shape that once again made him think of

185

Tasahre. This was a woman he'd whipped. His jaw locked. He struggled for words. *I'm sorry. I didn't want to. I had no choice.* But they all died in his throat. Sorry wouldn't take away the scars. Didn't want to? But he'd done it anyway. Had no choice? None at all? They both knew that wasn't true, not really.

She lifted her veil and her eyes were wide and sad. She stared at Berren and Berren stared back. He tried to remember Tasahre, to put the two of them side by side, and found he couldn't. The sword-monk's face kept slipping between the fingers of his memory; and sometimes he thought it was a wilful thing, that her memories had slowly chosen to leave him because of the awful things he'd done: for the old woman after the battle of the beach, for the bloody whipping in the castle yard of Tethis and for the guard under the castle whose throat he hadn't slit.

'My mistress says your name is Berren,' she said.

Berren nodded.

'Bondsmen don't have names.' Her eyes bored into him. 'But when I did have one, it was Fasha. Master Berren, I have not been truthful. I have not run away. I have come to humbly petition you on behalf of my mistress, Princess Gelisya of Tethis, daughter of the regent Meridian, for your aid.'

'My aid? In what?' He was staring at her. He couldn't help it.

Fasha's voice grew urgent. 'The warlock. He has touched my mistress. I fear for her. He will ruin her. He's touched you too.' She sank carefully to her knees and bowed her head. 'Master Berren, my mistress pleads with you: she begs you to help her. Will you do this?'

'Why ask me?'

When she looked up, her face was torn with grief. 'My mistress says you are the only one who can stop him. She says she has seen it, that it must be you. I will give you gold.'

'I don't want gold. Not for this. I'll kill Saffran Kuy out of spite.'

'You will help us?' Berren nodded. A moment later she was on her feet. She stood right in front of him, so close that they were almost touching and he could smell her skin, a slight tang of rain and sweat. She looked up at him, face brimming with hope. 'Truly? You will help us?'

'If the help you seek is the murder of Saffran Kuy, then yes.' When did it become so easy to be a killer?

She took a step away from him. 'Best not speak it aloud.'

'This is a war.' Berren tore his eyes off her. 'Wars are filled with vicious deeds. When it's done, I'll free you. Both of you. And I'll not take *your* gold, but I might take some from your mistress.' Her closeness was making his heart beat fast. Two years at sea and then another as a soldier and he'd almost forgotten what it was like to be close to a woman. What it had been like with Tasahre, standing among the stolen relics of the House of Cats and Gulls; but now he felt it again, a hunger and a longing almost too great to hold back.

'Thank you.' Fasha reached a hand to touch his face and Berren took it in his own, pressing her fingers against his skin. His other hand touched her hip, drawing her gently closer. She put a hand over his heart. 'If you will help us, I am to give you a gift.'

'I don't a need a gift.' But he did. His hand went from her fingers to her face, cupping her cheek, tilting back her chin, running slowly down the pale naked skin of her neck; and if she'd pulled away now, he wasn't sure he could have stopped himself from pulling her back, and what sort of monster was he for that? But she didn't. She pressed herself closer and his hand on her neck slipped to her breast and felt the stiffness and the beating heart beneath as she drew his head to hers and closed her eyes.

'Berren,' she murmured. 'Berren. Whisper your name to

me.' And he did, and she kissed him, slowly at first and then with a desperate passion, the both of them like starving men stumbling upon an unexpected feast. She moaned and cried out as Berren's fingers found her, and Berren gasped as hers did the same, as they tore each other naked and devoured one another, clawing and urgent and oblivious to the world beyond the circles of their embrace. And when their first throes of passion were done, Fasha took his face in her hands and led him to the bed and they lay down together, one beside the other, and simply stared into one another and stroked and touched and explored with fingers and tongues, all through the night until the first cracks of morning eased their way through the shutters on the window and the dawn roosters crowed.

'I must go.' The words brushed Berren's ear like perfumed silk. He let his eyes watch her as she dressed and then he called her to him and ran his hands over her skin once more. His fingers lingered over the scars on her back.

'I should never have done that to you,' he whispered. 'I'm sorry. I had no choice.' And he felt Tasahre's memory turn and walk away, sad and shaking her head. *There is always a choice, Berren. Always a choice.* And she was right. *Don't look to ease the harm, Berren. Look to do good. There is a difference.*

'You weren't the one who made me a bonds-maid.' Fasha closed her eyes. 'And I thought you were a warlock's boy. I knew what would come of what I did.'

He dressed. As he did, he caught a glimpse of something that lay under the bed, something that glittered in the candlelight. He reached for it and his fingers closed around something small and made of glass. He heard Fasha gasp and then he held what he'd found up in front of his face, a small vial. Another like the ones from Deephaven, with tiny words carefully etched into the glass, like the one he'd seen again in Tethis from the soap-maker's house: *The*

blood of the Funeral Tree, only this was one of the others.
His heart beat faster.

*Let them drink this and fall asleep. Whisper a name three
times in their ear, so that name may become the object of their
obsessions and desires.*

Berren almost dropped it. 'What? What is this?' He
stared at it and then at Fasha. She looked horrified.

'I ... I ... I did not ...'

'You tricked me! You ensorcelled me! And you call *me*
the warlock's boy!'

'No!' she cried. 'No, I did not! Look!' She lunged and
grabbed Berren's hand, forcing the vial up close to his face.
'See! It's full! My mistress ... she gave it to me, yes, and I
could hardly refuse it to her face. But I didn't use it! I *would*
not. And you agreed to help, freely. Please!' She clutched
at him. '*Please!*'

Berren shook his head. 'I would have hunted Kuy anyway.'

In a flash she grabbed the vial out of his hand and opened
it and held it to her lips. She looked at him and then closed
her eyes. 'Berren, Berren,' she breathed. 'Say your name if
you must. Say it for the third time.'

'No!' Berren grasped her hand and held it fast. 'Go!' he
said. 'Keep your freedom! Go and tell your mistress that
you've done what you came to do. And if you've got any
sense, you'll throw that potion into the sea.'

After she was gone, Berren lay still. He gazed at the ceiling, lost in a reverie of bliss and remembered sensation. He
only had to close his eyes and she was with him once again,
her face aglow with lust, her eyes wide with desire. He lay
there and dozed and thanked all the gods he knew, and
tried to forget their vicious little twist with Kuy's potion
vial. After all, like she said, she hadn't used it. She *hadn't*.

And then later he got up and walked away and joined the
Hawks as they marched out of their camp, as they turned

towards the south and towards the war that the thief-taker had made.

✣ PART FOUR ✣

THE PROPHET OF
THE BLACK MOON

24

THE TURNIP FIELD

The rains had made the roads hopeless for wagons, but Talon's mules didn't much care, and it seemed that the prince had quietly bought up every one of them for a hundred miles around. Each day the Hawks marched through rain and mud to the next nameless farming hamlet, and each one turned out to have half a cohort of men already shacked up in every barn, a mountain of dry firewood and enough food for the army to eat its fill. And so it went for a twelvenight and a day until they reached the outskirts of Galsmouth. By then word of their approach had raced ahead despite the rains and the atrocious roads. The garrison fled before them, and Talon had his first victory for nothing.

The people of the town endured the arrival of so many soldiers with a tired fortitude. Talon seemed in no hurry to move on, and his men were in no mood to argue about food and shelter and a few warm dry nights with a proper roof over their heads. Every building became a barracks and every house was soon bulging at the seams. This was his homeland, Talon reminded them, soldiers and citizens alike. His country, and so an uneasy peace reigned. Meridian sent out a cohort of cavalry, but since Galsmouth was brimming with food for the winter, there was little they could do. They tried to foul the river but the rain defeated them.

A week passed and suddenly, without any warning,

Talon ordered them on. Every mule and horse in the town was rounded up and loaded up with as much food as it could carry. He made a speech that was largely lost to the wind and the rain and then they marched again, with full bellies and dry feet and warm winter cloaks. Which, it seemed to Berren, was all that most of the soldiers cared about. They marched in the open, making no effort to hide their approach ever closer to Tethis, and it seemed for a while that they'd march right up to the castle gates themselves before anyone tried to stop them; but then, a day from Tethis, Talon led them away from the road, out into a sea of mud that had once been fields full of turnips. The Hawks formed up into their battle lines, shields locked together, spears held at the ready, and waited. Meridian was coming.

'Hold fast, lad,' muttered Tarn. Men pressed either side of Berren and behind him too, a battle line three ranks deep and more than a hundred wide. 'Keep your shield up. Keep your eyes open and watch your feet!' Meridian's line would be longer, Tarn had already said that, and now Tarn was standing right next to him and Berren's eyes were wide and ready to fight. 'If they come at us with horse, get down on your knees. Hold your spear steady and let the crossbows behind you do their work.' Not that he hadn't told them the same thing a hundred times, not that they hadn't practised it with the lancers. 'When it comes to the push and shove, watch your feet. You slip over and go down – and men will in this mud – you'll never get up. When they come at you, you stab them in the face with your spear or you stab them in the foot, because that's all you'll be able to reach. Your spear gets stuck, drop it and use your sword. Your life belongs to the men either side of you and theirs to you. Remember that.'

Berren's heart started to beat faster. He thought about how he'd always wanted to learn to fight, how he'd spent every day of his life in Deephaven yearning for it. But this would be no scattered chaos like the battle on the beach where every man had fought for himself; no, here was a real battle, the real thing, where men were crushed together, where it started with a rain of arrows or a charge of horse and all came down to who broke first, and learning swords had nothing to do with it.

Somewhere off through the rain he heard distant shouting. Talon rode along the battle line. Two hundred men lifted their shields and locked them together. The fear started to rise in Berren's throat. He had nowhere to go, nowhere to run. What use were quick feet and a flashing sword when there were men pressed in all around him?

And then Talon stopped in front of him. 'You!' He pointed at Berren. 'Out of the line! Now!'

Berren couldn't bring himself to look at the faces of the men around him as he stepped out. A lot of them were going to die. He was no better than them and they knew it – *he* knew it. He ought to be with them, facing what they faced, fighting with them, fighting *for* them, dying perhaps, and yet he was shaking with relief. Talon stopped again a moment later as he rode along the line, and then again, each time picking a man to come with him. The shorter men, Berren realised. The small ones. The ones who might be quick and fast but might not be as strong as the rest. The weak links! He almost gasped. That was him! For all his skill with a sword, in this battle line where everything would come down to strength and grunts, he was weak!

'Put your shields down,' Talon said quietly, voice half lost in the wind. 'You won't be needing those.' He handed each of them a crossbow and pointed through the rain. 'There's a farm half a mile that way. That's where Meridian will be. The lancers will come around the right flank towards it and draw out his reserve. You will circle around to the left. Do whatever damage you can. Good luck.' He saluted.

The other men saluted back but Berren just stared. Then Talon rode along the front of the Hawks' battle line, shouting rousing cries while the soldiers shouted back. In the lashing rain, men banged their spears and swords against their shields. The others Talon had chosen ran off into the sodden haze. Some, perhaps, were simply running away. Was that why Talon had chosen them? Did he know they were the ones who would break? Berren stayed where he was. He watched, creeping forward, keeping pace with the edge of the line. He couldn't simply leave, could he? Leave the men he'd fought with on the beach, the men he'd lived with through the summer?

Meridian's army emerged out of the rain like a wall of ghosts, banging their own spears and shields. Shouts went up from both sides: *The Hawks! The Panther! The Black Swords! For Talon! For Meridian!* Talon had three ranks to Meridian's five. Somewhere in the haze Berren thought he heard galloping hooves, or perhaps he felt them through the earth, for he certainly didn't see any horsemen.

The Hawks checked their advance – the front rank dropped to a crouch with their spears at the ready, revealing both ranks behind with crossbows. The strings were wet and sloppy, but the range was short, and four hundred bolts slammed into Meridian's wall of shields. Men fell. In the mud, soldiers tripped and slipped over the bodies of the fallen, but the wall of shields came on, and now they returned a barrage of their own. The Hawks rose to their feet. Another shout tore through the rain. Meridian's men began to run – not a flat-out charge, but a steady trot, keeping their wall intact. As Berren watched, the back ranks of the Hawks threw their crossbows away, high and over their shoulders. They readied their spears.

But not all of them. Along Talon's line tiny sparks of flaming light arced through the air towards the advancing soldiers. Even through the rain, light flashed bright enough to make Berren cringe. Fire blossomed along Meridian's line; men screamed and burned. Their charge faltered. The wall of shields wavered, and now the Hawks launched their own charge. They crashed into Meridian's line, its soldiers still reeling and screaming, the smell of singed flesh and hair mingling with the smell of rain and earth. The shield wall cracked and broke in a dozen places. Around the edge, soldiers broke away. Berren raced after them. He cut down one man who didn't even try to fight, just ran and wasn't quick enough, and then a second who tried to dart past him and slipped in the mud. The next one he let go. By then, everyone was so covered in filth it was almost impossible to tell who was who any more. And they were running – why kill a man who was already running?

He sighed, shook himself down and sheathed his sword. Somewhere out there was King Meridian. Perhaps Kuy too, both of them men Talon wanted him to kill. Quietly he applauded the Prince of War. Meridian had a cohort of men in heavy armour, two cohorts of longbow archers and around fifty cavalrymen. In this mud, in this rain, in this roiling mass of confusion, they were useless. It all came down to men in thick leather and old mail hacking and stabbing at each other with swords and short spears.

There were more of Meridian's men around him now, lurching through the mud, back towards the general direction of Tethis. Berren slipped in among them, but he'd barely gone a dozen paces when someone was running at him out of the rain, and Berren had no idea whether this was a friend or an enemy or just some irate peasant, letting him know what he thought of what was happening to his turnip field. All he could see was a madman covered with black mud, with wild white eyes and a great big axe.

'Cowards! Get back and fight or take what's coming to you!' The axe swung. Berren ducked and tried to jump away, but the wet earth took his feet out from under him.

He landed flat on his back, spattering mud in all directions as the axe split the air where he'd been standing. The axeman almost lost his balance as well. 'Vermin, all of you! Get back and fight! Afore I cut you all down like this one!' Berren tried to scrabble to his feet but he kept slipping. The axeman steadied himself. Somewhere underneath the layers of black goo was a skirt of hardened leather strips. He had braided hair and a spindly beard, both caked in mud.

He's from somewhere in the far south, *then*. The thought bubbled up from the storm of panic in his head. Berren pushed with his feet, trying in vain to find some sort of purchase. The mud was like a thick soup.

The man with the axe took a long hard look at him and braced himself. 'Deserter,' he hissed. 'You know what that means.'

Desperate, Berren threw a handful of mud. It caught the axeman squarely in the face. He shuddered, pitched over backwards and didn't move.

When at last Berren found his feet, the axeman was still lying there. Berren stood, waiting for his heart to stop racing, for his hands to stop shaking, for the urge to run away to fade. He dropped to his knees and threw up. Then he looked down at the axeman again, sprawled flat on his back in the slime. Already mud had started to ooze between the dead man's fingers. His face was covered in dirt and the tail of a crossbow bolt stuck out of his chest, punched straight through his mail shirt. Berren looked back the way he'd come, but all he could see was a handful of ghostly shapes stumbling through the mud, covered in it and almost lost in the rain.

His sword lay on the ground. He picked it up and wiped it clean. He'd never know who'd saved his life. His crossbow was soaking wet and covered in filth – though at least the rain washed the worst of the mud away. Whether it would still work, he had no idea. *Try not to get them wet*, Talon had said, and they'd still been laughing about that as they'd locked their shields together in the pouring rain with Meridian's soldiers rushing towards them.

He trudged on for a few minutes and then dropped to his haunches. He couldn't see any more deserters now. The ground here was firmer, the soaked earth not yet trudged into slime by a thousand marching feet. The turnips hadn't been crushed. Absently, he pulled a couple out of the ground and peeled them. They were sweet and ready for harvest. He peered through the grey sheeting rain for any sign of a building, a barn perhaps. That's where Meridian would be. Somewhere with a roof over his head. Somewhere dry where he could see what was happening, if only the rain would let him.

He heard a voice and then another, and then several at once, coming towards him. He dropped flat into the green shoots and the sodden earth. Since he was already covered from head to toe in mud, no one would notice one more body.

'... get out of this mud,' one voice was saying. 'This is a disaster!'

'... sound the retreat and get us out of here?'

'I thought he did!'

Berren wriggled, trying to turn his face toward the voices. The last one sounded strangely familiar. There was a pause. 'You told me he did!' said the familiar voice again. It had a shrill tone of outrage this time, one that Berren would have known anywhere, remembered from Silvestre's sword school in Kalda.

Lucama!

25
THE KING'S ASSASSIN

'I said he *should* have,' said the second voice.

'That bloody king probably won't let him,' said another. Berren wriggled again. There were at least four men now. Last he'd heard, Lucama had been fighting for the Mountain Panther. Made sense that he was here, but why *here* and not in the battle line being butchered with the rest?

'Even if they didn't call the retreat, so what? We've got what? Fifty men here? Let the Black Swords get themselves slaughtered. One less company to keep an eye on next year, that's what I say.'

Finally he caught sight of them, walking slowly out of the haze of rain.

'It's a shambles,' said the first voice. 'They had some sort of fire-throwers. *Our* cohorts managed to rally. Buggered if I know what happened to the Panthers. I think they broke. Then those traitor lancers came at us from the other flank. By the time we get back to the king, chances are we'll find the whole place overrun. Only thing that makes sense is we get back to the castle as fast as we can. What's left of us. Don't know why we left it.'

'Huh.' Lucama snorted. 'With archers and armoured swords, we don't need the rest. We could hold the walls on our own. And don't ask *me* why we came out here!' Which made Lucama a Black Sword now? Berren clenched his fists. Almost the first friend he'd made since escaping off that bloody ship, and now they were to be enemies across a battlefield?

'And what if the Prince of War has another trick up his sleeve?' asked the second voice. 'What if he's got some way to shake down the walls and make them topple back onto us?'

The feet trudged past where Berren lay. He watched them go.

'Don't be an oaf,' snapped Lucama.

'That fire seemed a pretty good trick to *me*!' snapped the other voice. 'And don't forget that the Prince of War grew up in that castle. If it has secrets then he knows them. They already did that to us once, don't forget.'

'And we were ready for them ...'

'And then there's the people in the town. What if they decide they want their old kings back?' The voices began to fade as the men walked away, but the last words caught Berren's ear: '... go tell that mouse-dick Meridian about that ... probably doesn't know.'

Right then. He picked himself up and sat on his haunches, watching the soldiers fade into the rain. When they were nothing more than hazy shapes, he wiped the mud from his hands and face and followed. More men passed him in dribs and drabs, coming the other way. Some of them were limping, some running. They slowly appeared out of the grey haze of rain, and slowly faded again, heads bowed between fearful looks over their shoulders. They were all headed the same way. Away. Anywhere but the battlefield.

Lucama and his friends led him to a hollow where half a dozen houses nestled together with maybe twice as many barns. Soldiers milled aimlessly to and fro, scores of them, or else propped themselves up under whatever shelter they could find. They looked bored and dejected and afraid. Covered in mud just like the rest of them, Berren walked into their midst without a single challenge. Lucama stopped at the largest house and exchanged words with two soldiers in long leather skirts who slouched by the door, then he vanished inside. Berren scratched his head. From here, in this weather, you wouldn't have the first idea what was happening on the battlefield. What sort of general was this, sat with his feet up, drying his cloak by someone's fire while his men were put to the sword in a sea of mud and rain? In his mind's eye he'd seen Meridian sitting on a horse atop a hill somewhere, watching the battle in horror. He'd seen himself creep through the mud, shoot him in the head, and that was the end of that.

Now what?

Another soldier hurried out of the house. Berren followed him with his eyes into a barn and then out again, a wine bottle in each hand, then back to the house. When he was inside again, Berren peeked into the barn. It was packed full of soldiers sheltering from the rain, but in among them were horses and mules. One of the horses wore an elegant harness in fine rich colours. The king's colours. He slipped out again and found himself a place to stand without being seen, between the barn and the house, out in the rain and away from the sheltering soldiers. He took the crossbow off his back, cleaned it up as best he could and settled to waiting along the path the king must take to his horse. Water ran in steady rivers over his face, trickles of it creeping down his spine, into his breeches, filling up his boots. He was soaked through to his skin and the cold had settled into his bones. Yet he waited, still and silent.

He almost missed them. Out of nowhere, three soldiers in gaudy cloaks and crested helmets walked swiftly towards the barn. They weren't muddy at all. An older man was with them, dressed in fine metal plates. He was carrying his helm under his arm, and he'd already walked past when Berren saw the golden crown set into it.

Meridian. It had to be. He didn't know what the king even looked like, but the crown was enough. As they passed, barely a dozen paces from where he stood, Berren lifted the crossbow. He took a moment to aim. Blood pounded inside him, urging him to hurry, but he it fought back, picking his spot with deliberate care. The string was wet, the crossbow would be weak, the man wore metal plate, but from this range none of that would matter.

The bolt hit the king square in the back of the head. Berren didn't see Meridian fall; by then, he was already gone, out of sight between the houses. He hurled the crossbow away, drew his sword and then gave in to the tautness inside him and ran, as far and as fast has he could. He had no idea where he was going. Away, as though there were a dozen men hard on his heel, maybe more. At first, he didn't even dare to look back over his shoulder.

And then he realised that no one was following him, no one at all. If anyone had even seen him go, they hadn't given chase. Behind him in the rain the hamlet was already nothing more than hazy shapes. He kept running anyway, until he couldn't see it any more, and then he ran further, in a different direction this time, until he was sure that no one who was looking for him could find him. Finally he stopped and caught his breath. Every part of him was shaking, trembling uncontrollably. He could hardly feel his fingers. They'd already been numb when he'd pulled the trigger.

I killed a man. He never saw me coming.

He saw Tasahre again, Master Sy cutting her down, face twisted with rage. And Radek, paralysed by Saffran Kuy's shadow around his neck as Berren smashed in his skull. The sailor, Klaas, the woman who'd earned him his name and the nameless soldier Syannis had killed beneath Meridian's castle.

After a bit he found a tree that gave him a vestige of

shelter. He huddled under it, cold and wet and shivering. The rain finally began to ease away as the early winter darkness fell. He could see the farmhouses again by then, or rather he could see the fires being kindled beside them. He could soon hear the men around them too, their rowdy singing and shouting. For a time he thought these must still be Meridian's men, camping for the night. But the fires grew more numerous, spreading out into the fields all around until Berren understood. This was Talon's army, not Meridian's. Talon had won.

He tried to run again then, to get back among them and back where there was warmth and friendship, but the best he could do was a stumbling lurch. He collapsed in their midst, sitting himself down beside one of the fires, rocking slowly back and forth, shivering. Someone passed him a bottle of something strong. He took a swig and stared into the spiralling flames. He could see his sodden clothes steaming, but he still felt cold and the shivering got steadily worse. Hunched under his cloak he watched the sparks from the fire rising up into the sky, mingling with the stars. A strange music started to fill his head. He looked around to see where it was coming from and everything began to blur together. He thought he saw Tarn grinning at him, and then the grin fading and a strange look in Tarn's eye. Someone passed him another drink, one that burned his throat. A soldier wrapped a blanket over his shoulders, and then another and another, layers and layers like sheets on an emperor's bed, but he was still achingly cold. The words and the conversations around him twisted into a blur of noise. He closed his eyes.

A smell of smoke and incense and fish and some giant was looming over him with hands that were neither kind nor gentle. He felt them touch his face ...

Dragons for one of you. Queens for both! An empress!

Daylight. He staggered along in line. They were going

somewhere. He saw Tethis. He remembered the place where he and Hain had buried their swords.

Gasping, watching a reflection of himself. The golden knife clasped in both hands. It rose and fell but there was no pain, no blood. In its swirling patterns he could see his other self, clutching and clawing, his face contorted with agony ...

He remembered shouts. He wasn't sure what they meant, but afterwards there was a warm place to lie down, and far off he heard men cry, *The king is dead! Long live the king!*

You have to keep it closed. Otherwise something will come through. He's making us ready. To let it in when the Ice Witch makes the Black Moon fall.

Someone whispering in his ear in the dead of night. A terrible smell of dead fish. *A true master makes a few tiny cracks in the stone just so, and then leaves time and wind and rain to finish his work.* And he saw them again, the faces of the dead – of Tasahre and of all the men he'd killed – and in his fever he was gazing through a tiny window out over the sea from the stern of a ship, watching Tethis as it receded into the distance, savouring a dull pang of regret. Not for anything he'd done, but simply to be leaving, and for what he knew would await him. He held a handful of sand and slowly let it trickle through his fingers to the floor.

See, whispered the voice of the warlock. *This is what happens to us all in the end.*

26

CRACKS IN THE STONE

Berren woke with a start. The last thing he remembered, the last thing that didn't feel like a dream, was sitting on sodden earth, staring into the flames of a campfire with half an army around him. Now he was alone in a big room, maybe a barn, but the roof was too low, lying on a hard pile of old straw. It was uncomfortable and scratched his skin. The room stank of sweat. When he tried to stand, his legs had no strength. He threw off his blankets and looked to see if he had some injury he didn't remember, but no. No blood, no bandages.

For a few seconds he couldn't think where he was. He'd killed a king, or what passed for one anyway. He'd run away and hidden shivering in the rain, getting colder and colder until he could barely feel his skin. Then he'd found the Hawks and their camp, the delicious warmth of their fires, and that was where his memories began to fray.

What came after that were fragments. Marching and marching and feeling tired enough to die. 'You've gone grey,' someone had said to him. There might have been another battle, but if there was then he didn't remember any of it. If there was, he was surprised he was still alive, because his arm barely had the strength to lift a sword, never mind wield it. But they must have won because the next things he remembered were more songs and drinking and more delicious fire. At some point he'd crawled away from the rest of them, stolen as many blankets as he could find and found a place to sleep, struggling to be warm.

Everything ached. When he walked to the door and opened it, he cringed at the brightness of the sunlight. He was standing in the yard outside Tethis castle, tents everywhere, surrounded by the sights and sounds of the Fighting Hawks. He sneezed. The winter sun shone through the clouds, warming his skin a little; still, he shivered.

'Berren!' Someone was waving at him. 'Light of the Sun! You were sleeping for the dead!' Berren squinted. Talon. The Prince of War came over and clapped him on the back. 'You missed all the fun!'

'What happened?' Berren sat down on a log. The ground was cold and soft under his feet from all the rain.

'You had the shivers.' Talon smiled and shook his head. 'Most of the lancers are down with it too. You Deephaveners can't take a bit of cold and rain, eh? So was it really you who killed Meridian?'

Berren nodded.

'You ranted something about it but you were all over the place. Stuff about Syannis and Saffran Kuy and a knife. Didn't make much sense. But we did find Meridian with a bolt through his head.'

'Kuy?' Berren shivered. Yes. In Forgenver he'd been set on hunting the warlock. He remembered that. Now ... Now all he wanted to do was to sleep. 'I don't know *what* I said.' He could barely keep his eyes open. 'But he was here, wasn't he?'

'I'm afraid so. But he's gone now.' Talon wore a big happy-cat smile. 'Aimes took one look at him and threw a fit. I didn't know he had it in him, but if Syannis hadn't been there to hold him back, I think Aimes would have ripped him apart with his bare hands.' He shook his head and laughed again. 'Aimes wanted his head and I'd have been more than happy to hand it to him too, but Syannis calmed him down until Aimes banished him instead. Syannis blames me, of course. He says Kuy won us the war and we should all be grateful. But he's gone, either way. No need to go hunting him after all.'

'Master Sy ... Syannis? He's alive?'

Talon's smile stayed where it was. 'Yes. Meridian kept him in the Pit. They weren't exactly kind but they didn't kill him. He's thinner than he was but he's not missing any limbs or fingers. After Meridian died in the battle and with us coming on to the castle, no one dared touch him, and in the end they let him out. If Meridian hadn't been killed then things might have gone differently. Syannis owes you for that.'

'Yeh.' He thought of Fasha, of what the thief-taker had promised. 'Yes, he does. But then I owe him too.'

'It's all over now. Radek and Meridian are dead. Tethis is ours. Aimes will be king in name, but now our father's sons will guide him, not some fat shopkeeper from Kalda.' His smile faded. 'Do you still want to go after him? Kuy, I mean. You don't have to. As long as he's far away, that's good enough for me.'

Berren shook his head, quietly happy. 'If he's gone, he's gone.' If he was gone then Gelisya was free of him and his promise to Fasha was met.

'I saw him onto the ship myself and then watched until it sailed to make sure he didn't get off again. Can't promise he won't come back one day of course. But if he does then I'll be waiting for him.' Talon sat for a while longer and talked about the battle. Meridian's army had broken before the storm of fire-globes. Hundreds of soldiers and king's guard had been killed or scattered, but half the army had eventually managed a retreat back to Tethis. The next day, as Talon prepared to assault the castle, they'd found Meridian's body. The mercenaries had quietly looted the castle and left. Outnumbered ten to one and with no one to tell them what to do, the last of the king's guard had melted away too. Talon and the Hawks had walked into the castle to find the doors hanging open for them, Syannis with the keys in his hands. 'The Black Sword cohorts and what's left of the Panthers are camped a little way outside the city,' Talon said. 'They don't have much interest in fighting. Syannis told me you were going to poison Meridian. Is that true?'

Berren shook his head. 'I don't know anything about any poison. I shot him in the back of the head with a crossbow. He owes me for that and so do you. The woman you had me flog. You owe me her.'

'I suppose we do. Are you going to sell her?'

'No, I'm going to let her go.'

Talon raised an eyebrow. 'Really? I've seen more of her now. She's probably worth more than most men would get in half a dozen seasons with the company. A well trained lady's bonds-maid, one who was trusted to royalty, no less … Sell her and you could buy yourself a farm or a shop in the city, or a passage back to Aria if that's what you wanted.'

'I'm going to set her free. It's wrong for one man to own another. That's all that matters. That and that men keep their promises.' He shuddered. Saffran Kuy's voice in his head was still as clear as a bell. *Kill him! Kill him now!* And he'd had no choice. Not a jot.

'She must have made quite an impression on you.'

'I hardly know her.' Berren held his head in his hand. He ached and he still felt terribly weak. 'Syannis had to give me some reason not to walk away and get on the next ship, and I couldn't think of anything else, and now I'll be damned if I'll let him break his word. Not this time.'

'Your sword-monk. This is for her, isn't it?'

Berren didn't answer. He didn't know how. Not that the two of them looked much alike, not once you stripped Fasha of her veil and saw her face. But he'd seen them both stand up for what they believed was right with no fear for consequence, one of them a sword-monk, one of them nothing more than a slave. 'Yeh.' He laughed at the irony. 'Probably is, too.'

Talon stood up. 'People sometimes do very strange things once they get what they want,' he said. 'They turn out to be not quite the people they were pretending to be.' A strained look flashed across his face. 'Go and tell Tarn you're fit to fight. King Aimes wants to see you – he's heard of the fearsome mercenary swordsman who looks like him – but that can wait a few days. We've all got plenty to keep us busy and I think it's time you joined your comrades. The Hawks are letting the taverns of Tethis know they're here.'

The days that followed were delicious, like his first days with Talon in Kalda but without the doubt and the fear. As soon as his strength was back, he worked for as long as the sun was up; in rain or snow, he didn't care. They built defences of earth and wood around the castle, preparing for the next summer when the merchant princes of Kalda would surely raise an army to avenge Meridian. In the evenings he drank with men who were now his friends, his sword-brothers, the men who'd stood beside him at the battle on the beach and in the shield wall outside Tethis. They'd seen who he was. They'd spilt blood together. He was the warlock's boy no more, but the Bloody Judge of the Fighting Hawks who'd crept inside the enemy's camp and killed their king and put an end to the war. The trouble still writ plain on Talon's face, shouting loud that all was not said and done, that was no longer Berren's problem. One thing alone was missing: Fasha. With every day he found himself thinking of her more and more, of their one night in Forgenver together, and what he hoped she might choose when she was free.

The summons came to bring him to the king's hall. The new king's guard – mostly Deephaven lancers – took his sword from him as he entered. He walked into what had once been Meridian's hall, the king he'd killed, and bowed before four thrones. At one end sat Talon, at the other sat Syannis, between them, Gelisya, fidgeting on her chair, and beside her ... Berren simply stared in disbelief. The king. Aimes.

'Berren of Deephaven, Your Majesty,' said Talon, loudly.

'You *do* look like me,' said the king happily. 'I thought you'd be giant or something like that.'

Berren couldn't answer. He'd never worn bright rich clothes like the ones the king had on. Nor had his hair ever been so long and lustrous. But beneath all that, stripped down to skin and bone, he might have been looking at his own reflection. Except for the eyes, for where Berren's eyes sparkled, the king's were dull and dead.

Aimes chattered at Berren and talked like a child, moving from one thing to the next on a whim, hardly seeming to notice whether Berren heard him or not, which was just as well because Berren was too busy staring. *Like having a long-lost twin.* When he was finished, he waved Berren away. Talon coughed loudly. A scowl crossed Aimes' face, and the king of Tethis stamped his foot and rolled his eyes. 'Talli says I'm supposed to give you a present for helping him,' he said. He looked none too happy about the idea. 'Is there something you want? As long as it's not the hawks or the falcons, because I like birds.'

Talon whispered something in the king's ear. Aimes' face brightened.

'You want that?' He pointed at Fasha, crouched at the foot of Gelisya's throne.

Gelisya squeaked, 'My maid? You can't have my bonds-maid! She's mine!'

Berren ignored her. He nodded. 'Yes, Your Majesty.' An idiot and a child sitting on their thrones? What sense did that make? But that was a question for Tarn, down in a tavern when they were both deep in their cups, not for now.

Aimes beamed. 'I like you,' he said. 'You're not greedy. I don't like greedy people. Greedy people aren't nice. Yes. You can have the woman. Talli, can we have lots of bondsmen now?'

'Of course.' Talon peered past Aimes at Berren and mouthed, *She's yours.*

Berren murmured some words of thanks but Aimes had already forgotten that he existed and was busy beaming at Talon. 'Uncle Syannis never lets me have *anything*.'

Berren bowed and began to back away. A slight whiff of bad fish tickled his nose. He looked around sharply. *Kuy?* There was no sign of him, but Gelisya caught his eye. A little half-smile flashed across her face, meant only for him.

'No.' Syannis rose suddenly. 'This bondswoman is the property of Princess Gelisya, little brother. She is not yours to give.' He turned and stared at Berren, and Berren felt a numbness filling his head. He stopped. He felt as though he was suddenly watching from high in the rafters, as though he wasn't in charge of himself any more but had become a passenger in his own body. He looked very angry, he thought, as he took two quick steps towards the throne. A voice that didn't sound anything like his own uttered a growl full of rage.

'You promised her to me!' He was pointing at Syannis, he realised. Around the room the new king's guard had their hands on their swords and some even had them half out of their scabbards. But Berren found he didn't care about that, not one little bit.

'You promised her to me!' he said again. 'I remember your words exactly as you said them. *When she's mine to give, she's yours.* On your knees, you made that promise to me, as payment for Meridian's death! Well, thief-taker, we failed that night, but I did the deed for you on the battlefield. Now honour our bargain!'

Syannis's lips curled back to show his teeth. 'But she is *not* mine to give you, *boy*.'

The part of him watching from the rafters saw the change in Gelisya's face. The smug grin freezing in place, her eyes filling with horror and surprise, her jaw falling slack. She jumped to her feet. 'You? *You* did it? *You* killed him?' She whipped around to Syannis. 'I want him dead! Dead! Do you hear me? Dead!'

Syannis shifted awkwardly. 'Your father fell in battle, Princess. No one can say for sure how he was slain. In honourable combat, no doubt.'

'He was skulking miles away, filling his face with wine, and he died with a bolt from a crossbow in the back of his head,' hissed Berren. 'You tell me if that's honourable, thief-taker. If you can tell the difference any more.'

Gelisya's rage turned into an apoplectic fury of hissing, of pointing and screeching. Syannis's face filled with a cold anger. 'Help the princess back to her rooms,' he said. 'Take the princess's bonds-maid as well so she might attend to her mistress.' He pointed to Berren. 'As for this one, throw him into the Pit. A few days there should calm him down.'

'Syannis!' Talon burst to his feet. 'No! You cannot—'

'*I* am regent here, *little* brother! Now *sit down*!'

In a flash, before any of the guards could get close, Berren reached for his swords only to remember they weren't there. Obscenities filled his head, waiting to be flung across the room at Prince Syannis, but his mouth was frozen shut. None of them were adequate. Talon had closed his eyes, head held in his hands. King Aimes simply watched him being dragged towards the door with a look of idiotic amusement on his face. As his own countrymen hauled him away, Berren's eyes never left Syannis.

'I killed a king for you!' he screamed.

27

TALON'S OATH

They stripped him naked and threw him into the Pit, the same one he'd seen the night he and the thief-taker had crept in through the secret caves. The lancers didn't seem to care, but some of the soldiers who made up the new king's guard had been Hawks. They threw him in because that's what they'd been told to do, but they didn't look happy about it. In the days that followed there were no beatings. The water they brought was clean, the food good. On the third day his clothes fell in and no one seemed to notice. Soldiers from the company came by from time to time. Sometimes things fell out of their pockets.

'It's making everyone restless,' Tarn told him one day when Berren had been in the Pit for a week. 'Talon knows it's not right.' He slipped Berren a thick slice of cold beef. The soldiers who were supposed to be guarding him were carefully looking the other way. 'Everyone knows it's not right. When the Hawks leave and the season starts again, you'll be out of here. Talon has sworn it on his father's soul.'

'When the Hawks leave?' Berren laughed bitterly. 'So much for *a few days in the Pit to calm him down* then.' In his mind he saw Syannis with a knife though his heart. *Bastard betrayer! To think I came back here for you!*

The days dragged to weeks. The soldiers guarding his prison were the same. Tarn and the others still came to visit, but to the rest of the world he seemed forgotten. When he asked Tarn about Talon and Syannis, Tarn only rolled his eyes.

'Talon paces the castle like a caged animal and can't wait to be away. King Aimes issues nonsense decrees. Prince Syannis does nothing but complain about money and insist that this, that or the other be stopped. Princess Gelisya's demands grow ever more endless.' He sucked a breath between his teeth. 'Whispers say it's her that's keeping you here. She's got her claws into King Aimes, that one, and she makes sure he won't allow Syannis to let you go, nor Talon either. She's not the child she seems. Oh, and that bondsmaid sends a message.' He handed Berren a crumpled scrap of paper and then watched with interest as Berren peered at it. He laughed. 'We didn't know whether you could read. There's not many of us can, but then there's not many of us who've been taught by priests. What is it you see in her?'

A broken promise, that's what I see, that's what he might have said, but Fasha's note killed the words right there in his mouth. The writing was neat and perfect. The Deephaven priests would have been proud. Still, Berren had to squint and read it several times, frowning over each word until he was sure he understood it.

I am a good slave and I do as I am asked.

I am carrying your child. In time it will show.

I must think for us both. I pray to the sun every night that all will be well.

Berren's foot began to twitch. 'What do I see in her? For a start, she can write,' he hissed. 'That's more than you can.'

When Tarn was gone, he paced back and forth, tempted to seize a sword from one of his guards, to run to wherever Syannis was and gut him. For a moment he wondered: would anyone actually stop him? They might wrestle him down, or try to, but what if they couldn't? What if it *did* come to swords? Would any of them try to take on the Bloody Judge?

A child? He'd be a father. Something he'd never had, not really.

As the first glimmers of spring broke winter's grip on the world, Talon and his soldiers quietly made their preparations to leave. There wasn't much to be seen at first except that their camp grew a little tidier, but the word trickled to Berren in his pit. One morning two fat-bellied ships sailed into Tethis harbour; later that day Berren looked up to see Talon gazing back down at him. *Prince* Talon now. The last time Berren had seen him had been in Meridian's throne room.

Talon whispered a few words to the guards. The soldiers nodded and one by one they left their posts until he and Berren were alone, one at the top of the Pit and one inside. 'Berren,' he said, and Berren glared back at him, 'I'm so very sorry for what happened. Syannis never meant you to think you could keep her, only that you would have her for a night.'

'I think you're mistaken about that,' Berren said slowly. 'I don't want to call you a liar, Talon, but I think Prince Syannis remembers exactly what he said and has simply changed his mind. Which makes him nothing more than a thief like me.'

Up above him, Talon took a deep breath and exhaled slowly.

'Or was Gelisya supposed to go with Saffran Kuy and have no need for a slave any more? Was that the deal that Syannis made?'

A shadow crossed Talon's face. 'I don't know who's been telling you such treasonous lies,' he said coldly. Berren kept silent. Talon probably didn't know more than a sliver of what passed between Syannis and Saffran Kuy. Probably no one did apart from the two men themselves.

'I just go by what I see. Does it matter? She's still here. Maybe that was another promise Syannis broke.'

Talon scowled. 'You must really like it down there.'

Berren's last sight of Syannis was a memory he'd carry with him for a long time. The look had been of murder and hate, and Berren knew he'd earned it for what his last words had done to the Princess, not for anything else. 'I've heard it's Gelisya keeping me down here. I don't know what she is, Prince Talon, but Saffran Kuy has had a hand in making her.' He lay down at the bottom of the pit, flat on his back and stared up at the darkness where the ceiling was. 'I killed a king for Syannis,' he said. 'Or maybe for you. Doesn't matter which, really. It wasn't so hard. Seems that kings are made of the same flesh and blood as the rest of us. I think I've learned a lot about kings these last few months. They don't seem to me to be so very special.'

Something flew out of the air and struck him on the chest. A purse with a few coins inside. 'When I found you, Berren, you were a runaway, a ship's skag. You had nothing. You could expect nothing. Everything since then you've had because I've given it to you. I gave you clothes and food and money. I gave you a sword. I gave you a life. I gave you respect and honour and a place in the world to be proud of. True or not?'

Berren's face burned. He couldn't answer because what he wanted to say was that no, it wasn't true, but it was.

'There is your payment as a Hawk for the winter. We will be leaving for clearer air shortly. I will tell you this for free, Berren of Deephaven: I am little happier about what is happening here in Tethis than you are, although our reasons are very different. So we will not be back for quite some time. You must decide whether you are a Hawk or whether you wish to leave my command. If you wish to leave then take your money and I will be gone. You will remain here as I found you. If you decide you are one of us then I will take you away, but you must first swear me an oath and accept one in return. You must swear that you will not seek revenge for any of this. Let it go. Let Syannis go. Let Kuy go. Give up on your bondswoman, or else, if you must have her for that babe of yours that she carries, do what you need to buy her freedom. Princess Gelisya is no longer a child. She will soon tire of her old bonds-maid and demand new ones. People always do, when they are children no more.'

For a long time Berren said nothing. 'And what's *your* oath?' he asked at last.

'To see, come what may of you, that the child is cared for. Your child, once it is born.'

Slowly Berren rose to his feet. 'And how much would it cost for a man to buy her? You told me, a week or two before Syannis broke his promise, that she was worth a half-dozen seasons in the company.'

'For a good bonds-maid, you'll pay in gold. For one who has waited on a princess, a lot of gold.'

'How much gold? I'll sell my sword. Everything I have.'

He watched as Talon winced. 'You had nothing when I found you and you have nothing now, save that purse I've given you. Everything else has been taken by Princess Gelisya to pay for the damage done to her property.'

'Damage?' Berren felt the blood running to his head. He shouted up at Talon, 'What damage?'

'Her slave is carrying your child. I thought you knew. It affects her duties.'

'Sun and Moon! She sent Fasha with a warlock's love potion to help her bed me! What else have I done? Am I to pay for the arrow I used to kill Meridian?' If Talon had been standing in front of him instead of looming over the top of the pit, there would have been blood. 'She was promised to me,' he hissed. 'A man can break his word as freely and as often as he likes, but he can never once *un*-break it. That was the payment I sought from Syannis: a word given and a promise kept. Just that.' He threw the purse back at Talon. 'And I made a promise too. I promised Fasha that she'd be free. I promised her that because of the flogging you made me give her; and I will keep my word, whatever it costs me now, and Syannis can shrivel up inside as he looks on. If I must now buy what was offered freely, let this be my payment. I have no use for it.' He started to pace in angry circles.

'It's not enough, Berren.'

'Then what is? How long, Prince Talon? How long should I fight for you and save every coin I earn? How long while I watch the rest of your soldiers go home with fat pockets to their waiting families or buy the land they so crave and start new ones?'

He heard Talon sigh, a long drawn-out sound. 'A year. Two. Maybe three, maybe four. Things will change here. Now the war is done, the coffers of Tethis will slowly begin to fill again. Syannis will come to his senses and see how poorly he has treated you. Princess Gelisya is already in her years of changing. She will shed her childish ways. All these things will come to pass.'

'A year, then. I'll fight for you for one year.'

'Four and I promise you she will be yours.'

'Is a promise from you worth more than one from your brother?'

He almost heard Talon wince. 'You'll have to decide that for yourself. Now, do I have your oath or do you want to stay down there?' The Prince of War moved to stand beside the ropes that would lower the cage down into the pit. Berren stared up at him. If he could have grown wings then he would have flown up and hurled Talon down to be in his place and then taken his sword and let the castle run red with blood. One king, two kings, ten kings, what did it matter? They all looked the same when they were dead.

But no wings came and slowly the cold truth spoke to him: Talon was the only reason he was still alive, and Talon had done him no wrong. If he refused this oath, if he stayed, then he'd be dead before dawn. When he spoke, his voice was calm.

'Very well then. You have my oath. I vow on the life of my child that is not yet born that I will never seek revenge for the wrongs that your brother Syannis or any here have done me. Be it one year or four, I will fight and I will kill for you until I can buy back what is mine.'

He watched the cage slowly descend towards him, glad that Talon couldn't read his thoughts, glad that the gloom hid the bitterness written over his face.

It will not be revenge. It will be justice.

PART FIVE

THE KING-SLAYER
AND THE CUCKOO

28

SEASONS AWAY

The Hawks sailed from Tethis. There were fewer of them than had arrived. Some of the men of Forgenver had returned to their homes. Others finally had the money to put their soldiering days behind them and a good few were dead. But though many had taken the king's coin to serve in the king's new guard after the war was done, not one of them remained in Tethis when Talon set sail. Syannis had made it clear they were not welcome, not wanted, disqualified by their loyalty to the Prince of War. Instead, he recruited from the soldiers who had fought for Meridian, from the Deephaven lancers, even from the old king's guard. Berren caught a glimpse of Lucama, decked out in the new colours of the old king. There would be trouble, Tarn warned. Radek and Meridian had allies and families. There would be more fighting, more battles, always more companies falling to the sword. Berren shrugged it away. Whoever sat on the throne, Princess Gelisya would be there with them; and as long as she remained, so would Fasha and so would his son or his daughter, whichever it turned out to be.

The company travelled far to the south, Talon putting as much distance between them and Tethis as possible. They met the Mountain Panther and his men once again; now the Hawks fought side by side with soldiers whom half a year ago they'd faced across a battlefield. Berren found himself among the legions of the sun-king, clad in glittering armour, facing wild horsemen who danced around the clumsy footmen and fired their bows and then wheeled and turned and fired again. He learned to brace a spear against a charging horse, how to advance behind a wall of heavy shields that the horsemen with their bows couldn't penetrate. He watched as massed ranks of armoured cavalry charged across the field ahead of him, as volleys of crossbow fire darkened the sky, as cohorts of battle-priests called down the sun to scorch the earth and rendered men into ash in the blink of an eye. He saw war machines he could not have imagined existing. The Hawks became nothing but a tiny speck in a vast engine sent by the sun-king to quell the rebellious west of his Dominion once and for all. Now and then Talon would tell them where they were heading or whom they were fighting, or what town or city lay ahead of them. Berren listened with care, but the names meant little. When he marched, he thought only of the battle to come. When he fought, he thought only of the victory that would follow. And when that victory came, he thought only of the dead and the treasures they might carry. Friend or foe, he looted them all, and in the nights when Tarn and the others were out gambling and drinking their plunder away, Berren sat alone in their camp, counting his coins as though they were days.

The season lasted long into the autumn, so long that Talon kept them together in the south for the winter. When spring came, they fought for the sun-king again, but some dispute had caused the battle-priests and many of the officers to leave, and that second year did not go so well. By the end of it, half the men in Tarn's cohort were dead or gone, their boots filled by olive-skinned men Talon recruited from wherever he could find them. They spoke in a strange sing-song accent that Berren could hardly understand, and they had never heard of Tethis, or of Kalda or

Aria. That year homes and tongues and skins all ceased to matter; all that counted was that a soldier fought and fought hard, that he stayed in the line and held his place, and that when the time came to run, they all ran together. They found the remnants of the Deephaven lancers, a score of them, and Berren found some comfort in talking to them of their home. They'd come from the same city and they knew its nooks and crannies and understood its beauty and its ugliness as he did. The lancer from Kalda was there, the man Berren had flattened after the rest of them had tried to kill Talon with their fire-globe. They eyed each other for a while, trying to remember where they'd seen one another, and then they talked and they drank and each apologised for trying to kill the other, but it was war and they'd been soldiers on opposite sides so there were no hard feelings to be taken. The Berren that had landed back then in Kalda, he would never have done such a thing, never even understood it, but that was a Berren who had never seen a real war, not the fields full of slaughter that the sun-king's armies left behind them, win or lose. The Berren he had become took the lancer to the nearest bottle of wine and drank with him and became his friend. A soldier was a soldier. Kings changed, alliances shifted, but the men who fought for them bore no grudges.

Now and then he heard whispers of Tethis. Aimes still sat on the throne and Prince Syannis still ruled in all but name, erratic and vicious while the kingdom simmered with discontent. No one had raised an army to seek revenge for Meridian and the little kingdom was at peace, but still, it was an uneasy one. He asked for word of Gelisya and Fasha, and eventually he had an answer. The queen's bonds-maid had given birth to a boy. What had happened to him since, none of them could say.

He had a son.

The lancers became his friends, twenty men lost in a

world they only half understood. They taught him to ride, to hold a spear steady in a gallop and how to look after a horse. Talon had been reluctant to take them at first, complaining of the cost of their animals. But after the sun-king's armies broke for the second time that season and the Hawks found themselves in the midst of a rout, he changed his mind. The lancers were imposing enough to deter the gleeful bloodlust of thousands of enemy horsemen towards easier targets, and the Hawks escaped what might have been their slaughter.

Towards the end of that second year, as the sun-king's armies nursed their wounds, Berren took to giving sword lessons as a way to fill the days. He taught men as Tasahre had taught him, and Syannis and Silvestre too. He taught them to be quick, to be dirty, to thumb their nose at honour and grace and cheat every way they could if it would keep them alive. His reputation spread – the Bloody Judge of Tethis – and by the end of the season soldiers from other companies, even officers from the sun-king's armies, were coming to him to learn.

He wintered again in the south. This time Talon went away. When he returned, months later, he wouldn't say where he'd been but Berren could see it in his face: he'd been home and what he'd seen had scared him.

'Your slave is alive and well,' he said to Berren one day as they prepared for battle once more. 'The child too. When this season is over, I promise you will see them again. It's been long enough now.'

See them, Berren thought bitterly. *Not touch them or hold them or feel them or talk to them. See them. Like promising a cup to man dying of thirst, but only the cup, not the water that should go in it.*

The battle-priests and the officers returned for that last year, and fresh legions came with them. The rebels crumbled and the sun-king's armies swept through them like fire. Berren saw cities that dwarfed Tethis burned to the ground, their entire populations crucified as a warning to others. The roads were lined with crosses; the air stank of death and decay, but he found it didn't bother him. At night, when there was nowhere better to seek plunder, he would cut down the corpses and search, in case the soldiers who had strung up the bodies had missed something. One late summer evening, with the war done and behind them, as the Hawks began the long road to the ships that would take them home again, Berren caught sight of himself in a puddle by the roadside. For a moment he paused, bemused. The man staring back at him was a stranger. Gaunt, with lines on his face that he'd never seen before and a badly trimmed beard. He had a dozen scars from three years of fighting and his whole shape had changed. But most of all he didn't recognise the eyes. They were cold soulless things. He looked at his hands, the calluses around his palm. They were forged for killing now, and when he tried to imagine them against Fasha's silky-soft skin, he could only see the horror in her face as she recoiled from their senseless touch. The feeling passed, but it was a while before he understood its meaning. He was afraid. After three years of fighting, a score of battles, after killing more men than he could count, he was afraid that something inside him had changed and was lost and would never be found again.

'Do I have enough?' he asked Talon as they made their way home, standing together at the prow of Talon's ship. The sun-king and his armies were gone, and Kalda was drifting towards them. It was exactly how he remembered it, how he'd seen it when he'd been a ship's skag four years earlier. It had even been the same time of year.

'I hope so.' Talon laughed bitterly. 'When Syannis takes one look at what you've become, he'll give her away for free if there's any sense left in him.' He looked Berren up and down. 'The Bloody Judge, the King-Slayer, the

Crown-Taker. How many men have fallen to your swords? You have become terrible to behold, my friend.'

Yet beneath the Bloody Judge lay Berren, not long a man. *And Fasha? And my son? What will* they *see?*

29

THE KNIFE OF CUTTING SOULS

They disembarked from the ship. Before the Hawks dispersed and went their separate ways, Talon took a roll-call of his men, of who would return to fight again next year and who would not. Most boarded new ships to take them home, wherever home happened to be. Others, like Talon and Tarn and Berren, let the city swallow them up, each finding his own comforts for the winter months. Talon took Berren and Tarn to the taverns they'd visited years ago. They got blind drunk together, passed out together, woke up the next day and did it again. Berren drank to numb the fear inside him. Talon ... Talon drank a lot when he wasn't fighting at the best of times, but there was something different now, some shared desire for oblivion that drew them together. Tarn drank to keep them company. Berren and Tarn had been tight as a sailor's cleat in the years of fighting; now Berren felt him slipping away from both of them. He and Talon each carried a burden that the other understood, ones that Tarn could never share.

'Did Syannis ever tell you what happened to Aimes?' Talon slurred one night, when they were both well into their cups.

Berren shook his head. Aimes wasn't right in the head, and if Berren hadn't known that already, it would have been obvious from the moment they'd met in the flesh.

'Didn't you say he was kicked in the head by a horse?' There was more, though, and it had something to do with Saffran Kuy. Syannis had let that much slip.

'Syannis always thought it was his fault. He'd been so used to the idea that he was going to be king one day. When Aimes arrived I suppose he couldn't help but be jealous. Then Kuy came. He always made the hairs on my skin prickle, but I was only a boy while Syannis was into his changing years. I couldn't tell you whether Kuy sought Syannis out or whether it was the other way around, but they became like thieves, always together, always skulking apart from the rest of us. I used to follow them around the castle, secretly so they didn't know I was there, but I wasn't very good at it and they usually caught me.' He laughed. 'It used to drive Syannis wild.'

Talon leaned closer. He glanced around as though he was worried they might be overheard. 'A couple of years later, there was the accident. Syannis has it in his head that Kuy somehow made it happen, that one of the warlocks did it so that Syannis could be king after all, but I know better. Aimes had a pony. He was starting to learn to ride. He loved the ponies and the foals. The big horses scared him, but he used to play around the stables, and that's where they found him. The stable master said he must have climbed through to the king's hunting horses and then slipped. Fallen over and cried out and spooked them. They knocked him down and one of them kicked him. After a decade of soldiering, I've seen enough people go funny from being thumped on the head.'

He covered his eyes. 'Syannis wasn't there but he always thought that Saffran Kuy had made it happen, and that he'd made it happen so that Syannis could be king. Thing is, *he* wasn't there but *I* was. I saw it all. I told Syannis too, but he never shook the idea that Kuy had cast some sort of spell on Aimes, or on the horses, or maybe on both. But there was one part I never told Syannis. See, it wasn't Saffran Kuy who arranged it so that Syannis could be king, it was me. My fault. Aimes didn't crawl in with the hunting horses at all. He was there because I put him there. He didn't fall; he was screaming because he was scared, and that was what spooked them. I saw him go down. Watched it and did nothing. I couldn't tell you which one kicked him. I never liked Aimes. I didn't mean for it to happen, but I can't say as I was ever particularly sorry.'

He stared into his ale and then drained it. 'It's all gone wrong, Master Berren. Syannis always said that once Meridian was gone and we had our kingdom back, he'd be able to fix it. Make it right, or else Kuy would. And then something happened. I don't know what, but it was before we fought Meridian. Something changed. When Aimes sent Kuy away, I thought it wouldn't be long before he was back. I would have killed the bastard too. But he went and he stayed gone for a long time and Syannis did nothing to stop it, and yet nothing is any better than it was before, and he can't make it right because no one can. Aimes is still a child inside and he always will be. There's no cure for that. Tethis is falling apart and Syannis too. He's so lost, Berren.'

Talon shook his head. Then he laughed. 'He had some wild idea, from the moment he first saw you in Deephaven, that Saffran Kuy had cut a piece of Aimes' spirit away to make him the way he is, and that whatever part of Aimes he'd had taken out, you had it. Just because you looked like him. Thought that for years, for all that time you were together in Deephaven and in Forgenver too, even when the two of you went to Tethis together. But in the Pit something changed. When he came out, he didn't believe it any more. He never talked about it, just said it had been a stupid fantasy and that he'd never really believed it in the first place, but I know Kuy got to him while he was in the Pit. Kept him alive, if you take Syannis's word for it, but there was a price for that, because there always is. Kuy took Syannis's hope.'

Something odd was happening in Talon's face, a desperation and a hopelessness that Berren had never seen there before. 'You've changed too, Berren. You're not the man you were when I found you either. Far, far from it.'

'You can thank your brother for that.'

'Are you sure?' Talon reached out. From beneath Berren's shirt he pulled the chain and the stone that Gelisya had given him on their first voyage to Tethis, back from the slaver camp. Then he let go and put a hand on Berren's arm. 'Try to forgive my brother. He's not himself.'

'Then who is he?'

Talon didn't answer. He stared at the chain and the stone hanging loose around Berren's neck now. 'Is it really possible? To cut out a piece of someone's soul and yet leave them to live? Is that really what Kuy did to you when you were with him?'

'I was never *with* Kuy. I was in his house once for a few minutes, that was all. The most terrifying minutes I'll ever know.' Berren's eyes glazed over. He could see the web of his soul right then, as clear as he'd seen it in Deephaven when Saffran Kuy had first cut him with the gold-handled knife. He could see the threads snapping, one after the other. Cut, cut, cut. And then he saw himself in Tethis, making the potion to pull Tarn away from whatever demons held him, filled with a knowledge he should never have had. He pushed the stone back under his shirt. 'Yeh,' he choked. 'Yes, he really did that.'

'Then why did he give it back to you, Berren?'

'I don't know. Maybe he didn't mean to. Gelisya never seemed that happy to let it go.'

'She could have taken it while you were in the Pit. She didn't.'

'But Kuy wasn't there then. You'd sent him packing.'

Talon waved another pitcher of beer to their table. 'After the accident Aimes didn't move. He didn't speak. It was like he was dead except his heart was still beating. Like Tarn was when Gelisya gave that to you. Aimes was like that for three days and then suddenly he was better. No one knew why. Sometimes that's what happens when you get hit on the head. Except Syannis once told me he saw Kuy go into Aimes' room late at night. After Meridian killed our father and scattered us, Syannis spent three years making sure we were safe. Then he vanished. He went halfway around the world looking for Saffran Kuy. Why? Why would he do that? We had so many other troubles and he left us to look for that bloody necromancer who'd brought us nothing but pain.' Talon's voice was slurring and his eyes were closing. 'And now ... we have to do something.'

Minutes later he was asleep, sprawled across the table. Berren lurched up the stairs. Talon had never been anything less than a friend. But Syannis? He looked inside himself to see whether there were any feelings at all. Eventually he found them, frozen in ice, trapped and caged. No, for Syannis he felt nothing. And nothing that Talon had said made any difference either. So what if Syannis was obsessed with Aimes? None of it would help him get Fasha and his son, would it? None of it would help him keep his promise. And if it didn't help with that then what use was it? None. The thief-taker had made his own troubles and now he could lie with them and be damned, and that was all fine, and ...

But then unconsciousness picked him up and hurled him into a sea of dreams. He saw himself as Aimes, trapped in a stable full of horses as big as houses, all of them angry and trying to stamp him flat while he desperately scurried out of the way, until one of them finally caught him and squashed him, pressing him down into the ground, ever deeper and ever darker to another place where even the sounds had bright colours running through them. He smelled smoke and incense and fish, and some giant was looming over him with hands that were neither kind nor gentle. He felt them touch his face, felt a sticky, bitter coldness at the back of his throat and a voice whisper in his ear: *Fasha, Fasha, Fasha.* Then the hands withdrew and clasped a knife between them, Kuy's knife, and cut him slowly open except there was no pain, no blood, only a numb relief as the tension and the hurt flooded away. *Fasha, Fasha, Fasha.* The whisper went on, only now the voice had changed; the words were no longer deep and long but high-pitched and childish. The giant hands became small and delicate and he saw that the figure looming over him was Gelisya. She held Kuy's knife so he could see it, could see himself in the blade as though pressed against a glass. And with him inside it, he saw Fasha too.

I have a piece of both of you now, said Gelisya, and she faded away into a deep and endless void.

The next evening, when Talon had finally sobered up, he told Berren what was really on his mind. 'I have a new commission,' he said. 'For as soon as the company can assemble.'

'I thought you were going back to Tethis.'

'Yes. That's the commission. I'm offering it to myself. I think I might accept it too.'

'We're going to fight for Syannis again?' Berren snorted. 'No, thanks.'

Talon looked sad. 'We're … we're going to fight against him.'

Now every part of Berren was suddenly awake and listening. 'Against him? For whom?'

Talon sighed. 'I want you to get rid of Aimes. Let him be dead.'

'You want to get rid of Aimes, let Syannis do it. All he needs is a bit of poison.'

Talon glared and growled. 'The *last* thing that *Syannis* wants to do is kill him. Sun and Moon, you can be a cold fish sometimes. Syannis wants to make him better, always did! He can't, but that won't stop him from trying. There are warlocks in Tethis again, Berren. He has it in him to be a good king, but not while Aimes is there, because at every turn the warlocks whisper to him. So I want you to kill Aimes, and I will deal with these warlocks once and for all. He can't just die, because then Syannis will fall to bits. He has to be killed. Murdered. You could do that. You killed a king for Syannis; you can do it for me. He'll hate you beyond words, but you can just get on that ship to Deephaven I kept promising all those years ago. He'll never reach you.'

'And why in the name of the four gods would I do that? What's Aimes ever done to me?'

'You'll do it for your slave and for your son and for all the gold you have and a sackful more, and because if you don't do it then I will, and then I cannot be there to make Syannis whole again. Aimes isn't fit to be a king and never was.' He shook his head. 'It has to end, and unless I turn my sword on my own brother, I can think of no other way.' He looked across at Berren. Half a smile twitched at the corner of his mouth. 'I suppose I shouldn't be asking you this, but I don't know who else might do it.'

'No, you shouldn't.' Berren shook his head. He closed his eyes and pinched his nose.

'Then say no and let it fall to me and forget that I asked. I'll not judge you harshly for that. I might even admire you for it.'

Berren looked up again. 'What you should be doing is the one thing you can't. *You'd* make a good king, Prince Talon. Get rid of them all, that's what you should do.' He shrugged. 'I've nothing against Aimes.'

'You had nothing against Meridian either.'

'You're asking me to murder your brother.'

'Half-brother.' Talon spat. 'And that's between me and my conscience, and I did tell you that I never liked him. You're the Bloody Judge, Berren. You've become that. Why is Aimes any different to all the other men you've killed? This time you could save a few.'

'Fine. I'll do it then. For Fasha and for my son, and for all the gold I have and a sackful more. A big sackful.' And for Tasahre, twisted as it was. Let Syannis feel the same pain.

'And then you'll be gone. Vanish. Back to where you came from. Too far away even for my brother to come looking. Because he will.'

'Like a ghost.' Casually, Berren smiled and leaned in towards Talon. 'You never did me any wrong, not yet. But like you said, I'm the Bloody Judge of Tethis now. If you cross me like Syannis did, you'd better kill me, because if you don't, I will cut my way through every single last one of you.'

'I have something for you.' Talon unbuckled his sword belt and passed it across to Berren, sword and all. 'Take it. I have others.'

Berren looked at Talon's sword. It was a fine blade, a proper Dominion fencing sword, a little longer than the blades he usually carried, but light, neatly balanced, with a basket hilt of curling coils of metal. 'Worth a bit, that.'

'As much as your bondswoman. Probably more. Think of it as part of your payment.' He closed his eyes. 'How did it come to this, Berren?'

Berren took the sword and the belt. 'Killing Aimes isn't what really needs to be done. But you know that.'

Talon only looked sad. 'You may be right.' He shrugged. 'But I'm not my brother. Either of them.' He got up and left, and Berren watched him go. He tried to see himself chasing through Tethis castle, slashing with Talon's sword at anyone who got in his way until he found the room where Fasha was waiting for him with his son, cowering in a corner and full of hope. But it wasn't Aimes he saw dead when he closed his eyes. What he saw was Syannis, with Talon risen in his place. Talon couldn't do it? Fair enough. Then Talon wouldn't have to.

30
LUCAMA

In the days that followed, Berren became surly and impatient, eager to return to Tethis and be done with it all. The fear he'd felt on the way to Kalda had grown, congealed into something solid that he carried inside him like a ball of ice wrapped up in his belly. As the winter went on, he dreamed of Fasha and Gelisya and Saffran Kuy and his knife. They haunted him more and more, sometimes night after night, and when they let him be, then it was the woman he'd killed after the battle on the beach. Over and over. Just her, lying on the ground and blood everywhere, and the wondering of why he'd done it.

'Do *you* have dreams?' he asked Tarn one evening. Tarn gave him a sour look.

'Depends what I've been drinking,' he said. 'Mostly not.'

'But when you do, what are they?'

Tarn cackled. 'Mostly women, and what happens is none of your business, dark-skin.' His face softened. 'Ships sometimes. If I dream of anything, I dream of sailing. A good strong wind, a sturdy ship, sails full, waves a little choppy, salt in my face. Moving swift and strong and sure.' He nodded. 'Nice dreams. I think maybe I'm meant to be a sailor if not a soldier. Pity, because I rather liked the idea of setting up my own little school and teaching people how to fight.'

Berren snorted. 'Sailing? Can't say I thought much of it myself.' But then maybe it wasn't so bad when you weren't

238

the skag. Maybe if you were the one giving the orders it was just fine.

After two winters in the south Kalda felt cold and bitter. The days ran together in a blur of impatience. Talon talked endlessly of Syannis and Aimes, about the times they'd had together as children and ever since. He told Berren about the war, of how when Radek and Meridian had invaded Tethis a strange illness had afflicted the king's guard. Some sort of poisoning, Talon thought. How after the war was won, Radek had scoured the world looking for Saffran Kuy and anyone who'd had anything to do with him. Mostly, though, he talked about Syannis and his obsession with the necromancer. Berren listened, not because he was interested, but because Talon was paying for the beer and their food and lodgings.

The weeks wore on and Berren found himself walking up to the rim of the city, one day, to the house of Silvestre the sword-master.

'I don't want you to teach me,' he said. 'But I've got a new sword. I need to get used to it. I need to practise.' *Against someone who fights like Syannis*, he added to himself.

'I've seen that sword before,' said Silvestre, but he didn't ask anything more. He set Berren against a few of his students but they were pitiful. Slow and clumsy and desperately predictable. In the end Berren trailed up the slope each evening and sparred with the sword-master himself, while Tarn, resting after his own day of fighting, looked on. After the fights Berren and Tarn walked back down in the dark together, filled with warmth, chattering idly about the old times in Kalda. Berren could feel his sharpness, the speed and power of his arm, the quickness of his thoughts; but more, he felt at peace, as he ever did when his sword was in his hand. It was a pity that the sword-master was old and past his prime. Silvestre tired too quickly to challenge him for long.

The first glimmers of spring broke through the winter air. The days grew longer, the air warmer, the last flurries of snow came and went, and the Hawks began to return. In another week they would be at sea and on their way. Berren hungered for it, for the day they would leave. As he walked back down from the sword-master, swapping jokes with Tarn about the other students Silvestre had this year, he wasn't even aware of the three men following until they were right behind him.

'Berren, aincha?'

The voice cut like a knife. The three of them stood a few paces away, two of them carrying long knives drawn and ready to fight, but he could see from their stance that fighting wasn't what they were here for. The third man was Lucama. He had his drawn sword in his hand. Tarn nodded to him. 'I remember you.'

Berren pointed to the man who'd spoken. 'Do I know you?'

The man shook his head. 'No. But I know you.'

'We're not here to fight,' said Lucama.

Tarn grinned at him. 'That's good for you, boys.'

Berren's eyes flicked across their naked steel. 'You have a strange way of showing it through.'

'We know who you are,' said the first man. 'You're the Bloody Judge.'

'What of it?'

'They're afraid of you,' said Lucama. He put his sword away. 'Very afraid. I wasn't sure I'd know you any more. The stories about you seem ... unreal.'

'I never kill without a reason,' murmured Berren. He could see it now – Lucama was as tense as a bowstring, and the other two men were ready to bolt at the first sign of trouble. 'What do you want?'

Tarn cocked his head. 'Who are you fighting for now?

From what Berren here tells me, you've turned your coat a few times since we last properly met.'

Lucama shrugged. 'Not your business, is it? There's someone here who wants to meet the Bloody Judge.'

'Who?'

'He can see for himself.'

Berren waved them away with a sneer. 'You want me to wander off with you to some dark alley where the rest of your friends are lurking? I saw you in Tethis before I left, Lucama. You were one of Syannis's guard then. Has that changed? Because I don't think he has much love left for me.'

A flash of anger crossed Lucama's face. 'The message I carry is from Princess Gelisya. And I'm here because I know you, and Her Highness wanted someone who wouldn't be killed before he could even open his mouth. She sends me to make you an offer.'

Fasha. His son. What else could it be? And for a moment, if one of the men had lifted their knives and run at him, he wouldn't have been able to do anything except watch himself be killed. When he found his voice again, the words came out slowly, dripping with danger. 'What offer? What have you done to my son?'

Lucama edged back a step. 'The message I have for you is this: Her Highness will give you what you want and give it freely if you will do one thing for her. She reminds you that whatever promises Prince Syannis has made, they are worthless, because what you want is not his to give. It is hers, and if you wish to have it, it is Her Highness with whom you must bargain.' Lucama paused, watching Berren closely, looking for any glimmer of understanding.

Berren gave a slight nod. Lucama shook his head. 'It's just the message, Judge, and I'm just the one carrying it. There's more, but ...' He glanced at Tarn. 'You'll have to come with me. There's someone else who carried the rest. You have my word you'll not be harmed.'

Tarn snorted. 'No, he won't, because I'll be coming with him, and you won't be taking our swords either.'

Lucama's eyes narrowed a little. 'You may keep your swords, and if anyone lifts a weapon against you, you will have mine as well.' Something in Lucama had changed since they'd been students together. He was master of his own temper now, and if he hadn't been one of Syannis's king's guard, Berren thought he might like him better than when they'd once sparred together. So he followed, with Tarn at his side, as Lucama and his two nervy henchmen led the way to the harbour. They took him to one of the fine guest houses that promised to keep visiting sea captains and merchants and other travellers of quality away from the riff-raff of the docks, and stopped outside. It reminded Berren a little of the Captain's Rest in Deephaven, although not as grand.

'Is she here?' he blurted.

'Princess Gelisya?' Lucama laughed. 'Prince Syannis would never let her out of his sight. I don't think she's been allowed to leave his side since they were wed.'

'Syannis married her?'

'Oh yes, almost as soon as you and Prince Talon were gone.' He snorted. 'Well that's what kings are like, I suppose. Maybe she was still a child when you last saw her. Not any more.'

Lucama took a deep breath. He turned to face Berren and a half-smile twitched around the edges of his mouth. The other men slipped into the guest house. 'Quite a name you've made for yourself. The Bloody Judge. The Crown-Taker. They say you're fearsome and terrible. They say you killed Meridian. If I'd known, I might have watched you a little closer when it was just us and Blatter. Bet he'd shit his pants if he met you now.'

Berren didn't reply. Every soldier lived with fear and each one dealt with it in his own way. Lucama had been the sort to deal with it by going into a frenzy. Others talked to themselves as they fought, or took tokens from the men they killed, or whispered prayers to their gods. Older soldiers learned to put their fear away until later, until after the battle; and then when all was said and done they could be found squatting among the corpses, weeping or drinking or dancing. For Berren, none of these things mattered. Fear had abandoned him in Syannis's pit. He remembered the axeman in the turnip field, remembered puking his guts up because he'd been so scared and the panic after he'd killed Meridian, but all those memories were distant, as if they belonged to someone else. In the south he strode across the battlefields with a strange sense of calm, as if he no longer cared whether he lived or died. In the sun-king's wars nothing had mattered except the plunder he took from the bodies of the fallen.

The men came back out and stood with Lucama while Berren and Tarn waited a little apart, just far enough away to be out of sword range. They were on the wide road that ran from the docks towards the heart of Kalda, and it wasn't so late that they were alone. Small groups of men and women made their way past now and then, or else a wagon laden with goods for one of the ships would come the other way. Half a dozen of the harbour watch loitered nearby, quietly watching. Lucama had chosen his spot well.

Two men approached from the dockside. Berren's eyes ran over them. One was simply a soldier, quickly dismissed, but the other ... For one juddering moment he thought it was Saffran Kuy. The man wore the same robes, a hood hiding his face in its shadows. But this man was too tall; he had no limp, and when he drew the hood back, the face was someone else. Yet there were echoes there, and the same tattoos that Berren remembered, and a warlock was still a warlock, and there was something familiar …

That very first day in Tethis when he was looking for what he needed for the potion to save Tarn. Before he'd even started. The Mermaid. The tall man with the elbows who'd been stealing glances at him. And now he was a warlock?

Berren stared. The warlock was carrying a bundle carefully cradled in his arms. The bundle wriggled and shifted and then settled again. For the second time that night Berren froze, his whole body flushing numb. The warlock was carrying a child!

Lucama's hand flew to his sword. Tarn stepped away and did the same. The other soldiers drew back and Berren was shocked to find his own blade already an inch out of its scabbard. He slid it slowly back, reluctant to let it go.

'Berren Crown-Taker,' said the man in grey.

'Is that my son?' hissed Berren. Out of the corner of his eye he could see the harbour watchmen eyeing them closely.

'Princess Gelisya sends her salutations,' said the man in grey. 'We have heard much about you, Crown-Taker. What a penchant for killing you have.'

They stared at each other. The watchmen were slowly easing themselves closer. Berren wondered if he could he kill this warlock before they arrived. Probably not. He had too many men around him. If the others fled, he could do it, but if they stayed to fight then he'd never get past them in time. Lucama, he was sure, wouldn't run. The others … would they? And what about Tarn? Would Tarn have his back if he just launched himself at these men out of nowhere?

But the warlock had his son, and killing a warlock was never easy. He'd seen that. The moment passed. 'What is it that you want, warlock?'

'Warlock?' The man laughed. 'I make soap, Crown-Taker.'

'Then you're Saffran Kuy's brother Vallas, and your life hangs by a thread as slender as spider silk.'

A little smile played around the corner of the warlock's mouth. He looked into the bundle he carried. 'We are all Saffran's brothers. Princess Gelisya of Tethis has not forgotten that you murdered her father. She sends you a warning and the offer of a bargain. She will never, ever sell her bondswoman to you. Never. For all the sun-king's gold, still you will not own her, nor will you own your son, and if you try to take either by force then she will have them killed, instantly. But she *will* give you the woman and her child freely and forgive your murderous past if you will perform one small service for her.'

'And what service is that, warlock?'

Vallas tossed a stone to Berren's feet. A tiny scrap of paper was wrapped around it. 'They say you can read and even write. Unusual for a soldier. But it's your sword and your willingness to use it that Her Highness wishes to purchase. It won't be difficult for you. It won't be difficult at all. I think you might even enjoy it.' He glanced down to the stone lying at Berren's feet and then pointedly at Tarn. 'You might not wish to share. But that's up to you.'

Slowly Berren nodded. He picked up the stone and un-wrapped it. The words on the paper were few and simple, the language plain. *It is my will to rule, Crown-Taker.* 'And if I refuse?'

Vallas Kuy shrugged his shoulders. 'Then Princess Gelisya will have you hunted down and killed for the mur-derer that you are, and your son will fall to me.' With that, the warlock, soap-maker, whatever he was, turned his back and walked away, taking his men with him. For a moment Lucama remained. He hesitated, then approached Berren and put a hand on his shoulder.

'I like to think we were friends, back when Sword-Master Silvestre was teaching us both.' He seemed to struggle with himself for a moment. 'I know the child he means. I suppose everyone does. He's back in Tethis, fit and feisty. I don't know where the one he's carrying came from and I don't think I want to, but we brought no children with us when we sailed. Perhaps it's best you know that.' He stepped away, saluted and followed the others.

31
THE SACKING OF TETHIS

Berren crushed the paper in his fist. Later he threw it into the fire. It was something Talon could never see, nor Tarn, nor the other Hawks he called his friends. He stared on into the flames long after the paper was ash. *It won't be difficult for you.* Berren watched the embers flicker and die and begged to differ. There would be a price, there always was. *I think you might even enjoy it.* He had no illusions as to what she meant. She wanted Syannis dead.

'Why me, though? Why ask me?' The flames and the embers that followed them had no answer.

'I'm afraid of what will happen,' he said to Talon one night. Talon had seen the change in him as clearly as if his skin had turned red.

'As am I, Master Berren, as am I.' He looked far away and Berren knew they were talking about utterly different things. He felt a sudden urge to take Talon by the shoulders and shake him and tell him that this was all wrong. Tell him that no one was to be trusted, not even him. Tell him of the warlock and of Gelisya's offer, everything, and then make him stop, or else do the one thing that would save them all and take the crown of Tethis for himself. But he couldn't. When he opened his mouth, the words refused to come. Why? Because of Fasha? Because of a woman he barely knew who'd shared his bed for one night three years ago? Because of a child he'd never seen? He should walk away, just as he should have walked away years ago, but he couldn't, and still for the same reason. Syannis and all that lay between them. Even Talon, who was so astute on the battlefield, whose tactics and strategies were the stuff of legend among the free companies, had a blindness when it came to his own brother.

Three days after Vallas Kuy had given Berren his choice, sixteen cohorts of men sailed for Forgenver, and Berren was with them. The old camp outside the town was still there. The tents were gone but the wooden huts remained and a tiny shanty town had sprung up. The place stank and Berren felt a wild urge to race into its midst and burn it to the ground, to chase off everyone who would flee and slaughter the ones who would not and give it back to the ghosts of all the men he'd once known but would never see again.

They marched from Forgenver down the south road towards Galsmouth and Tethis. Berren rode at the front of the army on a horse he'd stolen from some officer of the sun-king who'd found himself on the wrong end of a javelin. He could have had his own cohort if he'd asked for it but he never did, preferring his own company. In the south he'd fought with Tarn, or with Talon, or wherever else he thought he could make a difference. Where the enemy was strongest, or weakest, or simply the easiest to reach. Today he rode with what was left of the Deephaven lancers. There were a dozen of them now, the rest dead or drifted away, and he was as much one of them as he was anything else after the last season in the south. And besides, he didn't want to be with Tarn for this. Not with a friend he might see killed for such a sour and selfish business. Everywhere he looked, he saw reminders of the last time he'd come this way. The anger, the hunger, the hope, the desire. They'd come to free Syannis, to free Fasha and

Gelisya and to kill Saffran Kuy, and for all their victories they'd done none of that.

At least there was no endless rain this time, no need for carefully prepared caches of food; now they lived off the land. As they reached Galsmouth, half the company, the half made up of the veterans who had fought against Meridian, marched openly towards the town, welcomed with open arms by the soldiers that now made up the garrison there. The rest, Berren, the other foreigners and southerners, the men with strange faces and sun-darkened skin, skirted the town and vanished into the hills. They left behind their colours and their badges, took on new ones and became the Thousand Ghosts. A forgery of renegades whispered in the winter winds in Kalda, masquerading beneath carefully planted stories of brigands and rapists, of looters and pillagers.

Talon's plan was absurdly simple: the Thousand Ghosts were a story carefully made and spread over months. For one night they would become real. They would throw themselves on the city of Tethis and for a few perilous hours it would seem as though the town stood on the edge of destruction; then Talon and his Hawks would arrive in the nick of time, the wicked brigands would flee and all would be safe once more. Everything would happen in a blur of confusion, too quick for anyone to count the Thousand Ghosts and realise they were more like a hundred. It would be over in a night. In the chaos Talon would sweep away the warlocks, and in that blur kings and princes would die.

On the last day out from Tethis Talon slipped away from his men too. He put on a helm that covered his face, hid his colourful cloak and banner behind leathers and furs, and joined the Thousand Ghosts. They waited all through the night, until before the first gleam of dawn on the horizon. From the light of the stars and the moon, they could all see the castle where king Aimes was doubtless sleeping, little more than a bow shot away.

'You know where to go.' Berren nodded. Talon turned to the three men who would lead the charge on the castle. 'And you? Sure you know what to do?' They nodded too. 'Smoke and noise, friends, no more. This is my home.' Maybe it was the moonlight, but Talon seemed to have turned pale, almost white as though he'd seen a ghost. Finally the Prince of War took a deep breath. He gave the sign and the Thousand Ghosts began to creep in silence towards Tethis and the castle that loomed before them.

'Let it begin.' He sounded grim.

Berren mounted his horse. He waved to the lancers and rode towards the river and its gorge. In the time it took for the Thousand Ghosts to rouse the castle guard, Berren would come from another way. They would leave their horses at the top of the gorge and slide silently into the castle, following the same path that he and Syannis had used years ago. He had no key this time, but he had a dozen men and he had a small ram. They'd appear inside just as he had done before. He'd slip through the darkness and find Aimes and kill him for Talon and then open the gates and the castle would fall. Except his own plan was a little different. He would not search for Aimes but for Gelisya and for Fasha and for his son. He'd take them all, and then, and only then, decide who he would allow to live and who would die.

They reached the top of the gorge and there everything started to go wrong. There were king's guard, a dozen of them, maybe more, already making their way along the river and into the fields. They couldn't possibly have come so far from the castle unless they'd already left before the attack had begun, and there was only one thing that could mean.

Syannis knew.

The soldiers sent up a cry of alarm; the lancers, who knew no better, rode them down. Berren screamed after them and charged in their wake. The lancers scythed down half the guards on their first pass and turned hard for a second. Berren watched, lost for words. Most of the survivors broke and ran. The horsemen chased them down. In the middle someone was still standing. Whoever it was had his back to him. Berren lowered his spear and cut him down.

The lancers dismounted and drew their throat-cutting knives. For all Berren knew, Aimes might be among the dead here, Syannis too, perhaps both of them. When the Deephaven soldiers were done, he forced himself to stare into the faces of the fallen, and there was Aimes with his head smashed in. King Aimes. Dead. He wasn't wearing anything to mark him out, no crown, no golden sword, nothing. If he hadn't had Berren's face, he could have been anyone.

But no sign of Syannis. Berren wasn't sure whether to feel glad or afraid; all he wanted right now was the same as he'd wanted for years: Fasha and their child. And then he'd be gone, away with the gold he'd saved from the seasons in the south. The dead staring back at him made it possible. For better or for worse, more by accident than intent, he'd done what Talon had wanted of him. There would be no more killing. He'd take his son and go somewhere far away, where Syannis and Talon and Gelisya would never find him. To Deephaven, or to some other part of the empire. Syannis might chase him to the ends of the world for what he'd done here, but however far he went Berren would simply go further.

He took a moment to look at Aimes, that face that was so nearly his own, the face that had changed his life beyond all reason, and closed the dead king's eyes, glad that he'd not been the one to deliver the killing blow. Then he turned away, because what mattered now was to get into the castle, to find Fasha and do it quickly; and then to the harbour and away, never to see Tarn or Talon or any of the others again. He'd miss them, he knew. Some of them.

They left the bodies where they lay and cantered back to the gorge, dismounted at the top and ran down the path that Syannis had once shown to him. He missed the cave at first and wasted ten minutes searching for it. They lost another five smashing down the grate. By now he was late, terribly late – the sun was rising and he should have been inside the castle almost an hour ago – but there was nothing to be done about that. They stripped off their armour and swords and swam the sump, Berren first. The Pit lay beyond, empty and dark today. They paused long enough to arm themselves again and then ran up the steps, through the cellar and into the guardroom, to the place where he and Syannis had last raised their blades together.

It was empty. The king's guard were out on the walls. In Talon's scheme Berren and his lancers would take the castle gates from behind and let the Thousand Ghosts inside. They'd ransack the place and Aimes would die. And then, in the thin light of the dawn, the Hawks would come. But Aimes was already dead, and Berren was afraid of what else that might mean.

He knew we were coming.

He tore open the door to the armoury, but the secret panel at the back had been bricked shut. No way through. He cursed. 'Out. Quietly. Take down anyone in your way and get the gate open. Quick now.'

He left the lancers to it and ran from the guardroom deeper into the castle. The place was deathly quiet. No soldiers anywhere. No shouting. He kicked down the doors to the kitchens. Empty too. Except for the soldiers out on the walls, the castle seemed abandoned.

And then it came to him: Gelisya wasn't here! And why would she be, when she knew what was coming?

The Hawks had made no secret of their march south from Forgenver. She'd known days ago. Syannis had known too. *That* was why he'd found the king's guard taking Aimes away to safety. They knew it all, Talon's whole charade, and now it was just a farce.

No. Not *all*. They hadn't known that he'd come down the gorge with a squadron of horsemen. They *obviously* hadn't know that part.

The lancers did their job. The gates were opened and the Thousand Ghosts poured in. The surrounded guards threw down their swords and surrendered without a fight. Berren counted. Sixteen of them left. Sixteen men to defend a castle? He pushed through them, looking for Lucama, but Lucama wasn't there.

No Gelisya. No Syannis. No slave. No son. And he would go after them, and Syannis would stand in his way, and one of them would have to kill the other after all. There was no other way any more. 'Princess Gelisya?' he asked, breathless.

A guard glared at him. 'Not here.' That was all he got.

'Where? Where's Syannis? Where are the servants?'

'Gone. All gone.'

Gone. But the Bloody Judge of Tethis didn't lose that easily. Gelisya would be near. He could almost feel her presence. She'd be here to see everything happen as she desired it. And Syannis too – he could have held off a dozen men on his own and rallied the rest – yet the guards had thrown down their swords as soon as the gates were opened. As though they knew what was coming and it was what they'd been told to do.

There was a clenched fist inside him. He paced the castle, desperate with frustration, trying to work out where Syannis and Gelisya might be, then climbed the wall overlooking the city. He stared down as if hoping to see them somewhere, staring back at him, but nearly all of

Tethis was hidden beneath the cliffs. Where the coastline curved away he could see some of the fishing villages on the edge of the town, little more than grey shapes in the early morning light. Too far. No one there would be able to see what was happening; probably they wouldn't even be able to see the smoke. No, Gelisya would be closer than that, but where? The only part of the city he could see was the market, where it spread up the far side of the gorge, and even there all was still.

As he stared out across the sea, he suddenly knew the answer was right in front of him, in the dull shapes out among the waves. He couldn't see the harbour from the castle, but he remembered how it had been, sailing into the city, sitting in a longboat and looking up at the cliffs. She wasn't in the city at all. She was on a ship. Safe and out of reach and there to see it all.

He jumped down from the wall and ran out of the castle into the brightening dawn. Eyes followed him but no one made any move to stop him. He was the Bloody Judge, after all, Talon's trusted right arm. He sprinted down the steep road that wound around the side of the gorge and into the market district. Half the Thousand Ghosts were ahead of him, screaming and shouting and burning. The air already carried the taint of smoke.

There was more than one ship anchored out in the bay. He had no way of knowing which one might be hers, but that didn't matter. If that was where she was, that was where he'd find her, even if he had to search ship by ship. Syannis? Well, no need to look. Once the thief-taker knew what he'd done, he would come.

32
A FAIR REWARD

Berren ran down through the city to the harbour. He had blood on his sword now from some fool who'd taken him for a looter and come at him with a knife. For a moment, through the smoke, he'd thought he'd seen Syannis, face stained with tears and carrying a body. But it couldn't have been, and when he'd looked again it had been some stranger, lost and confused, carrying a bundle of sticks in a blanket.

From the waterfront, he knew exactly which ship must be Gelisya's. A fast sloop lay anchored only a few hundred yards from the shore. It was the ship he'd seen years ago outside the slaver camp where he'd shot Saffran Kuy, and the colours she flew were the same colours that flew from the castle, the colours Talon had worn on the day they'd killed Meridian. Down here, amid the sprawl of the docks, the pall of smoke over the market looked distant and small, the noise from the castle muted and indistinct. A few morning drunks stood grouped together, gawping at it, raising their fingers to test the wind, idly taking bets as to which way it would turn and how the fire might spread, but otherwise the sailors and teamsters and wagoneers were already about their normal business, the air tantalising him with the smells of fish from the smoking houses and hot grease off the braziers.

He found himself a longboat, gave a couple of pennies to

a pair of burly sailors who didn't seem to have much to do, and they rowed him out to the sloop. He'd imagined he'd have to fight his way on board, yet as the boat drew close a voice from the deck shouted directions and a rope ladder was thrown down. He climbed aboard, hands always floating beside his sword. On the deck a dozen or so king's guard watched him. He saw Lucama and they exchanged a cautious nod of greeting. A few sailors sat idly around, staring out at the city and the blot of smoke that hung next to the castle. Neither Gelisya nor Syannis was on deck, yet none of the guards seemed surprised that Berren was there.

'Fasha!' he shouted. 'Where's Fasha?' The shouting made the soldiers stir uneasily. 'Princess Gelisya's bondsmaid! Where is she?' As he moved to search the ship, the scrape of swords half drawn brought him to a halt. 'Aimes is dead!' he shouted at them. 'The king is dead. The king you were supposed to protect.'

Lucama regarded him with a puzzled look. Then a door to the inside of the ship flew open, and Vallas the soapmaker emerged into the light. Berren bared his teeth. 'No little child to hide behind this time?' A dozen guards. He couldn't take them all, not at once, but he could hold them off for long enough to run a length of steel through a warlock. His hand gripped the hilt of his sword.

Vallas was smiling at him. Berren had seen a warlock stabbed by a sword once before. Even with the blade sticking right through him it hadn't been enough. The soapmaker beckoned. 'Come inside, Master Crown-Taker. If the king is dead, come and claim your reward.'

'Where's Syannis?'

'He will come. Your slave is here.'

Berren took a step closer. He drew his sword and held out in front of him, straight at the soap-maker's face. 'I still might kill you, warlock.'

'You might as well draw a knife across your slave's

throat then. But try it if you wish.' He turned his back and Berren him followed into the bowels of the sloop, sword drawn, point inches from the warlock's skin. The guards made no move to stop him. Vallas led him down almost to the bilges, into a low cargo hold. Crates and sacks and boxes lay scattered about in the gloom. A dozen candles flickered, making a circle of dim light. The air was hazy with their smoke and Berren's eyes burned. In the middle of the circle Gelisya sat, legs crossed, looking at him. She was holding a knife, the golden-hilted knife, the thief-taker's knife, the blade that Saffran Kuy had used to cut a piece out of Berren's soul. Lit up by the candles as she was, Berren could see how much she'd changed. The girl he remembered had become a woman.

'Hello, murderer,' she said, and even her voice had changed. Where her words had once sounded sharp and petulant, now they were languid and fleshy.

'Aimes is dead,' Berren said shortly. 'You have what you wanted. Now give me what I came for.'

Gelisya smiled at him. 'No, no. Aimes is not enough and you know that perfectly well.' She cocked her head. 'I tried so hard with Syannis. I sent my slave with a love potion to make you do what I wanted, but you said you'd do it anyway, so there it was, left over. After you killed my father, I fed it to Syannis. I whispered my name three times in his ear to see what would happen. I could see how much it pained him to refuse me anything after that, but he still wouldn't get rid of Aimes. I tried to have him poisoned with the stuff you left for me, the paste you used to make your friend better, but he caught me. I hadn't realised how clever he was. He couldn't do anything about it, of course, but he still wouldn't let me get rid of Aimes. I suppose he'd spent so long thinking that Saffran was going to put his little brother back together one day that he couldn't let go of the idea. Poor little Sy. Even with Saffran gone, even

257

after he knew that he'd been lied to for all those years, even when he was on his knees, begging and pleading and weeping for me to forgive him, he *still* wouldn't let me get rid of Aimes.'

She made a show of inspecting the knife. 'Then I found that he had this. Saffran has one just like it. He told me about it once, what the star-knives did, and now one of them was right in front of me. So I made Syannis give his one to me and after that I had to start cutting. Little pieces. I thought, maybe, if I cut the right piece out, he'd do what I wanted.' Her eyes met Berren's again. 'So much cutting and still nothing. Then I thought of you, murderer. I think of you a lot actually. But I thought of you in a new way on my birthday, you see, because I was ready to be a queen, and no one had given me what I wanted. Did you really kill Aimes?'

Berren nodded. 'He's dead.' His head spun. Syannis deserved every sour twist fate could give him. Berren tried to shake it off, throw it all away, everything Gelisya said she'd done. The two of them deserved each other. But he couldn't do it, not quite.

'Then I suppose you've as good as killed Syannis as well. Aimes was really the last thing holding him together.' She looked at the knife again. 'You might as well finish the job.'

'Where's Fasha?'

'She told you her name? She shouldn't have. I must have her punished. Would you whip her for me again?'

Berren snarled at her. 'Where is she?' *I fed it to Syannis and whispered my name three times in his ear to see what would happen.* 'That potion you sent with her – you're lying. You'd already fed it to Syannis before Talon ever marched south. While he was in the Pit.'

Gelisya smiled again. 'Very good, murderer. Very astute.'

'And that's why he wouldn't keep his promise. Because

you wouldn't let him. All these years I've hated him and it was you!'

'But you still hate him. Don't you? Vallas, please show the murderer his slave.' The soap-maker bared his teeth. Gelisya held the knife up to the light. 'After everything I've taken from him, there's more of him in here than in his head now. I always know how he's feeling, and so I know that you're telling me the truth and that Aimes is dead, because Syannis has found out. I can feel his desolation. I wonder who told him.' She pouted and gave a little shiver of exhilaration. 'Pity. *I* wanted to be the one to tell him, but his despair *is* delicious. Come come, Vallas, show the murderer his prize.'

Berren thought of the guard he'd hacked down. Could that have been Syannis? The last man standing, the one who hadn't fled. But if so then why hadn't they found his body?

The soap-maker disappeared for a moment, vanishing behind a stack of crates. He emerged again dragging a body dressed in white. Fasha! For a moment Berren thought she was dead, and before he knew what he was doing, the blade of his sword was at the soap-maker's throat. Vallas dropped her. He looked more annoyed than scared.

'Don't hurt my warlock!' snapped Gelisya. 'That would make me angry. I gave her Safansa water to make her sleep. *You* know what that is. It's there if you look for it. In the stone. In that little piece of you. I never *did* want to give it back, you know, but Saffran said I had to. She's not hurt, not yet. See for yourself.'

For a moment Berren still stared at her. 'If you were always Saffran's, why did you send her after me and ask me to have him killed?'

Gelisya pouted. 'Can't an apprentice have a little falling-out with her master now and then? When she doesn't get what she wants? *You* know what that's like.' She giggled.

'You're mad.' Berren knelt down. Fasha lay on her back, breathing peacefully, fast asleep. He put his sword away and lifted her gently in his arms. 'And the boy? My son?'

The soap-maker went back behind the crates and returned holding a boy, a few years old, sleeping like his mother. Gelisya smiled. 'They won't wake for hours. We've been waiting for you. I knew you'd come, you see, but I didn't know how long it would take you. The knife tells me things, but not everything. Saffran said you held it yourself, once. Did it talk to you?'

'Yes, it did.' Berren swung Fasha over his shoulder and picked up the boy with his other arm. 'You don't need me for Syannis. You can clearly deal with him yourself.'

'You're right.' Now and then when she spoke, there were sing-song traces of the child he remembered. 'It's almost better this way. I might even thank you.'

'Aimes was a mistake. An accident.' He gave Gelisya a nod and made to leave. 'But you got what you wanted. All debts are paid then.' Warlocks. Tethis. This little girl-witch. Syannis. He despised them, loathed them, all of them, and the sooner he was away the better. Far, far away.

'No.'

He stopped and looked over his shoulder. Gelisya was still sitting in her circle of candlelight. She was pointing the knife at him. Her eyes were large and black.

'No, murderer,' she said. 'All debts are far from paid. And I still have a tiny little piece of you in here. Which makes me pleased because it means I can do whatever I like!'

Her fingers tightened around the knife and an unearthly pain split Berren's head in two, white-hot and unbearable. He sank to his knees. Fasha slipped from his arms.

'You killed my father,' whispered Gelisya. 'You murdered him. You shot him in the back of his head. So no, murderer, all debts are *not* paid. Vallas, Syannis is on his way here. Go up and guide him to us. And tell your brother he can stop skulking and hiding. This one's all his whenever he wants him.'

Dimly, Berren saw the soap-maker bow. He'd got it all wrong. She wasn't their puppet, she was their *mistress*! 'Who are you?' he croaked.

'I am the Princess Gelisya.' The pain grew stronger. She smiled. '*Queen* Gelisya now, thanks to you. You can call me Your Majesty if you like. For as long as you're alive.'

Berren gritted his teeth. 'You're not a queen yet.' Then every nerve inside his head shrieked at once and the world went mercifully black.

33
THE CUTTER

When Berren woke up, the pain was gone and so was his sword. His hands were bound together. He was still in the hold exactly where he'd fallen. Fasha lay on the floor beside him, murmuring softly in her sleep.

'Look!' said Gelisya.

Berren craned his head to see her. She was sitting as he remembered, but now there was someone else inside the circle of candles with her. Syannis. Lying curled up with his head on her lap while she stroked his hair. Berren stared, struggling to believe what he was seeing. 'Sun and moon! What have you done to him?' He looked terrible. Gaunt and ragged and utterly, utterly lost.

'Look,' said Gelisya again, 'look, my little puppy. I woke the murderer up again. What a long sleep! We all went up on deck to see what was happening at the castle and we only just came back. Imagine, you might have woken all alone. Oh!' She put on a mock frown. 'Wait! But the knife wouldn't let you. Not until I say so. Syannis, why don't you help him to his knees?'

As though in great pain, Syannis rose. He stepped out of the circle and hauled Berren up. The candles, Berren realised, had nearly burned out.

'You shouldn't have hurt my beloved,' he said. '*We* shouldn't have hurt her. Either of us.'

Berren stared at him, filled with fury and fear and bloody-minded disbelief. 'I didn't touch her!' he spat. He didn't recognise this man at all. The thief-taker he'd loved and hated and feared and admired and envied, that man was gone. What was left was a shell.

'We took her father away.' His face was a mask of anguish.

Berren tore his eyes away from the thief-taker's empty face. 'What have you done to him?'

Gelisya smiled and showed her teeth. She pointed the knife and Berren felt a slight tingle inside his skull, enough to make him flinch. 'I told you. A little cut here, a little cut there. Poor Syannis, you so nearly understood, but all the time you thought that Saffran was going to make your little brother better for you, and it was always a lie. Wasn't it, Saffran?'

An old familiar shape pushed out from the darkness behind her. Not the soap-maker this time, but Saffran Kuy. 'You!' Berren was shaking.

'Hello, little Berren-piece. Do you still wear my crystal nice and tight and close?'

Berren pulled at the ties around his wrists. 'I will kill you, warlock. I will.'

Kuy let out a little cackle. 'I've already seen who will kill me, little Berren-piece. I told you, years ago. Not you.'

For a moment Gelisya glared. 'Saffran knows how to make the knives work *properly*.' She bared her teeth at Berren. 'Stupid Aimes sent him away before he showed me, so I had to work it all out for myself.' She shrugged. 'It would have been the easiest thing in the world to get rid of you when you were in my Pit, but he just wouldn't do it, even though he was so, *so* in love with me!'

She clapped her hands together and made a face. 'But now Saffran is back and so are you, and it's all the way it was supposed to be, and Syannis is my little puppy again, aren't you, my love? You do what I say. We'll get it done right this time. No need to be rid of you after all. But we *will* need to deal with that other brother. I'm afraid you'll have to do that. He's going to come here.'

A coldness spread through Berren's gut. The anger he'd nursed all these years thinking Syannis had betrayed him, and it hadn't been Syannis at all ...

'You *do* love me, don't you? Of course you do.' Gelisya smiled again, then her face hardened. 'Now kill my servant woman! I don't like her any more.'

Berren's heart nearly stopped. Syannis looked up at Gelisya. 'Why, my love? What is her crime?'

'Does it matter? Do you have to question *everything*? I said kill her!' she snapped. 'Make it bloody. She told him her name and let him have her. I don't want her any more and I want him to see her die. Have Vallas weigh her down and throw her into the sea and her little bastard too. Make him watch. But send the guards below decks. I don't want them to see you do that – they won't like it. And then ... No, wait!'

Her eyes widened and she waved the gold-hafted knife so that it made patterns in the air, then squealed with delight. 'No, not the bastard. Let Vallas make him into soap! And you, Crown-Taker, you get to watch and then you can be Saffran's little plaything. He has plans for you, don't you, Saffy? Had them for a long time. You're going to be someone that matters. Or what's left of you, once the Black Moon is inside you. And we all know what you did, *murderer*.'

Syannis turned to Berren. He looked desolate. 'You killed Aimes,' he said.

Berren nodded. Syannis's hands were quivering above his swords and Berren knew how fast he could be. Behind his back, Berren's hands strained at the ropes that bound them.

'I thought you were him,' Syannis said. His voice was slurred. 'Back at the start, when I found you in Deephaven, I thought you were him. Saffran said he'd put him inside you to keep him safe, and that's why you looked so alike. But you weren't. You were a nothing, a nobody whose face simply looked the same.' Instead of a sword he drew out another golden knife, exactly the one Berren remembered, the exact twin of the knife Gelisya still held.

Syannis looked at his knife. His face was an abyss. 'I thought I needed this to put Aimes back together. That's all I ever wanted. To make up for wanting him dead.' He shoved Berren back, knocking him to the floor, and then he turned away and faced Gelisya again. 'And now, finally, he is,' he said.

'I know,' she cooed. 'And I know how much Aimes meant to you. I know your pain.' She gripped her knife. 'I feel it, beloved.'

'Dead and gone.'

Gelisya's face turned petulant. She waved her knife at Berren. 'Yes, and *he* killed him! And you were there, right there, and you didn't stop it. You *failed*! Now make him suffer for it!'

'He killed Aimes. And you told him to.' He took a step forward and then shuddered to a halt as Gelisya shifted the point of the knife and squeezed.

'Kill my slave!' she hissed. 'Kill her or you will never touch me again!'

'No.' Syannis breathed a little sigh and stepped forward again. 'I love you more than life,' he whispered, 'but not more than my brother.'

One hand still held the knife. The other suddenly held a sword, swinging in a blur towards Gelisya's face. He struck downwards, but before he could finish the blow, every muscle in his arms and back froze solid. His left hand went limp and the gold-handled knife dropped to the floor.

Berren scrabbled back into the shadows. Gelisya lunged. She didn't dive away, as she might have done; instead she stabbed forward. The knife in her hand ripped into Syannis's belly. He staggered. His sword faltered. For seconds it seemed they simply stood there, Syannis with his sword in the air, Gelisya on one knee with her knife in his guts.

Gelisya pulled away and stabbed him again and then again. He began to sway. Then she was on her feet, stabbing and shrieking, but there was no blood, none. *For this is no knife that you would understand, Berren. This blade cuts souls and now I will show you how ...*

For a moment it seemed that everyone had forgotten Berren. He curled up into a ball and struggled and strained at the ropes around his hands until he wriggled his wrists around his feet and had his arms in front of him. He looked for the knot so he could work on it with his teeth.

'You stupid, stupid thing!' Gelisya was screaming. *'You do what I say!'*

'Princess!' Saffran Kuy took a step towards her; she waved the knife at him and he shrank hastily back.

Syannis slowly crumpled. Gelisya watched him fall and stood over him, her chest heaving. Then she dropped to all fours and very slowly pushed the knife up under Syannis's chin, up, up inside his head, until his eyes rolled back and closed and each twitching finger fell still. She turned to look at Berren. Her eyes were black with rage. She raised the knife again, but Berren leaped at her, lashing out with a foot. He felt his head split open with the same pain as before, but then they crashed together and the knife flew from her hand. As it did, the pain in Berren's head vanished like the light from a snuffed-out candle. He sprawled to the floor on top of her, rolling through the circle of flickering flames and then away, dazed by the fading sense of an iron spike smashed through his skull.

'Saffran!' Gelisya squealed. 'Make him stop!'

Saffran Kuy smiled. Berren rolled, scrabbling to get to his feet. There was nowhere for him to go, and all the warlock had to do was open his mouth just as he had in Deephaven on the night Tasahre had died. *You. Obey. Me.*

Gelisya's knife! Still with a piece of him inside, she'd said! Berren snatched it up. For a moment he and Saffran Kuy stood still, their eyes locked together.

'Put the knife down, little Berren-piece,' said Saffran Kuy, still smiling. The force of his words roared in Berren's head, but this time there was something new. Something that kept them at bay. The knife. This time it was his.

The warlock's eyes changed and grew wide. The air around him began to shimmer, a swirling of something that had yet to take form. Berren saw Gelisya rising, saw her glance towards Fasha. He sprang and lunged at Saffran Kuy before either of them could act. The knife buried itself up to the hilt in the warlock's chest, as though Kuy was made of nothing more than smoke. A look of horror and dismay stretched across his face, while a pulse of fire swept down Berren's arm. For a moment he was blinded, his vision filled with ghostly faces. He could see one Kuy before him, and he could see another: one made of skin and bone, the other a shimmering spirit made of something else. He could see two Gelisyas too, two Fashas. And someone else, standing next to Syannis's corpse. Other faces and forms swarmed around his head, ones he'd never seen before. They filled the room, swirling shadows howling in his ears. And inside the ghostly second shape of Saffran Kuy he could see the web of the warlock's soul, an endless tangle of threads. The knife could do almost anything, almost anything at all. It had the power of a god inside it, lurking just out of reach; not yet his to command but there *was* one thing he remembered, one thing he knew he could make it do.

Tell the knife! Make it your promise. And then cut, Berren, cut! Three little slices. You! Obey! Me!

With each stroke the knife sliced a little piece of Saffran Kuy away. As Berren cut, he could see it working, see how each thread mattered. The knife showed him all of it, exactly as it was and would be, exactly as he'd seen it before.

He withdrew the knife when he was done. The second Kuy shrank and collapsed into nothing, sucked into the shimmering blade. The ghostly forms faded and he saw clearly again, and what he saw was the Saffran Kuy of flesh and bone staring at him in horror, and Gelisya crouching over Fasha, looking at him with a mad glee. In her hand she held the other knife. She pointed it at him. A terrible smile spread across her face. But then nothing happened. No pain. Nothing at all. For a moment they glared at each other as Gelisya's grimace of victory crumbled to ash. She had the wrong knife.

'What did you do?' Berren hissed. 'What did you do to her?'

Gelisya shrieked, 'Saffran!' but Kuy was already running, wailing, towards the steps from the hold as fast as he could go. Berren snatched up Syannis's sword. He hurled himself after the warlock and bore him down.

'You. Obey. Me!'

'No!' The warlock's scream was silent. 'You cannot! I have seen my end and it is not you!'

'Then you saw wrong. Now do as you're told and die.' He drove Syannis's sword through the warlock's heart, and now the warlock's scream was real. He writhed and arched, every part of him. Black blood ran out of his mouth and became black smoke.

'Not. Good. Enough,' he hissed. His fingers and feet were starting to dissolve. Berren watched, transfixed. Tasahre had done the same with swords made of sun-steel, driven both of them right through him, and the same thing had happened. And he was right: it hadn't been enough.

Gelisya bolted. She ran like a deer chased by a leopard, jinking back and forth, careening off crates and stacks of boxes. Berren chased after her but his hands were still tied. They slowed him and she jumped up the steps, a moment too quick for him, and was gone. On the floor Kuy was a writhing black mass.

The knife. Without thinking, Berren plunged the golden knife into what was left of the warlock, ripping open his soul for a second time. He cut and cut and cut again, and slowly he shredded the warlock into ribbons until there was nothing left at all, and the last black smoke wafted and thinned and vanished.

'Good enough now, warlock?' But Saffran Kuy was gone. Ended, and now the hold was dark and still.

Without haste, Berren cut the bindings that held his wrists. He gathered his sword – the one Talon had given him – and the one gold-handled knife that was left, and then his eyes turned to Fasha and to his son, lying still and peaceful on the floor. He almost didn't dare to look. Were they dead or quietly dreaming? How could they be made to sleep through all this? Would they wake up again and if they did, who would they be? Gelisya had done something, he knew, in the moment when he'd first struck Kuy. He'd seen it in her eyes as she crouched over her bonds-maid. He lifted Fasha's veil. She was still breathing. Something, at least. They were all alike now, every one of them. When he'd cut Saffran Kuy and the air had filled with spirits, he'd seen the hole in Gelisya's soul. A tiny one, but still a hole. Someone had cut her too, once, and now Fasha would be the same. Each one of them with a piece missing.

He looked at her face and almost wept. She was a stranger, a woman who had given herself to him for one night so that he would kill for her, and finally, after all this time and far, far too late, he'd honoured that promise. All these years he'd thought of her, and yet he knew almost nothing about her. He stroked her cheek and her hair. She could have been anyone. Maybe that was the point.

He let her down gently to lie on the wooden deck and squatted for a moment beside Syannis instead. The thief-taker was dead. More than dead, if such a thing was possible. He was slumped against a crate, tipped over sideways. It looked an ungainly way to lie. Awkward and uncomfortable, even if you *were* dead. Berren shook his head. Stupid, after everything else, but he had tears in his eyes. He dragged the thief-taker away from his crate and laid him flat. Closed his eyes and crossed his arms over his chest. There was no blood anywhere. Now he looked almost as though he'd died in his sleep.

'You were a right selfish arrogant prick.' The tears were rolling down his face now. He knelt beside Syannis and took the dead thief-taker's hand and pressed it to his cheek. 'She got away, but I'll not go after her. I've seen what that's like. That's a lesson you taught me well.'

He looked away and shook his head, trying to clear his eyes, trying to clear his thoughts. Two deep breaths, one after the other, and he replaced the thief-taker's hand on his chest. Berren turned and rose and went to look at the face of his son for the very first time. He'd be another dark-skin, but he'd be handsome and strong, that was what mattered. The boy looked peaceful, sleeping in whatever stupor Gelisya had put him. They would wake up. He suddenly had no fear of that.

Above him, on the deck of the sloop, the dozen guards were still there, and he couldn't fight that many at once. So, in the gloom of the hold, he clung on to Fasha and her warmth, cradling the son he'd never seen until today and listened to the creaking of the wooden hull. He waited as the candles, one by one, flickered and guttered and died. Sooner or later, someone would come. And then they would see.

270

EPILOGUE

It seemed to Talon that everything had started well enough. The castle fell. The Thousand Ghosts swarmed through the streets making mayhem – late, but they did it. He had them sack a few houses of people he didn't like. When he led the Hawks to drive them valiantly out of the castle and seize it for himself, word quickly came that Aimes was dead. Eventually the lancers brought back his body.

And then it started to go wrong. He searched the castle but there were no traces of the warlocks he'd come to kill. He dashed back out to the city and joined the Hawks, rounding up the last of the Thousand Ghosts and noisily chasing them away. Still no warlocks. And Berren, where was Berren? Nowhere, and suddenly Talon had a terrible knot of doubt growing in his gut. He muttered silent curses to himself. A pall of smoke sat over the market. *That* was never meant to happen. His soldiers were scattered. He screamed and shouted at anyone he happened to see, trying to restore some order before the whole town sank into looting and anarchy, or else simply burned to the ground. He thought he saw Berren running through the streets once, but when he looked again it was only smoke, and he had bigger problems than one missing sword.

By the time the early spring sun was a yard over the horizon, he was back in the castle and a little more sanguine. The mockery that was the Thousand Ghosts had fled and a good part of the Hawks were off across the countryside, making a big show of pursuit. A ragtag militia of angry citizens and a few of the king's guard had coalesced towards the end and gone after them too. Talon left them to it: if they wanted to wander aimlessly across the fields and hills around the city for a day or so, that was their business. The Thousand Ghosts would vanish back into everyone's imagination just as easily as they had sprung forth.

He turned his mind to Saffran Kuy and the warlocks, the real reason he was here. If they weren't in the castle then he'd just have to winkle them out of their holes. He dragged Tarn into a quiet corner and asked him about Berren, because if anyone would know about warlocks and where they might hide, it would be the Judge.

'He was looking for the princess.' Tarn was all frowns today. He didn't care for this, any of it. 'Didn't like the look on his face either. Far to eager.'

'Princess? You mean Gelisya?'

'Yes.'

No one knew where Berren had gone after he'd left the castle. No one had seen Syannis either, but the king's guard knew enough for Talon to know where to start. He glanced across the harbour to the ships anchored there. Yes. He knew *exactly* where to look, for Berren and for his warlocks too, and so he grabbed a handful of soldiers and marched them straight through the town into a pair of longboats and out to Gelisya's sloop. He'd half expected to have to fight his way on board, but the guards on the deck lowered a ladder without any fuss. If anything, they seemed happy to see him. He thought he heard *Crown-Taker* whispered once or twice, and perhaps *the Bloody Judge*, which brought a nasty smile to his face. With a bit of luck he'd find Syannis here too. They could end all this right now. They could have a trial, here on the ship. Some warlocks would die and then maybe he and Syannis could at last put everything behind them.

He marched into the cabin at the back of the ship and there was Gelisya. She flung herself at him, clinging to him as though for dear life. 'Prince Talon, thank the gods you're here!'

Talon ripped her off him and flung her away. 'Get off me, you witch!' he spat. 'Where's my brother?'

A flash of fury crossed her face, quickly hidden behind her mask of frightened little girl, but not quickly enough. 'In the hold, Prince Talon. With the Crown-Taker. I'm scared. I think the Crown-Taker has killed him.'

Talon snapped out orders to his men to search the hold. As he did, Gelisya slipped her hand into a pocket and pulled out a tiny vial. *Blood of the Funeral Tree*. When Talon turned back, her face was downcast. 'What have you done?' he demanded.

Gelisya sniffed and rubbed her eye. She stared at the floor, her hair cascading down to hide her face. 'Syannis found out what the Crown Taker did. After that ...' She started to sob and shake. 'Aimes meant everything to him.' Through her curtain of hair, she watched Talon's shoulders slump a fraction. He looked flustered.

'No one leaves this ship,' he said.

Gelisya nodded again and watched as he paced round the cabin. His soldiers were out on the deck. She waited for a minute or two. With a bit of luck, the Crown-Taker would kill the men Talon sent down to the hold. She idly took a few steps to where a jug of wine stood on a small rimmed table and poured a goblet for herself. She took a sip, careful that Talon saw her do it, although he would never see her swallow.

Enough to kill six men. And it was no secret that Talon liked his wine. She didn't look at it though, nor at the remaining goblet beside the jug. Just looked at Talon and cowered like a little girl from his anger, lifting her own shaking goblet to her lips and yet never drinking, until at last he poured one for himself without even thinking and drained it. He was in the middle of waving his fist, telling her how everything was going to change and be put right – she nodding because yes, that was exactly what would happen – in the middle of telling her how she was a witch and how she had brought ruin on Syannis, when his eyes went very wide. His mouth fell open. His face turned a shade blue and his fingers grew limp. His cup slipped between them and fell to the floor.

Gelisya stood a little straighter. She smiled and offered him her goblet, and then dropped that one to the floor too, still full. A dark stain of wine spread over the wood. 'Yes,' she whispered in Talon's ear. 'You're right.' She put her arms around him and caught him as he sank to his knees. 'All gone now. All done. All finished.'

His eyes rolled back. She dropped him onto the floor and screamed. 'Murder! Help! Hawks! Guards!'

The first men into the room were three of the Hawks Talon had brought with him. They stared dumbfounded, stunned for just long enough for two of her own guards to arrive before they understood what they were seeing. One drew his sword.

'Help!' Gelisya looked straight at the onrushing king's guard and pointed at the mercenaries. 'They've come to murder me!'

As the room filled with fighting, she slipped away, not waiting to see who would win. She ran out onto the decks. 'King's men!' She called. 'To me! The mercenaries are traitors and murderers! Take them all!'

And then she watched as the Hawks and her guards killed each other, and her heart raced with the thrill of it. Saffran would have chided her for this, but the sight excited her. The Hawks didn't die easily either and she lost half of her guards before it was done; and then more of Talon's men emerged, the ones he'd sent to the hold, the ones the Crown-Taker hadn't killed after all. They rushed out, swords drawn, and for a fleeting moment she tasted fear. One of them broke through and ran at her. She drew out the golden knife to cut his soul and make him hers. It fumbled through her hasty fingers and dropped to the deck.

But the soldier paused as a flicker of doubt crossed his face; she was barely more than a girl, after all. And then blood bubbled out of his mouth and he collapsed. Lucama offered her a little bow. Gelisya steadied herself against him. She liked this one, she thought. A quick count – three of her guards left standing, that was all – but Talon's soldiers were dead now, every one of them. She started to laugh. Aimes gone, Syannis gone, Talon gone, all of them out of her way.

Then she saw him: Berren. The Crown-Taker. The murderer. Standing on the deck by the hatch to the hold with a sword in one hand, her bonds-maid over his shoulder and the little bastard boy tucked under his other arm. She flinched away, even though the whole length of the sloop was between them. She looked over her shoulder for her warlocks. 'Vallas! Saffran!' But Saffran Kuy was dead and the soap-maker was nowhere to be seen.

Lucama forced himself to breathe steadily, the way Silvestre had taught them. Nice and slow and pushing the fear and the bloodlust both away. Three of them left, one on either side and him in the middle. And here was his old friend the Bloody Judge, staring back at them, cold and unyielding. The Judge bared his teeth and hissed. Either side of Lucama, the two other guards stepped back a pace.

'My name is Berren!' he said. 'They call me the Crown-Taker. I've killed more men than I can remember, and I took joy in none of it!' He took a pace towards them.

Lucama saluted and took up his guard. 'I don't want to fight you, Berren,' he said.

'I bet you don't.'

'But you will not pass.'

'Kill him!' screamed the princess. 'He killed the king! Do your duty!'

'Stand aside, friend,' the Bloody Judge growled. 'No need for you to die.'

One of the other soldiers moved forward. Lucama put a hand to his shoulder, stopping him in his tracks. 'I was there in Kalda, Berren. I know what the queen's message said. I brought it to you after all. You should go. You have what you were promised. Take them and leave.'

Princess Gelisya screamed again. 'Kill him! King's guard! Obey me!'

For second after second Lucama and Berren stared each other down. Then the Bloody Judge stepped back one pace and then another, and with each step Lucama backed away in turn, taking the other soldiers with him. Behind him his princess howled, screaming curses.

She's afraid of him. We're all afraid of him.

Without taking his eyes off them for a moment, Berren Crown-Taker, the Bloody Judge of Tethis, backed away to the ladders still slung over the side, to where Prince Talon's longboats bobbed in the water. He sheathed his sword and climbed carefully down, carrying his burdens with him. Lucama watched him go. *We could rush him*, he thought. *One man carrying a body over his shoulder and another under his arm, and he's only got one sword, even if he really is that quick*. But he didn't move. Instead, he let his eyes linger on the ladder, watched it shudder with each step that Berren took towards the water, until it finally went limp.

Gelisya was screaming something about crossbows, but Lucama knew they didn't have any. He didn't tell her; and when she vanished into the cabins to look for one, he strolled to the side of the ship. He watched Berren row slowly away to the shore. After a bit he took hold of his badge, the badge of the king's guard, and tore it off his chest.

'Good luck to you, thief-taker's boy,' he murmured. He tossed the badge into the water and turned away. Then he put his hand to his sword and went looking for mad Princess Gelisya.